I0819954

I MAY NOT BE PERFECT BUT
I'M IRISH

Chapter 1

“I’m going to kill you, Joey.” My three year old sister Katie picked up a small hand gun that was lying on the bed and pointed it at me. The gun looked real. I tried to grab her arm.

“Let me see that.” Her finger was on the trigger. She startled and jerked away from me. The gun fired. It missed me. The sound scared her and she started screaming hysterically. My immediate concern was for my little sister. I held her close to me and tried to calm her.

Jane, my stepmother, rushed into the bedroom, slapped me hard along side of my head, and tore my sister away from me.

“Joe, what the hell are you doing? Where did you get a gun?” She hit me again. It was then that I became terrified. Unknown to me at the time was that Jane had spent hours with the child teaching her to point and fire the gun. She had threatened to kill me many times before. This was for real. You don’t accidentally leave a loaded gun with the safety off out where a child can get it. This was no accident. This crazy bitch was trying to kill me. I had just turned fourteen two months earlier.

My father never wanted or liked children. My mother didn’t use birth control and believed that having a child would save her marriage. She sensed that my father was seeing another woman. I was born and I was a fact whether my father was ready or not. My mother Linda was just seventeen at the time.

I was born with the proverbial silver spoon stuck up my ass. Too young to appreciate the fact, I was born into the privileged wealthy élite. My father Joseph John Kennedy Jr. was a young attorney with a prestigious Chicago law firm and my grandfather Joseph John senior was a well liked and respected superior court judge. My father was a brilliant young man in his early twenties with degrees from four leading universities, Notre Dame, Loyola, North Western, and De Paul University. The family was ruled with an iron grip by my grandmother Anne. I was her first grandchild and I was loved and adored. I wanted for nothing. At two years old I had 105 suits of clothing and this was during the Depression years.

My brother Shaun was born in 1937. I was two years old. Still my father did not want or like children. He resented my mother for bearing us. A cold and uncaring man by nature he drew increasingly apart from my mother. He was a hard drinking man, prone to drinking to excess, but never to the point where it might interfere with his law career. His career seemed to be the only thing he cared about. My father never abused my mother or us. He just ignored us and grudgingly paid the bills. Unbeknown to my mother he would slip gin into my baby bottle to keep me quiet so he could get a good night's sleep. Needless to say, I slept like a baby and in later years acquired a liking for gin.

Until the age of five I was loved, spoiled, and pampered. Then disaster struck. My grandmother died. My father quickly divorced my mother and married a woman named Jane. My mother devastated, moved in with her sister temporarily taking me and Shaun with her. She did not try to get alimony or child support. Understand my Irish Catholic father would have never divorced while his mother was alive. My grandfather? He retired and withdrew from reality full of deep sadness and grief for many years until he remarried a wonderful and remarkable woman who became my step grandmother. But my life as a privileged class citizen was over. Our 22 year old mother was broke, uneducated, and hurt. She felt somehow it was her fault but she didn't have a clue as to why. She was without a job at a time when there were no jobs and she had two children to take care of. It wasn't until years later that I could appreciate the sacrifices this proud beautiful woman made.

So my little sister tried to kill me. It was nothing like the beating Jane gave me afterwards. She made me take off my clothes, tied me with tape, gagged me so the neighbors wouldn't hear, and beat me with an electric ironing cord so viciously that I fell unconscious. When I came to I was lying naked and bleeding on the day bed , locked in the enclosed front porch, covered with a blanket. I remember while I was being beaten, Jane was in a wild rage, and yelling accusations at me. This was the worst beating I ever had by her. I heard my father come home. I remember it was a Friday.

They went into the kitchen where I could barely hear them. What I did hear was hardly reassuring. Jane was telling him what a terrible person I was and told him I stole her gun and gave it to the baby. I could have killed my sister. I was a liar, a thief, and she could no longer put up with me. My father started drinking. She raved long into the night. Finally she unlocked the door and set a plate of food on the floor. "Eat, you ungrateful son of a bitch." She left and locked the door. My father did not even look in on me. I was resigned to the fact that I was a dead man. My stepmother was crazy, no one cared. There was no escape. Little did I know then that the worst was yet to come.

Monday morning I was allowed to dress and leave to enroll in Sullivan High School on the North side of Chicago. Up until this time I had only gone to a private school out in the country. As the school was not accredited I had to take a series of test to see if I was eligible for high school. Despite the fact that the private school was for throw away rich kids that no one wanted, I did manage to get a good education. I passed the tests and was admitted. It was my first experience in public schooling and the first time I was close to girls.

One should appreciate that my step mother hated me and was insanely jealous of my mother. When the only job my mother could find was in Michigan she went to court to get full custody of Shaun and me. The court awarded custody to my father. Jane felt that she could hurt my mother most by taking us away from her. She didn't want us and put us both in a private school which to this day I considered to be a combination reform school / orphanage for throw away children from broken homes. We were simultaneously beaten and terrorized into behaving. While abused, we still managed to get a good education. If we did not learn we didn't eat. I was a tall skinny kid and my only goal was to grow big enough where people would stop beating on me.

By the time I entered high school my mother had remarried and had two more children. The man she married was Roderick D'Angelo, an uneducated, hard working father of two children by a former marriage. In his spare time he was an auto racer. A colorful, good looking man he attracted women like flies and no doubt cheated on my mother at times, but he was basically a good hearted person who loved his family and took his obligations seriously. The court had awarded my mother visitation rights and it was negotiated that my brother and I spent half of our vacations and holidays with our mother. When I started high school I was to spend every other weekend with my mother and step dad. It was the only sanity had in my life.

When I tried to talk to my mother about how I was mistreated she refused to listen. She had her own life and problems. My father was a rich lawyer and as far as she was concerned it was the best place for me. I had advantages and I was to consider myself lucky. Her last born child, my half-brother Chaz, was born with Cerebral Palsy. The medical bills were overwhelming. Rod D'Angelo was the sort of man who when he won a race would buy my mother an expensive fur coat even if it meant that two days later there would be no money for food. My mother had taken up drinking and smoking, something she had never done when she was married to my father. A good housewife and mother she wasn't but somehow everyone survived. Rod at least had a steady job running an auto repair shop rumored to be owned by the mob.

I was fascinated by girls but I was awkward and extremely shy around them. The all boy's private school had not prepared me with any social skills whatsoever. I saw girls occasionally when we drove into town to attend church when we weren't snowed in. They sat on one side of the room and us boys on the other. I self educated myself about women by reading books and looking at pictures of women in their underwear in the Sears Catalogue, and topless black women in the rare National Geographic magazines. I acquired a longing for black women that I have to this day.

Jane didn't allow me any time to myself nor was I able to have any money. If I was not home from school by her specified time, I was beaten. Upon arriving home I was locked in the porch room which served as my bedroom. The blinds were kept closed so I could not see out and I was not allowed to do any homework or read. No one spoke to me except in third person and then it was always a curse word. I was allowed out of my room only to use the toilet and to eat dinner after the rest of the family had eaten. It was my job to do the dishes which were closely inspected. Needless to say my grades suffered and I had no friends.

It was during my English class. The teacher instructed us to write an essay on how we spent our summer vacation and the fun we had. I sat there frozen. Tears started flowing from my eyes. The teacher asked me what was wrong. At first I couldn't speak. Then I finally started crying and blurted out "I didn't have any fun." I was sent to the principal's office. He asked me what was wrong.

No one in my entire life had ever asked me what was wrong. I broke down and told him. He sent me to talk to someone else. It was a physiatrist. Again I told this man everything. He listened but I could see that he didn't believe me. I was put into the nurse's room and told to lie down and rest. They gave me a pill and I fell asleep. When I got home from school I didn't say a word about what had happened. I was terrified I would be killed or worse.

The school requested my father to come to school. Of course, he couldn't be bothered and sent my step mother. She thought she was talking with the principal but she was actually talking to the physiatrist. To the outside world she could be very charming and convincing, but he sensed something was terribly wrong. Whether it was true or not, he could tell that I was terrified that Jane was going to kill me and Jane resented me and seemed to hate me. It was a dangerous situation at best.

It was at this time I went to my mother's house for the weekend and told her that I couldn't go back. She explained that Rod didn't want me, the house was too crowded, she had my little brother to take care of, and I was so much better off with my rich father. I couldn't get through to her. I was afraid to go back. Jane would kill me. The two days passed quickly and my mother kissed me goodbye and gave me money for car fare and an extra two dollars. I left but I couldn't go back to my father.

I didn't go back. It was winter. I had no friends and no place to go. The first night I spent under a porch covered with a piece of canvas I had found trying to keep warm. Monday morning came. I was unbelievably cold. I spent what little money I had on a steaming hot cup of coffee and phoned my mother. She cried and begged me to go back to my father. She was worried sick about me and made me promise to call her at one o'clock. When I called back she told me that she had retained an attorney and begged me to call him. I had no choice. I called him.

The attorney told me that they were going to court to file for custody of me. He told me to go back to my father and that nothing would happen to me as it is now a matter of public record. He didn't know my step mother. I was a dead man. He said he had spoken to my father who assured him that no one would harm me and that I would be all right. My father was not aware of any problems but he would look into it. Big deal! I was a dead man. Jane would find a way to kill me and make it look like an accident. I had no choice. I went back.

My father had an apartment on the North Side. I never was allowed to have a key. I entered the lobby to wait until my father came home. I was afraid to ring for my step mother. The warmth of the lobby soon lulled me to sleep. I woke up to my father shaking me. He did not look too happy. He marched me upstairs to the apartment where I had a bath and was locked into my room. Late into the night I heard my step mother running me down to my father and for the first time ever he was drinking on a week night. They remembered to bring me something to eat. I wasn't good enough to eat at the table.

The next morning I got up and dressed for school. I still hadn't seen my step mother. My father unlocked the door and said "You're not going to school today. You're going downtown with me." He would not look at me directly and avoided eye contact. My step mother was no where around. I left with my father. I didn't see my step mother again for four years.

My father took me to the court house, found an empty room and told me to wait there. Someone would come and get me. He pulled out his wallet and gave me a twenty dollar bill. "Here, you might need some money." He turned and left.

About an hour later a big giant of a man came in and asked if I was Joe Kennedy. I said yes and when I stuck my hand out to shake hands, he handcuffed me. You're coming with me." I could see that he had a gun. My God, he was a hit man and he was going to kill me. My father was rich enough to do anything and get away with it. He took me to reformatory where I was locked in a solitary cell. It was warm and I was fed. My hit man was an officer of the court charged with delivering me. I was handcuffed so I wouldn't rabbit.

The next day they told me I was being processed. When I asked to make a phone call I was told I was not allowed to phone or write anyone. I told them that I could not see without my glasses. They let me send a postcard to my mother asking her to send me my glasses, nothing else. At least now she would know where I was. Actually, I could see just fine. No one told me anything. I was scared. As a minor I evidently had no rights whatsoever.

What I didn't know at the time that was I was being railroaded into an insane asylum. At the time, in the State of Illinois, a minor child could be committed to a state insane asylum on the recommendation of a private physician. My father had a doctor in his back pocket. He was getting rid of me once and for all. At least I wasn't dead yet. There was nothing I could do. I was resigned to my fate.

When I didn't show up Monday morning for school, they were concerned and contacted my father directly. Whatever he said only heightened their suspicions that something was terribly wrong. When they called my mother she did not know anything until she got my postcard and called the school. Between the school and my mother's attorney they forced my father to admit to where I was and why. The State of Illinois Board of Education demanded that I be tested before I was committed and the court agreed.

Meanwhile nobody told me anything. I was interviewed by several doctors who asked me many strange questions. I was tested and retested. I was totally confused. I was moved from solitary confinement to the general population of minors waiting to go to court for disposition. Several older thugs decided to hold me down and rob me. I fought back and pushed a kid so hard he cracked his skull and was taken to the hospital. I was left alone after that but it did not look good on my record. They were constantly observing me. I did the best I could and answered all their questions and submitted to their tests. I was there for weeks. One day I was released. My mother was there to take me home with her.

"Damn, the sons of bitches. I'd like to blow them all up…" My mother was shocked. I had never spoken like this before. For a moment she seems a little frightened of me. On the drive home she told what had happened.

When the custody case was heard, the presiding Judge called my father before him and asked what exactly did he claim was wrong with me. My father named four things, any one of which, if true, was cause to have me locked up. The Judge said "Mr. Kennedy, I have your son's report before me. I could only hope that a son of mine could have as fine of a report as your son has."

"In that case, your Honor, I drop my petition. The mother may have custody of the child." My mother won and was awarded $10 a week child support. The good old boys network still prevailed. We went home.

If Rod didn't want me, he sure didn't show it. He welcomed me like I was his long lost son. He seemed genuinely happy to see me again but I didn't trust him at first. I couldn't trust anyone. I was to share a room in the attic with Tom, Rod's son who was one year older than me and built like a Sherman tank. Like his father he wasn't all that smart but he was big! Tom went to CVS, a vocational school, and I transferred to the local high school named Fenger where the girls outnumbered the boys two to one. There wasn't one black person in the entire school. I thought only girls were virgins but I was one too.

Life was good. There were no restrictions on me whatsoever. I could pretty much do what I wanted. I had a strong interest in the girls but I was too shy and uncomfortable to do anything but look and admire. I was 6'4" tall and weighed 135 pounds. I was one skinny boy and I thought I was ugly. With no social skills, I focused on learning. I was naturally intelligent and was able to learn very quickly.

In my third month of high school my father pulled my brother Shaun out of private school to live with him and Jane. It lasted about one month before he told mother he wasn't going back when he visited us for the weekend. My father gave up without a fight and Shaun came to live with us. Mom got a whole extra $10 a week for his support. My brother and I were always close as all we had were each other but now that I was older I didn't want him hanging around me. For a little kid he was the toughest person I ever knew. You would have to kill him before he would let you see him cry.

We lived on 123rd street on the South side of Chicago which was about as far as you could live and still be in the city limits. At that time black people lived pretty much North of 65th street and didn't venture too far into our turf. The neighborhood was made up of mostly 1st generation Italian, Polish, & German hard working immigrants from the old country. They all wanted their children to have a better life than they had. The Italians were mostly Catholic and their daughters went to Catholic schools. Without exception all the girls had big brothers who would kill you if you touched their sisters. Of course, they didn't mind touching everybody else's sisters.

Most of the boys hung with a neighborhood gang that protected you and gave you a sense of belonging. I went along to get along but for a long time I just didn't fit in. I was basically a loner who didn't trust anyone. The girls that showed any interest in me were out of luck. I was too scared of them to hold a decent conversation. And then I discovered alcohol. With a few drinks in me I could talk with anyone, dance with any girl, and fight anyone. I was a giant and there was no stopping me. It was then I discovered the completely wonderful world of sex. This was what I was born for.

The older group of boys I hung with drove to Calumet City on weekends to visit a whore house just outside of town called the Black Oaks Inn. For $10 you could buy sex with a woman. I couldn't wait to get $10 together. I never wanted anything so much in my life before. If only to get it over with and experience what it was like. You just didn't have sex with nice girls until after you were married. I couldn't try an easy bad girl because I couldn't admit that I didn't know how. I had to make some money. I was too young to get a job without lying about my age. I didn't even have a social security card. I couldn't go to my mother and ask her for money to get laid and I was too chicken to steal. It looked like I was going to be a virgin for the rest of my life.

I found a job by lying about my age and using a friend's social security card. I became Arthur S. Baker and I was an usher at one of our leading movie houses where I wore an elaborate uniform of grey and wine with gold braid. My boss knew who I really was and how old I was but for $5 a week paid under the table he kept quiet and let me work. It took me two days to get my first pay check cashed as I did not have identification under my false name. That weekend I went with the gang to Black Oaks. I had to chip in two dollars for gas.

You entered a large room with a jukebox playing and half dressed women standing against one wall. You were supposed to pick one out. Thank God I was half drunk because I could hardly look at these women. My friends all picked their dates and left me alone. I pretended to be listening to the juke box. Finally a blond girl about 23 years old came over and took my hand. "Do you like me?"

I followed her into a small room consisting of a bed, small table, and a chair. On the table there was a basin of warm water, "Take your pants off, Baby." She unbelted my pants and slid them down with my under pants. She took my throbbing rock hard penis in her hand and started to wash me. I came all over the place. I couldn't help it. I swear I came so hard I must have hit the ceiling. I almost cried. "Is this your first time?" she smiled softly. I just nodded. "It's all right. It will be better next time. Just ask for me. Betty. I'll take special good care of you." It was over. Of course, I couldn't tell anyone what had happened, ever. We drove back to Chicago. I was still a virgin. Was I a complete jerk or what?

Drag racing was a big deal in those days. The guys would block off the streets with their cars and we would have speed contests. As I hung around with an older crowd that had cars I was usually there. My good friend Billy Thorton was one of the consistent winners. He had an older Ford with a stick shift that he worked on himself. Billy was a handsome lad who could get any woman he wanted by snapping his finger and could care less. His claim to fame was his fast car and the shirts he wore. He never wore the same shirt twice and they were always expensive. You might say that he was my best friend.

Billy had a stepfather that mistreated his mother and tried to tell Billy how to live his life. Billy swore that some day that he would kill the son of a bitch. Billy was also one of the best street fighters I ever saw. He was fearless. Men liked him and girls adored him. He was lucky in gambling and seemed to always have money. I felt lucky to have him as my friend and tried to be more like him. There could only be one Billy. He was an original.

I was growing up wild. I did what I wanted and no one cared. I really had no purpose in life except to live it. I was growing stronger and tougher. I had sense enough not to get too involved with the real bad kids who had only two ways to go, dead or in jail by the time they turned twenty. That wasn't for me. I didn't know what I wanted or what I wanted to be but it had to be something better than this. I didn't know it at the time but I was going to experience life as most men never had. I felt I could do anything, be anybody. Life was mine for the taking. It was all good until it turned bad.

In the second year of high school my stepfather bought me a car with a three quarter race engine with a high speed rear end. It was a 1937 4-door Dodge painted my school's colors, fire engine red and Kelly green. I always wore his old racing jackets and lied about being part of his pit crew. I was fearless, reckless and a show off. This car was really fast. One day I picked up 12 traffic tickets at one time. My mother said Rod would take away my car. This was unacceptable. I decided to run away.

I packed everything I owned in the car plus two bottles of whiskey I stole from the pantry and took off. I hadn't the faintest idea of where to go. Night fell and it was bitter cold. I sipped whiskey all night to keep warm. I had never opened the car up to see how fast it would go. At first light I drove to a filling station and filled my tank with high octane gas and checked the air pressure in my tires. I was in the middle of nowhere, somewhere in the county side of Illinois. The highway was deserted.

There was no traffic in either direction. I was probably a little drunk for it all seemed so unreal. I floored the gas pedal and I flew. The speedometer only went to 100 mph. I hit that and the car kept gaining even more speed.

Suddenly the front tire blew up. I panicked and hit the brakes. The Dodge started skidding from one side of the road to the other. The left side of the road was a level cornfield with a barb wire fence, while the right side was a deep ditch. Just as I thought that I had the car under control, I went off the road on the ditch side. The car hit the bottom of the ditch so hard that the impact crushed the right side flush against me. It made a complete turn in the air and landed on the flat side. All the windows just shattered. I felt pinned in. I had no feeling from the waist down. I was slipping into unconsciousness. Thru my blood, out of the corner of my eye, I saw flames. I forced myself to stay awake. With my hands I managed to pull myself out of the driver's side window. I wasn't trapped as I had feared. As I hit the ground my legs buckled and I rolled away from the car. There wasn't an explosion, just a quiet whoosh, and the entire car was in flames.

A truck driver had stopped, climbed down the ditch and pulled me to safety. On his ham radio he called emergency. The ambulance and the police arrived at the same time. It was unbelievable but I was unhurt. Except for a few cuts I was fine. I was taken to jail where my parents were called. They were there in a couple of hours to take me home. There were no criminal charges. The car was totaled. One spare tire that had flown out of the trunk at impact was saved and one door handle did not melt. Everything I owned, including school books, were gone, as well as my shoe I lost getting out of the car. My parents were not as mad as they were concerned. They were relieved that I wasn't killed. Rod told me later that if my mother had seen the car before she saw me, she would have had a heart attack. He told me that as a race car driver he had seen many wrecks but he had never seen anyone walk away from one as bad as this one.

On first impact my watch was broken. At the same moment back home my mother yelled hysterically that something had happened to me. When I lost control of the car I remember what Rod had taught me, if you are going to be in a crash, relax don't tense up. As I went off the road I grabbed a Saint Christopher medal I had hanging from the car mirror that my mother gave me. In truth, I think being half drunk and just dumb luck saved me. God had more shit to put me through. It just wasn't my time.

I liked Rod but he just wasn't my father. Aside from knowing cars I thought he was dumb. When he was young he left grade school to work. Times were tough and he had to help out. He never did get a formal education. He would never admit it but he could barely read. I was clueless about mechanical stuff and actually ruined a car that Rod gave me by being too dumb to check the water and oil. I was the only Army ROTC high school student who, after four years of training still couldn't dissemble and reassemble a M1 rifle. Rod didn't have much use for me but he treated me mostly OK.

It was in my third year of high school that I joined the Illinois National Guard, 33rd Infantry Division Artillery, Medical Detachment with a friend of mine. It gave me another source of a little money. My training was to be a

Medic. I had elected to join the high school Army ROTC in lieu of gym classes. The draft was in effect and we all expected to be drafted at 18. We were fighting in Korea at the time and in a cold war with Russia. When I was drafted I wanted to be ready and in the back of my mind I was hoping for Officer School.

Chapter 2

I finally had a little time for myself. I didn't date any girls as they all seemed too young for me. I was uncomfortable around girls my own age. I hung with the older crowd, drank too much, and pretty well did what I damned pleased. I pretty much coasted thru my third year and kept out of serious trouble. I got in a brawl with a huge German kid from another school and somehow we ended up being best friends. Karl Welhelm Rheinhardt was a little strange but was smart as a whip. He predicted another war with the Germans who were going to conquer the world and he promised that I would always have a job polishing his boots. Just to play it safe he was studying Russia. His parents were nice and didn't seem to realize that they were raising a perfect little Nazi. Karl was a good friend to have. Everyone was terrified of him except me. While I didn't beat him in our fight, I didn't lose either.

Summer vacation came and Karl invited me to join him for a trip down South to visit with some of his relatives. Karl hated cripples, black people, Jews, and most everyone else who didn't believe as he did. I thought he was a little crazy but he did love his mother. I refused to argue with him so I was tolerated. It was a road trip to remember.

Our first stop was to visit his cousin Beau in Franklin, Kentucky. Beau introduced us to the wonderful world of "White Lightning", a clear deceptive liquid aka "Shine", sold for one dollar in a heavy glass quart mason jar. Beau drove us around in his car showing us the sights as we sipped the liquor in the back seat. He was not drinking as he had to work later that night. Suddenly Karl yelled for him to stop the car as he had to take a piss. There was no moon that night and it was pitch dark. We were out in the country driving a back dirt road to avoid the law.

Beau braked the car to a sudden stop. Karl who was more than a little drunk opened the back door and like a soldier marching off to war he stepped boldly out into the night and totally disappeared. From a distance we heard a tremendous cursing. He missed the running board and stepped off into an eight foot muddy ditch. He was too drunk to get up, his pants had fallen around his ankles, and he had wet himself. I couldn't stop laughing. Later on the threat of death I had to promise to never tell anyone. I never did.

Our next and last stop was Nashville, Tennessee, to spend two weeks with his aunt and uncle. I never met such warm, loving, gracious people in my life. I found it impossible to believe that Karl was family. I was accepted as if I were one of their own. I never had so much and wonderful food in my life. For the first time in my life I felt as if I belonged. This must be what Heaven was.

Their next door neighbors were the Brown family whose father was a deacon in the Church of Christ. Deacon Brown had a 15 year old daughter Susan Mae. It was love at first sight. Susan was everything a man could ever dream of having. She was so beautiful that it hurt just to see her and not hold her. The best part of all was that she liked me. To the amusement of the grownups we spent most all of our time together. The two week passed quickly and we had to leave for home. We pledged our undying love to each other and I finally got to kiss her. She pressed her entire body against me and I nearly passed out with pleasure. I never should have left.

We stopped in Franklin on the way back for a couple of days. I wanted to take some moonshine back to Chicago for my friends. In case we were stopped by the cops I poured the shine into two large Windex bottles. In less than an hour the plastic spray tubes dissolved. Karl refused to drink any of it but not me. I always knew I was tougher than he was.

A few things about down South bothered me. I couldn't help notice that the toilets and drinking fountains were marked "white only" and "black". This just didn't feel right. When I was walking down a Nashville street, an elderly Negro stepped into the gutter to let me pass. He averted his eyes. This was 1952. Karl and I were drinking in a beer bar when some Reb yelled "I think I smell a Yankee in here."

I whispered to Karl, "Let's get the hell out of here. They're still fighting the Civil war." We made it back to Chicago without incident.

My fourth year of high school began. I was getting a little tired of paying for sex. I worked too hard for my money. It was during my last semester at Fenger High that I had to leave home for good. It was Mom's wedding anniversary. Rod phoned from the shop and told her to dress up nice as he was going to take her out for dinner and dancing to celebrate. Mom got dressed and waited.

Rod didn't show. Around midnight she started crying softly. He staggered in about three in the morning, drunk, his pants unzipped, and his face marked with lipstick. When Mom asked him where he had been, he hit her. I got out of bed, pulled on my steel toed engineering boots, and went down stairs.

Mom was really crying as he was about to hit her again. I grabbed his arm and slugged him hard. I chased him into their bedroom as he tried to get away from me. He was too drunk to defend himself. I pounded on him for a while and he just glared at me drunkenly. It's no fun hitting a man who won't fight back so I quit. I went to comfort my mother. I asked why she didn't leave the son of a bitch. She told me that she had to take care of Chaz , my half brother with Cerebral Palsy, who was about 3 years old at the time. I gave up and went back to bed. I didn't sleep too well. The next morning I was having breakfast with the family before going to school when Rod came into the kitchen. He looked like hell and had two black eyes. "Don't be here when I get home." He went to work without so much as a cup of coffee. I had just lost my happy home.

I packed my few belongings, tried to calm my hysterical mother, and left. She gave me the $10 child support my father had been sending for my support. I went to the YMCA and rented a room for eight dollars a week. I now had two dollars a week to live on. I was sixteen years old and I had promised my mother that I would graduate from high school. It was not easy.

I scored a job in the high school cafeteria as a busboy during lunch hour for one free meal a day, no wages. That took care of five meals a week. I took to hanging around with my friends after school, staying long enough, that their folks would invite me to stay for dinner. Next to the YMCA was a White Castle where you could buy a dozen hamburgers for a dollar. I tried everything I could to make a dollar or two. It was hard but I survived. Once a week I would check in with my mother and pick up my $10.

About the fifth week of this, Rod came home early and caught me. He told me that all I was doing was upsetting my mother and don't come to the house anymore. There went my rent money! I called my father the big time lawyer and asked him to send me the money directly. He informed me that if I wasn't living at home he was under no obligation to support me and hung up. I was out of options.

I didn't have many adult friends and pretty much kept my problems private but there was one teacher I could confide in. My English teacher had a friend who knew a friend and I was offered a job washing dishes six nights a week for a dollar an hour and food. Having my back to the wall I took it. I still didn't have a social security number but the owner took out withholding nevertheless. Every day I would come to work at 4 o'clock. While the dirty dishes were piling up, I had to hand peel a hundred pounds of potatoes, before I could tackle the dishes. Around eleven it was my job to clean up the kitchen. I hated it but I gritted my teeth and did it. I was the best dishwasher they ever had.

The downside was I had no time for myself or study. I was usually tired. I had to give up all my special activities. I dropped off the swimming team, the school news staff, the band, and the chess club where I was the president. I had no time for dances, parties, or girls but I did get a Monday off to go with the boys to the whore house in Indiana. I was a regular and always went with the same woman, Betty. She seemed genuinely touched when I brought her a present for Christmas but I still had to pay ten dollars. I kept the dishwashing job and got to be pretty good friends with the owner but he was careful to keep his family away from me. I took my vow to my mother seriously and I was determined to graduate if it killed me.

I had signed up for a required math class in Trigonometry. A requirement was that I had to have a slide rule, but it was too expensive. After the first day I never went back. I was too ashamed to admit that I was poor. I thought back to my first year of school when I wanted to play trumpet. I had joined the band at the time because of a very cute girl who played violin. If you wanted to play trumpet, you had to supply your own.

I was working as an usher at the time and could afford lessons. I also bought a trumpet on time payments from my instructor. I ended up in the hospital with double pneumonia and my trumpet instructor came to visit me. I thought it was nice of him as he was my only visitor. When he left he took my trumpet. I was only two payments behind. As the fingering was basically the same and I was large enough they offered me the chance to play the Sousaphone. I played in the band but I never did ask the girl for a date. I wasn't a very good musician but good enough to get by. I got in all our football games free.

I excelled at swimming and won my school letter in my first year but I never could beat the top swimmer on our team. I usually took second place unless he was out. Then I usually won. No one could beat me to the end of the pool but I could never perfect the turn for the second lap. I tried out for the boxing team. I was pretty good as I had long arms and could take a punch but I had zero coordination. I got booed out of the ring when I used a back handed blow to keep from getting my ass whipped by this short aggressive boxer. He was knocked unconscious but they gave him the win. I never fought in the ring again.

I aced most classes without doing much studying which was good when I started working steady and had so little time. I resented the fact that I had to work so hard when I came from such a wealthy influential family like the Chicago Kennedys. On the other hand, I didn't have to kiss anyone's ass. I knew that someday I would be rich. Being broke was just a temporary situation. I thought that when my father died, I would have it made. When he did die, he didn't leave me or my brother a dime. It all went to my step mother Jane.

Two years of a foreign language was required to graduate. I had absolutely no aptitude whatsoever. I managed one half year of French, one year each of German & Latin. In all three classes I passed only if I promised to never come back. It seemed that to graduate you had to complete two years of the same language. By not showing up for the one math class and not doing the required homework for a sales class, I was in real danger of not graduating with my class.

Because I had promised my mother that I would graduate, I was going to graduate, even if it meant going to summer school when the semester ended. There was what was called a GED test one could take to graduate and I always did especially well on tests. Everything came easy to me except money and women. When I drank enough, women were no problem. Life wasn't good but it wasn't too bad either. I was growing up tough and street smart. I finally grew big enough that people quit beating on me, with one exception.

I was walking a girl home from school when her boyfriend and three of his crew grabbed me. Eddie Bautz, a German giant of a lad who towered 6' 7" tall, held me from the back while the other three boys beat me to a bloody pulp. They left me lying on bleeding on the sidewalk. The girl had run into her house. Evidently her father seeing the number of boys was too frightened to come out and try to stop them. After the gang left, her father came out and turned a water hose on me to wash some of the blood off. When I was able to stand, he told me that I had better not hang around his daughter. Then he went back in the house. I was lucky I made it to work that night. God, I hated to peel those potatoes.

Of the three boys that beat me I only knew one. It was Sammy Esposito of the Esposito brothers and was reputed to be a Golden Glove Champion amateur boxer, star football player, and one of the best all around sport champions our school ever had. He excelled in every sport he played and was rumored to be one of the toughest boys on the South Side. Nobody beats me up like that, not anymore. I had to challenge him when he was alone. I took a tough kid, Karl Rheinhardt, with me and waited by his house. I brought Karl along so

Sammy wouldn't kill me. Sure enough Sammy came riding up on his bicycle. He skidded up to me and sarcastically asked if I was back for more and started to get off his bike. I hit him and he went down with his bike. He got up and the fight was on.

The sucker punch was the only advantage I had. He was the better fighter but I was Irish mad. We went toe to toe for about 4 minutes. My arms were starting to tire. Sammy wasn't even sweating. I was resigned to getting another beating when his mother came out, made him stop fighting, and told him go into the house immediately. It was over. The next day in school two of his football buddies tried to hassle me in the men's room. I just pushed my way past them. Fighting the toughest kid in the school enhanced my reputation and I was pretty much left alone after that.

Eddie Bautz the giant who held me helpless while the other kids beat me was on the swimming team. Later we got to be great friends but he never did speak of that day or apologized. He came from a German family where the father worked hard with the dream of sending his boy to college. Eddie felt awkward around most people because he was so freakishly tall. He was one hell of a swimmer and mastered the back stroke. I don't think anyone ever beat him. He was offered to try out for the Olympics in his last year. A prostitute picked him up in the bar of the hotel where they were staying and he played all night. The next day he could barely walk let alone swim. The Olympic dream was ended.

Eddie was offered a 4 year swimming scholarship to Loyola where he graduated and became a successful engineer. He treated himself to a new Jaguar as it was the only sports car he could fit into. He was the first one in his family to graduate from college. His mother and father were proud. His father never could have saved enough money for his education painting houses in Chicago. Hell, I was proud for him. His parents were nice people.

Percy Malone Smith was a frail, rather small boy who worked the school lunches with me as a busboy. Percy was a gifted piano player who happened to be gay. His father had thrown him out of the house when he was fifteen and like me he had a room at the YMCA. Unlike me, his parents felt guilty enough to give him enough money to live on. They just never wanted to see him again. As far as I know Percy never engaged in improper sexual behavior, he just liked buys instead of girls. I didn't try to understand. I just accepted him as a friend. He didn't have many.

After we completed our lunch room duties, Percy and I usually went outside to play some catch before the next classes started. One day, the football team who ate together at one table, pushed their table out to block Percy's bus cart from getting by. I had enough of these jock jerks. I walked around Percy, shoved the table back with my left hand and slugged the kid sitting at the end. I hit him so hard his tooth came out and lodged in my hand. He was on the floor and we were both bleeding profusely. Down we went to the nurse's office and then to the principal's office. I was expecting to get expelled.

I was mad. I told the principal the whole story, how Percy was always getting pushed around because he was different and wouldn't fight back, How the entire football team thought they were better than everyone else, and how they tried to get me in the men's room and rip my pants off. I told him how Sammy Esposito beat me bloody with his two thugs while a third one held me helpless. School was hard enough without putting up with this kind of bull hit. I don't back down from anyone, not anymore. I got suspended for the two days before the weekend.

Something was gnawing at the back of my mind. I could do anything and not worry about it as I knew I was not crazy. What I didn't get was that with all the pressure I had been under with my step mother, why wasn't I crazy. It seemed to me that a normal person would be driven nuts. It bothered me so much that I went to see the doctor who had tested me and said I was sane. He explained that I had a sense of humor that acted like a safety valve. When pressure built up and things became impossible, life became ludicrous to me and I had to laugh. It kept me normal. It was his story and I was stuck with it. All I knew was that it was a powerful feeling to be a teenager and positively know that you are not crazy.

When I came back to school no one bothered me. "Don't mess with Kennedy, he's psycho!" I thought of it as a sign of respect. Of course, the girls all thought I was crazy and would have nothing to do with me. It could have been funny but it was a little sad. My friends still hung with me and to Percy I would forever be a hero. I didn't know it at the time but Percy had a small collection of hand guns he was going to use on his tormentors, his parents, or even himself. I never knew what happened to Percy but I believe that some of the long talks we had kept him balanced enough so that he never killed anyone. One day he just disappeared. No one talked about him. No one seemed to notice or care.

I like to believe he went somewhere where there were people like him and that he found someone. I never did know.

I was starting to hear disturbing stories about my brother Shaun. He was going to the same high school as my step brother Tom and was hanging with a pretty rough crowd. When I left home, Shaun pretty much withdrew into himself, and spent his time building up his body. He was a loner and pretty much stayed to himself. I was surprised to hear he was running with a gang. They were known to seek out, beat up, and rob gays that they found in city parks. I felt Shaun and I should have a talk.

I arranged a meet and laid down the law. No brother of mine was going to end up in jail or killed in a gang fight. Thank God, he still looked up to me and listened. He wanted to leave home like me but I made him promise to stay until he graduated high school. I let him know in no uncertain terms just how tough life really was. I think I cinched my argument with the 100 pounds of potatoes I had to peel every night. I didn't like my life very much at the time and I guessed it came through.

I don't know where it came from or how it happened but I got it in my head that I wanted to be a priest. I was never a religious person but I was Irish and I came from a Catholic background. I recalled that several years ago Shaun got caught in an undertow at Bass Lake. I did not know how to swim at the time but we were alone and I plunged into the water after him. I managed to find him and pull him out somehow. He was cold, pale, and unconscious. I called on God and promised that if he saved my brother I would serve him. Maybe this was payback time.

I talked with a priest and started training to prepare for the Seminary. An inadequate knowledge of Latin was a stumbling block to my new career but I was a bright lad. Since I started high school I had one year of Latin, one year of French, and a half year of German. I had passed each course by promising that I would not continue and embarrass the teacher. With a new perspective I felt I had a true purpose in life. I almost gave up drinking and the weekly visits to the whore house. The time to quit was when I actually started the seminary.

Graduation day was approaching fast. I had written a story about my brother almost drowning for an English assignment named "Give To Me My Brother". Unknown to me, the essay was submitted by my English teacher and I was awarded a four year English scholarship to a small college. Because of my financial situation I was offered a Pullman Foundation money Scholarship to the college of my choice. I declined them both secure in the knowledge that the Church would take care of my education.

"Give it to someone who really needs it. The Good Lord gave me two hands to work. If I can't work my way thru college I don't deserve it." Was I a total jerk or what?

I was given four tickets to my graduation. I sent two for my mother and Rod, one to my boss, and one to my father. It was an impulse. I wanted him to know that I made it without his lousy ten bucks a week support money. As it happened, he was the only one that showed up. I graduated. My father invited me out for a cup of coffee. It was the first time I had seen him in four years. I told him I didn't drink coffee. He took me out and bought me a beer. I didn't believe it but there it was.

For a man who never wanted or liked children, he seemed interested in what was happening in my life. Hell, I told him. He sat quietly, listening intently, and occasionally asking a question. When I finished speaking he spoke.

"I think you are going into the Seminary because you feel you have nowhere else to go. I don't have a problem with the church but I don't believe anymore. I'm convinced that there are some major flaws in their thinking. You really should get more education before you make this kind of a decision. You seem like a very level headed young man. I would like to help you if you will let me."

He hit the nail on the head. I would probably flunk the admittance test to the Seminary. I had it with working full time and going to school. I liked sex and drinking way too much to be a priest. "What do you have in mind?"

"I'll pay your way for four years of any college you want. You work for spending money during summer vacation. I'll even help you find a job. There are some fine Jesuit colleges if that's what you want. I don't care. I just want you to have a fair start in life."

"What about Jane?"

"I talked it over with her and she's in total agreement. You don't have to make up your mind now. Come to the house for dinner this Friday and you can give me your answer then. Do you want another beer?"

"Yes, please."

Dad ordered another beer for me and stood up to leave. He held out his hand. We'll expect you at seven." We shook hands and he left. It was strange. He looked like he was glad to see me, he never once mentioned the past. Nor did he apologize. I had a lot to think about. It was three days to Friday.

Chapter 3

I had made the decision to take my father up on his offer. I felt it was my birth right. It was with apprehension that I rang the bell that Friday night at his home. He lived on the North side of Chicago in the Roger's Park District.

My step-mother Jane answered the door and hugged me. "Look at you. You're all grown up now. Come in, come in." She was all smiles and looked normal I'd be working in Chicago during the summer and Jane would be at the summer home in Bass Lake, Indiana with my little sister Katie. Father would drive down on weekends. I figured I would only have to see her two days a week at the most for the two months until the start of college. I was a lot bigger and tougher now and I was no longer afraid of her or anyone. Katie was very shy but seemed glad to see me.

We sat down together at the dinner table for a delicious home cooked meal. It was a perfect picture of one big happy normal family. If anything it was a little too normal. My father was animated and talked more than I had ever remembered. He was always a serious silent stern man of quiet demeanor. I fully expected to hear him laugh. I had never heard him laugh before. There was red wine on the table but my father drank his usual gin and soda. After dinner the three of us went into the study and Katie went to watch TV in her room.

"I take it that you've decided to let me help you?"

"Yes, thank you, sir."

"I'll restate my offer. I will pay your full tuition and room and board in the college of your choice as long as you maintain a passing grade and you are to make your own spending money. Is that agreeable?"

"Yes, sir."

"Have you decided where you want to go?"

"Chicago North Western, where you and Grandfather started."

"Excellent choice, I've got excellent connections there. Now some good news for you, Jane found you a job. It's construction work, the pay is good, and it's at Bass Lake. You can stay at the cottage free. You will be able to save all your money for school. No sense waiting. We can drive by the "Y" on our way down to the lake, pick up your things, and you start Monday. How's that for fast? I'll even get you enrolled in school."

This was way too fast for me. My head hurt. The die was cast and I was going to have to play the hand dealt me. I felt that my life was spinning out of control but I did not see a choice here. How bad could it be? I agreed. I'd have to watch my step but damn it, I deserved a chance at the good life for a change. I looked at Jane. She was smiling...

The cottage was a large two story house with a basement that opened out to the lake and about 20 feet from the shoreline. There were 2 acres of woods undeveloped, on one side that my father owned and four other lakefront homes on the other. Our home was about fifty yards from the road with a dirt driveway to the cottage. I had my own bed room on the second floor next to Katie's room. The master bedroom was at the end of a long narrow hall. Bass Lake was a rather small lake about two miles wide and three miles long. The nearest town was about two miles away.

Monday morning I started my new job. I was to work in a gravel pit on top of a iron bar grader. The crane would dump a load of stone on the grader. My job was to jump down and pull out the larger rocks and throw them into a pile to be picked up later for crushing. It was hard, dusty, & hot work but I was being paid $20 an hour which in 1953 was a decent wage. I had to constantly get out of the way when the crane spun around to release his load, and try not to pass out from the heat bouncing off the stone walls in this hell pit. I thought I would die the first week but it passed in a daze. It became a little easier.

A savings account was set up for me to deposit my pay check into for college and I was given the grand sum of $10 a week for personal spending money. I stayed out of Jane's way the best I could. The first hitch came when she insisted that I do chores for my keep. I did not argue and did all she asked. It was when I was cleaning the master bedroom that I discovered her gun in the dresser drawer that was partially left opened. It looked like the same gun that my sister had tried to kill me with four years ago. I don't know why but I took it out and unloaded it. I put the bullets under some clothes in the same drawer. I never told anyone.

I remember a strange story that my mother told me about my step mother that I never could quite believe because I never thought of my father as being a stupid man. Jane previously had been a notorious madam, she had a nervous breakdown and was committed to an asylum. She was released only to be recommitted. The third time she was committed they would not release her, but she hired my father's law firm who did manage to get her out on probation. My father met her, dated her, and left my mother. Jane was insanely jealous of my mother and wanted to hurt her by taking her children away. As I resembled my father, it became Jane's obsession to destroy me. I never knew how much if any of this story was true.

Because of probation Jane was not allowed to have a gun. The gun was in my father's name and was given to her for protection. I remember seeing her shoot a bird out of a tree with one shot. For the distance, with a small hand gun this was good shooting.

I knew something about guns from my reserve training as I had excelled in rifle competition. I had sent a letter to the Illinois National Guard requesting a discharge on the grounds that I had moved out of the state. This was one of the few legitimate reasons allowable. I didn't mention that I was planning to move back to Illinois to attend college.

My first day off I took our motor boat and headed into town. I met a few local boys about my age who were duly impressed with me being from Chicago, a Kennedy, and working what was considered a dangerous job. Like always I kept my personal business to myself but I loved the attention. The one bar in town served me without question and I felt like quite the man. It was here that I picked up on some disturbing rumors. It seems Jane was the lake whore. While men partook of her favors they were all a little afraid of her. Several times she had walked in on me when I was nude and once she let me see her completely naked. I pretended it was nothing. In truth it was more than a little disturbing.

I'm sure my father knew nothing about what was going on. When he arrived on Friday nights he was already drunk and he stayed drunk the entire weekend. Evidently his drinking never interfered with his job. He was considered one of the best attorneys in Illinois. What he ever saw in Jane I never knew. It had to be some strange sexual attraction. She was really built but I didn't find her attractive at all. She was too scary and had weird eyes. I remember five years previous when she was insanely beating me half to death and the phone rang. In an instant she changed from a raving insane person to a calm pleasant housewife. "Why, how are you? I'm so glad to hear from you." No one could tell from her voice that just seconds before she was beating a tied and gagged child with an ironing cord. What was I doing here? I must be as crazy as she is.

Sometimes life puts a little whipped cream on your shit life. Helen Rock fell into my life. Helen was from East Chicago, Indiana and was visiting her grandparents in Bass Lake for the summer. Their house was the house next to ours and I met Helen sunning herself on our shared beach. Helen was two years older than me. The previous year she was Miss Indiana and tenth runner up in the Miss America Pageant. She was the most beautiful girl I had ever seen in my life. I fell instantly, madly in love with her. She liked me and for the rest of the time we had together we were inseparable. I could tell her anything and soon she knew my entire life story, except for the one thing I never told anyone.

In my first year of high school while I was still living with my father and Jane I had a heart attack. It seemed that when I was three years old I had rheumatic fever that damaged my heart somewhat. I never knew it but there it was. Stress, fear, or the beatings I endured probably contributed to the sudden attack, but I collapsed while carrying two bags of groceries in the middle of an intersection while crossing the street. I came to in the Cook County hospital where my first thought was that Jane was going to kill me for losing the groceries.

The family doctor told me that I was going to be an invalid for the rest of my life. When I was released and returned to school I had to walk slowly, climb stairs one at a time, and no gym. I was excused from getting to classes on time and I became an object of pity. After a week of this crap I decided that I didn't want to live anymore. I didn't tell anyone. I went out alone to the deserted football field after school and started running as hard and as fast as I could. By God, I ran until I fell. I got up and ran again. I kept it up, blood flowing from my nose, until I collapsed from exhaustion and could run no more. I was crying uncontrollably. I didn't die. No big thing. Jane would probably kill me when I got home. I was over an hour late.

Jane took one look at me and said nothing. I was sent to bed without dinner. The next day I went to school. I never allowed myself to be an invalid again. If that running didn't kill me, my heart was OK. The next weekend I went to my Mothers and told her I couldn't go back to my father's house. When she finally got legal custody of me I never told her. I never told anyone. I lived my life to the fullest and never worried about a weak heart again. Maybe God wasn't through with me yet.

Helen Rock was the closest I ever had as a soul mate. I knew she felt that I was too young for her but she was kind enough never to mention it. I never tried anything with her. At the time I had two narrow views of women. Good women, on a pedestal, untouchable, Virgin like, and bad women who did any and everything sexual, dirty, and otherwise. The good women were never to be touched until they were married. In theory I had no definition for my stepmother. She was too divorced from reality. Jane was more of a monster than a woman.

One moon filled evening after Helen went home I stayed up all night walking on the beach and wrote a song for her, "I Guess Maybe, I'm in Love with You"

Nights are endless, days far too long.

Time passes slowly. I wonder what is wrong.

I guess maybe, I'm in love with you......

Everywhere I look I see your face

I try to read a book. I always lose my place.

I guess maybe, I'm in love with you.....

I take a walk ‘most every night
Each shadow reminds me of you.
The winding path, the soft starlight
Seems to whisper, I love you....

Spring is in the air. This is the season.
Music's everywhere. There must be a reason.
I guess maybe, I'm in love with you.....
I know...Baby; I'm in love with you.....

I had written some poetry in school, but this was the first song I ever wrote. I was in love like some crazy sap. No excuse, except I'm Irish. Helen thought it was sweet and like the perfect lady she was she kissed me on my cheek. I wanted to throw her down on the sand, rip her clothes off, and ravish every inch of her. My rock hard penis was almost bursting out of my bathing suit but I was a gentleman. I guess that is part of being Irish also. For many years afterwards I regretted not trying to seduce her. I never knew how she really felt or might have reacted. Damn it, being so young and inexperienced. I just didn't know what to do with nice girls. Sober I didn't have a clue. Just give me a bad girl every time and I can more than handle it, and they come back for more. But nice girls now, they're a different breed. What did I know? All was not wasted. It was a decent first song.

One weekend my father asked me if I still played chess. I was pretty good and in my third year of high school I was president of the chess club. My brother Shaun could never beat me until he got so frustrated that he got books on chess from the library, studied them faithfully, and beat me. I never won another match from him for the rest of my life. I played my father who beat me in five moves, then lost the next two games badly. He was brilliant. He took pity on me and showed me two moves known respectively as the Fool's Checkmate and the Scholar's Checkmate. I can't remember anything else in life he ever taught me.

When I entered public school I needed a letter from my parents for permission to play football. My father would not sign as he claimed he had spent too much money on my teeth to risk having them knocked out. In his college years he was a pole vaulter and I heard he was very good at it. Summer vacations he worked as a head lifeguard at Chicago Lake Michigan beaches. Johnny Weissmuller of Tarzan fame and Olympic Gold Medal fame worked as a lifeguard under him. My father never was a lifeguard himself but with his father's connections he was the boss. He met my mother in his final year of college and was quite smitten by her. She was a girl acceptable to the family, a promising new lawyer needed a proper wife by his side, and of course she was Irish.

With all the advantages of wealth, position, influence, and power my father had it made. He had a degree from Great North Western, Loyola, Notre Dame, and De Paul University. He interned at one of Chicago's most prestigious law firms, was soon made an associate member, and finally a full partner in a short period of time. He wanted for nothing and he was well on his way to becoming a Judge. During the Second World War he served on the draft board, avoiding being called into the service himself. He did not want or like children and was adamant about not having any. His work was his entire life. He was cheap in the small things but wore expensive tailored business suits and handmade shirts. He would not buy a drink in a bar as he felt the markup was too high. He bought gin by the case, made his own soda water, and drank at home. Like many Irish men he was a hard drinker with a dark moody soul. He drank far too much but he never let it affect his work. He was a man always in tight control.

I remember being in his office one time when his partner Frank came in. “Excuse me, Joe. I’m billing Jones & Hampton and I remembered you helped me.”

“Hell, all I did was look up something in a law book. It took three minutes at the most.”

$75?”

“That’s about right.” Wow, was I impressed. $75 for 3 minutes work. My dad explained it to me.

“It’s not the actual time. It’s the knowledge of knowing where to look.” I think I learned an important message there. But it didn’t seem to be something I could use at the time. I filed it away in my brain for future consideration.

The first week after I graduated high school and moved to the lake my father had his serious talk with me. “I know you are going to be drinking and that is OK. Here is the liquor cabinet and here is where I keep the key. You can help yourself anytime you want. I don’t want you drinking away from home and I never want to see you drunk. That being said I want you to know that we trust you are old enough to exercise good judgment." Jane and he drove to town for the weekly shopping. When they got back I was passed out drunk under the dining room table with a bottle of gin in my hand. So much for my excellent judgment...

I heard my father laugh once in my life. It was at the lake and I was upstairs sleeping when I heard a loud bang followed by insane laughing. I went downstairs to find my father in his shorts sitting at the breakfast table drunk as only the Irish can get. He would pound this gin bottle on the table and laugh, again and again. Each time he hit the table he would start another uncontrollable spell of laughing. It was weird but he seemed to be having the time of his life. I never knew what he found so funny and he never spoke of it. I wish I knew. It was the only time I saw him happy. He quit laughing after two hours and passed out. Now it was his snoring that kept me from sleeping. It sounded like a man dying.

I took Katie and Helen out for a ride in the motor boat. Katie was now seven years old and she worshiped me. I was her big brother again and probably her only friend. Against the rules I let Katie drive. We must have hit something because the motor fell off in about ten feet of water. I immediately anchored the boat, calmed my hysterical sister, and dived down to locate the outboard motor. It took quite a while but I found it. I rowed the boat closer and dived for it. I managed to get it to the surface but without leverage I could not get it into the boat. Helen attempted to help me get it in the boat but it was too heavy and awkward for her. When she tried to help me the boat listed to one side and started taking on water. This was an impossible task. I refused to give up.

I tried again and again. By the time I got the motor to the surface I was out of breath. I tried to rest a little by holding on to the side of the boat with one hand and lift the motor with the other. Time and time again it slipped out of my grasp and sank to the bottom. It was hopeless. I was turning pale as I became exhausted. Katie was crying and Helen was afraid I was going to kill myself. But I wasn't going to quit. I had to get that motor back. Every so often I would pull myself into the boat to get a little rest. The last time I almost didn't make it. It was starting to get dark and it became harder to see underwater. Suddenly I had an idea. I dove down and dragged the anchor over to the sunken motor, tied the rope around the motor, got back in the boat, and hauled it up. It worked! The engine wouldn't start and I had to row back but I saved the engine. We got yelled at but I explained the engine quit and I had to row back. The truth never came out. Helen claimed that I was the most stubborn person she had ever met in her life. I could tell she admired me for it.

My savings account was really growing fast. It was in my father's name so I could not get to it. The job was hard but it wouldn't last forever. Bernie Small was the dynamite man. About three times a shift we would pause working while Bernie set a charge. This Charge would blow down part of the quarry wall for the crane to dump on my grader. During these down times I became friendly with Bernie and he would show me the how to set and handle the explosives. If anything happened to Bernie I wanted to take over his job. He got paid $50 an hour. Besides you never knew when knowing how to use dynamite could come in handy. I might want to rob a bank some day or something.

It was late Friday afternoon when I caught something out of the corner of my eye. The crane instead of swinging to the left after dumping a load had swung to the right. When the crane operator realized his error he swung back over my grader to the left. With quick reflexes I managed to jump out of the way just in time. I would have been killed instantly if he had knocked me off the grader. Climbing down angry I jumped on the crane and flung open the door. I could smell the liquor. The son of a bitch was drunk. I was so mad I could have killed him with my bare hands. They pulled me off him and I was sent home for the rest of the day with pay. The crane operator wasn't fired. He was all they had. Monday morning we met with the big boss, shook hands, and went back to work. He apologized. I later wondered if he was one of the men who were having sex with my stepmother. Excuse me all to hell. I wasn't paranoid. Someone was trying to kill me again. It only seemed to happen when Jane was around.

I had pushed my previous life with my step mother out of my mind. I didn't trust her and I watched her like a hawk. I tried to do nothing that would upset her and did every unreasonable thing she asked. As to her running around on my father, I felt it was none of my business, and the less I knew the better. I was fixated on my goal of saving as much money as I could and going to college in the fall. I knew the value of a good education and the difficulty of obtaining it alone. I was old enough to know that people were not perfect, and smart enough not to give a damn, but the near accident at the quarry brought back a lot of repressed memories.

Before Jane taught with my little sister to aim and shoot a gun, there were hints of madness. One of her rules was that we always had to eat everything on our plates. As she was always gathering wild mushrooms in our forest, she would tell me that I would never know if she accidentally fed me the poisoned kind. She always laughed like it was a big joke but it wasn't funny to me and my brother. Her laugh was strange and she had a weird way of looking at us.

Shaun and I came to live with my father and Jane several years after their marriage. Shaun was very high spirited, hard headed, and would not obey anyone other than our mother. Jane could do nothing with him. You could kill Shaun before he would cry one tear. He was the toughest child I ever knew. Secretly I was proud of him. Unable to control him she had my father put him in a private school that was on a farm in down state Illinois. It was named the Rolling Hills School for Boys. I didn't see my little brother for several months. He finally came home on vacation. It was "Yes, Sir, No, Sir, Thank you, Mama' and if you should scratch your head, he would jump a foot. He wouldn't look anyone directly in the eye. His spirit was completely broken. Wow! Wasn't this great. It was just the perfect place for both of us.

Off we went to where I was condemned to spend the last five years of grade school in what I can only describe as a combination orphanage/ reformatory with the worst traits of both. Rolling Hills School for boys was a working farm located about a mile down a dirt road from the small town of Gilberts, Illinois. It was far enough away from anyone to hear the terrified screams of the 30 or so children who were the helpless victims of the sadistic headmaster. When he hit Shaun in the back with an iron frying pan and kicked him down a flight of stairs, I swore that someday I would return and kill the son of a bitch. His name was Big Tom Klempler who sweated too much to be normal.

All of us children had certain things in common; we were all from rich families, unwanted, and had no one to turn to except each other. It was a large farm with two dormitories for the students. Only the main house had running water and inside toilets. A handy man came in five days a week but it was mostly the children who ran the farm and did all the chores. Shaun's job was taking care of the chickens, while I taught the younger children. We all took turns at kitchen and laundry duty and during harvest time we often worked 14 hour days. An outside teacher came in one day a week to teach us English.

We were all throw away kids and our parents or legal guardians paid $7 a week to keep the lid on. The rules were strict, equally enforced, and misconduct equally punished. It was the first time for many of us to have a structured life and we learned. By God, we learned or we were not fed. We were made to write one letter home a week which was always censored and woe to anyone who dared complain about anything. We were only allowed two visits a month for two hours on the second and fourth Sundays. Jane and my father never came once during the five years I was there. My mother and Rod made it about one out of five times. Many children had no visitors ever. On our rare vacations we spent half our time with our mother and the rest with our father. Some children had nowhere to go and never got a vacation except from school work.

I survived and somehow got a good education. I escaped my troubled life by reading anything I could get my hands on. Lucky for us, the school had a lot of donated books. I don't know the scam he was running but somehow we were always getting donations from strangers. It was here that I developed my first goal in life. Just to grow big enough so people would quit beating on me. The dark feeling of being totally helpless lasted years. I could never understand why it was that the people who were supposed to love you could hurt you so much. Neglect, not caring, often hurt as much as the physical beatings. I had no way of knowing it at the time but some serious damage was being done to my emotional makeup. Was I being rewired into some kind of monster?

The few times we ever saw girls was when we weren't snowed in during the winter and rode into the church in Dundee, Illinois. The girls sat on one side and we were required to sit on the other. We never had the chance to talk to one another. Big Tom was too cheap to supply toilet paper in the out houses and we had to use pages from a Sears & Roebuck catalog to wipe our pink behinds. Woe to the poor soul who had a brown stain on his underwear at the weekly laundry inspections. Pages of women in the underwear section was carefully preserved and passed around to all. My absolute best thrill was looking at the bare breasted natives in the occasional National Geographic magazine. That about summed up my sex life at the time.

Chapter 4

Big Tom lived with his wife and plain looking daughter of about 16 who was much too fine to associate with us animals. She had a habit of leaving her drapes open at night and undressing slowly in the light, to the delight of us older boys who watched in the dark from a hill side level with her window. Bless her dark little soul. She was the first naked girl I saw and she actually had what looked like a little hair between her legs. We had to be very careful. All the dormitories were wired with two way speakers. One never knew when Big Tom was listening or would call for an answer. We had our little ways with prearranged signals if he called unexpectedly. We may have been prisoners but we weren't stupid.

Classes were held in a small one room school building with a wood burning stove at the front of the room. Big Tom presided as our teacher four days a week from a huge desk behind us. He had a small hard rubber ball that he would throw with shot gun accuracy and hit the back of the head of any boy caught misbehaving. He never missed once in the years I was there. All the grades were taught in the same room which was especially hard on the younger grades who did not understand what was going on. Math and English were pretty much all we were taught. If we didn't learn we didn't eat.

The food was good and healthful but not very large portions. We were mostly always hungry and it really hurt to miss a meal. Being on a working farm there were ways of getting extra food from the crops or the fruit trees. We older boys managed to steal from the store room once in a while and we had a stash of food supplies hidden in the barn that Big Tom never found. We were tough. We could survive almost everything but the beatings were the worst. Big Tom had a wood paddle with holes in it he used on our backsides. He had a small horse whip he used when he was really mad. What I hated most was when he forced us older boys to punish the younger ones and sometimes we had to fight one another. I kept it to myself but I knew that someday I was going to come back and make this bastard pay for what he did to us.

Helen, bless her, kept me focused on my college goal. I had one week left to go before my enrollment and the summer vacation was over. I was feeling sad about Helen as I felt I might not be seeing her again. One afternoon after work we walked to town and went into the only bar where I was going to have a cold beer. Jane was in there drunk sitting with a man at the bar. He had his hand up her short tight dress. She saw us and a look of pure hatred clouded her face. She screamed at me. “I told you to stay home and watch the baby.” My sister was 7 years old.

“I’m sorry. I forgot. I’ll go check on her now.” I grabbed Helen’s hand and we left. When I got home Helen came inside and we talked. “I don’t know how much more of this I can take.”

“Joe. You got what, six more days? You can tough it out. She’s been drunk before. She’ll probably not come home and when she does she’ll sleep it off. She probably won’t even remember.”

I calmed down and we talked for what seemed like hours. Jane came home. She didn't say a word. She just glared at me. Her face was pure evil. "I'm going to walk Helen home. I'll be right back." Jane didn't say a word. I walked Helen next door, pulled her close to me, and kissed her. I walked back to the house to find the screen door locked. Jane was lying on the floor. Katie was screaming. I thought Jane was having an attack. I tried to force the door open. Jane got up, ran to the door, and ripped it open. From behind her back she pulled out her gun and stuck it in my face'

"I'm going to kill you, you, Son of a Bitch." She pulled the trigger. Nothing happened. The gun was empty. She was totally confused. She kept pulling the trigger and jabbing the gun at me. She reached in her pocket and pulled out some bullets. She was shaking as she tried to reload the gun.

I backed away slowly, keeping me arms at my side in a non threatening way, and slowly backed down the three wooden steps keeping my eyes on her face. I was paralyzed with fear. She got the gun loaded. I turned my back on her still walking real slowly. I kept thinking that no one would ever shoot someone in the back. Out of the corner of my eye I saw she was holding the gun with both hands, trying to sight in on my head. She was trembling. I kept repeating to myself. "Don't shoot....don't shoot."

The gun fired. The bullet whistled past my right ear. I fell to the ground as my legs gave out. I forced myself to roll in the dirt road. She fired two more shots at me but missed. I managed somehow to get up and started running. She fired two more shots into the air while laughing like a crazy person. I ran into the woods and ducked into some undergrowth. I started shaking uncontrollably. I tried to hold my breath but I burst out in large gasps. My heart sounded like a bass drum. I felt that she could hear me and would kill me.

She trashed around for a while calling for me to come out. She screamed that she would find me. It was getting dark and then it was quiet. I felt that she was hiding somewhere waiting for me to move. After a while I got up slowly and took a few steps and quickly hid behind some bushes. It seemed a long time before I got up the nerve to put some distance behind me and the house. I couldn't think. I did not want to endanger Helen by trying to see her. I only had a few bucks and some change with me. I decided to go see my friend Bernie Small from work. I had to talk with someone normal. This was too unreal. Thank God, Bernie was home.

Bernie gave me some whiskey that helped to calm me. We talked for a while and on his advice I called my father. He said Jane was going through a change of life and was apt to act a little strange at times. She was probably firing blanks at me as some sort of joke. He asked me if I had enough money to take the train to Chicago where he would pick me up. We would drive down the next weekend and get everything squared away. Don't worry about the job as the boss was a good friend of theirs and he would take care of it. Above all don't say anything to anyone and just get home as fast as I could.

Bernie drove me to the station and gave me enough money for the fare. I took the train back to Chicago. My father met me and took me back to the apartment. He claimed Jane hadn't phoned him and that he hadn't talked with her. He said that he had no complaints from her about me and that she was glad for the company. I didn't tell him about her running around with men. I didn't say much of anything. It was Wednesday night and we were to drive down to the lake Friday night. I wasn't looking forward to it.

Dad and I had an uneasy truce for the next two days with neither one of us saying much of anything. I decided to myself that I would be happy to settle for my money and my clothes. I would consider myself lucky if I never saw her again. I had always thought of my father as being an intelligent man. Now I had lost all respect for him. Anyone who would give up a beautiful person as my mother for this psycho bitch had to be as nuts as she was. For a moment I almost felt sorry for him. Friday afternoon he called me from his law office.

"I've been discussing the matter with my partner Frank and he thinks it best that I go down alone first. I want to be sure everything is all right and I'm sure it is. You can take the train down tomorrow. I'll call you tonight. Don't worry. It will be fine. We'll get you off to college next week and this will all be forgotten. Stay close by the phone for my call. Is that all right?"

I was tempted to say no but I agreed to his terms. I had totally lost control of my life. I waited for his call. It didn't come until 3:30 AM. He was completely drunk.

"You are no longer welcome in my house. Get out now." He hung up. That was it. I checked my resources. All I had was a little change, less than two dollars, and the clothes on my back. I searched the apartment. I couldn't find a penny. Katie had a partly filled piggy bank in her bedroom but I didn't have the heart to take my sister's money. My first thought was to burn the place to the ground but what was the use. My father didn't want me. What else was new? Well I didn't need him either, his loss. I'd make it somehow. I didn't have a plan except to get out of there quickly before he had me arrested or something. I left. It was raining and I didn't have a jacket. That's all I needed...pneumonia.

Back before my fight with Rod D'Angelo, my stepfather, when I was still living at home I would sometimes go downtown and work day labor at a place called Manpower's. I needed the money, exercise, and I was interested in learning how a man ended up on skid row. I had dreams of being a writer someday. It was hard physical work and paid a dollar an hour. You picked up your pay at the end of the day in a bar next door. If you cashed your check in the bar you would get a free 15 cent glass of cold beer. I heard many hard luck stories from the winos that were still well enough to work. The one thing that they all had in common was that somewhere along the line they gave up on themselves and life. They drank to ease the pain of reality.

Mike, not his real name, after a hard day's work at the office, came home to find his wife of 27 years gone. There was no note. All the furniture, rugs, window coverings, her clothes, everything was gone. Their bank and stock account were closed, the money gone. There was no argument, no harsh words, not a hint of anything being wrong. Mike didn't know if she had a boyfriend or was unhappy about anything. He was a medical doctor that worked hard and long hours. He started drinking and ended up on skid row, a hopeless drunk.

Mike wasn't bitter, just empty inside. He was a good worker for an old man but all he lived for was to get the small check and buy a bottle. They took out withholding and the checks were small for the jobs we did. By closing the office and making us pick up our checks at the bar, many men didn't make it out of there after the free beer. I finally quit going there. It was too heart breaking. I can see where a man might give up. I was almost there myself.

It was a long ride across Chicago from the North Side to the South Side where I had gone to school. I looked up my friend Karl Rheinhardt. He was home and I borrowed $100. I bought a suit, belt, one shirt, tie, pair of shoes & socks and got a haircut. I went downtown Chicago to a private employment agency and was hired the same day. I was to start the next day as an insurance underwriter trainee for the Inter- Insurance Exchange of the Chicago Motor Club. The employment fee was paid for by the company. Now all I had to do was to find a place to stay, keep clean, and eat, before my first paycheck. A lot easier said than done.

I moved back into the YMCA, lived on White Castle hamburgers, and the occasional dinner at my various friends house. I washed my one white shirt in the bathroom sink every night and pressed my pants by putting them under my mattress at night and sleeping on them. The office was closed Saturdays so I worked day labor back on skid row to get a few dollars. Finally I got my first paycheck and opened a bank account. I bought some more clothes and life was easier. I decided to see my father about the money I had earned during the summer working construction in the quarry. I did not call him first. I just dropped in his office during my lunch hour.

He was busy but I waited. Finally I was let into his law office. It was obvious that he didn't want to see me. I kept it short. I told him I was working but I needed the money from my savings account. He mumbled something about room and board, took out his check book, and wrote me a check. Nothing was said about Jane or what she had told him. He looked haggard and beaten and wouldn't look me in the eye. I got out of there fast. I looked at the check. It was for a hundred dollars. My rich cheap big shot lawyer robbed me, his son. Screw him. I paid off Karl. Now I didn't owe anyone anything.

My job was going along great and everyone seemed to like me. It was a long trip to and from work every day on overcrowded public transportation but I was getting paid a decent salary. Harry Cohen who also lived at the YMCA had gone to school with me. We were pretty good friends and decided to rent an apartment together. Harry was a rather small Jewish kid who had a club foot which left him with a slight limp. He worked in a local department store selling men's wear. He was an intelligent quiet lad who made it his business to blend in and never cause any trouble. My friend Karl instantly hated Harry, probably because he was a Jew. I didn't care. Karl was wearing as a friend. He seemed to hate everything.

A month had passed and I decided to try and find Helen Rock. I knew she lived in East Chicago, Indiana, but I didn't have an address. I got the phone directory from the library and called all the people with the last name of Rock. "Hello, my name is Joe Kennedy. I'm a friend of Helen Rock who I met at Bass Lake and I lost her phone number. I'm trying to locate her. Do you know her or where I might find her?" Bingo! The 14th call did the trick. Helen got on line and she agreed to meet me the coming weekend. That Saturday I took a train to East Chicago. One look at Helen and I knew this was the girl I wanted to spend the rest of my life with. She was that beautiful.

Helen, of course, did not know what had happened to me. I met her parents. They were very nice people but I was surprised that they were so plain looking for having such a beautiful daughter. Helen and I talked late into the evening catching up. I caught the last train back with the promise of a beach party date for the following Saturday night. I was ecstatic. Helen didn't mention that she had any boyfriends and she asked me out where I would meet her friends. She was a few years older than me but it didn't seem to make a difference. I was mature for my age. I had a good job with a future. It was a long trip back but I was floating on air.

I hadn't had sex since the previous June when I went to the house in Black Oaks. I never had sex with a nice girl or when I was sober. I was still extremely shy around women unless I was high. Harry had introduced me to a girl who worked at the Department Store. She was willing to have sex with me but I would have to use a condom. I had never used one before, didn't know how, afraid to admit it, and too embarrassed to buy one. I had her naked several times in the apartment on the couch but no matter how hard I tried she wouldn't put out without protection. She soon became frustrated with me, gave up trying, and stopped coming over. When Harry asked me what happened, I told him. It was then that he told me that he always kept condoms in the bathroom and I could help myself. I was too tough to cry.

There was a short busty girl named Ann that worked in the office with me. She took it upon herself to introduce me around and always included me in business related functions. She seemed to like me well enough and I was interested but afraid to mess around with women where I worked. Then Jackie exploded into my life. Hired as the personal assistant to the CEO and part time office receptionist she made Helen Rock look like a little girl. She was tall, dark, slim with the biggest breasts I've ever seen on a woman. She wore tight sweaters that clung to her fabulous chest like the fuzz on a ripe luscious peach. She had the most beautiful deep brown eyes I ever saw in a perfect face. Every man who saw her lusted for her. She wasn't a flirt and was a quiet warm person. Everyone liked her including the office women. I suspect most wives didn't. I seemed to be in perpetual heat. I could hardly wait until the date with Helen. I promised myself that I would make my move.

It was a memorable beach party. It was celebrating the end of summer. It was mostly an older crowd. I was probably the youngest one there but I was with Helen and that made me a somebody. Helen wore a bikini bathing suit. Beautiful as she was for the first time I didn't see her as a Goddess. After meeting Jackie, I realized that Helen was just a woman. like every other woman. There was a roaring fire, beer, and plenty of good food. As it got darker, most put on sweat shirts, and wrapped up in blankets. Helen and I lay together under a blanket and kissed. We started some heavy petting. I rolled over on her getting more excited by the minute. Several times I tried to pull her bottom down but she stopped me every time. I started rubbing against her with my rock hard erection. Helen was moving with me like a cat in heat when suddenly I exploded. Four months of hot pent up cum exploded in my bathing suit. At the same time a terrible foul odor came from my armpits. Helen was holding me tightly and still grinding against me. I forced myself up and ran to the outhouse to try to clean myself up. Try as I might I couldn't get rid of the terrible odor. I was ashamed to go back but I did. I couldn't wait to get out of there and away from Helen. I would probably never be able to have sex again. Correction, I would probably never have almost sex again.

That foul odor bothered and scared me at the same time. What the hell was it? It had never happened before. I kept dreaming about Helen. I vividly remembered her grinding against me and how close I came to getting her pants down. I had to try again. I called her. She claimed that she wasn't feeling well and was going to stay home for the weekend. I didn't believe her. It was the big kiss off. I remembered how at the beach party her friends were so surprised that she was with me. There were hints of a boyfriend but I was so focused on Helen I let it slide over me. Now, bits and pieces came back. She had a fight with her boyfriend and was probably using me to make him jealous. I was starting to get mad. I'd kill the son of a bitch. I'd kill both of them. I borrowed a gun from Percy. I was one bad ass and now I had a gun. I could do some really damage. That son of a bitch would never touch my Helen again. Joe Chicago has spoken. Joe Chicago was born that night.

My friend Harry sensed that something was wrong and got the story out of me. He tried to talk me out of it but I would not listen. I told him I was taking the gun just to scare the boyfriend. He didn't believe me, of course, and insisted on coming with me to East Chicago. He kept talking to me on the long train trip. He made sense and I was starting to feel a little foolish but I felt at least I deserved to know the truth. I wouldn't give him the gun. We arrived at Helen's house and I hid in some bushes across the street. I really didn't know what I was going to do. Harry kept trying to talk me into forgetting it and go home. Night fell and it got dark and cold. About ten o'clock I decided to call it off but before we left I wanted to leave her a note, just to let her know I had been there. I rang the doorbell and Helen came to the door. She had been home all evening. I introduced her to Harry and she invited us in for some coffee.

When I sat down on the coach I flinched. I forgot putting the gun in my back pocket. Helen noticed and asked what I had. I wouldn't tell her. She put her arms around me and grabbed at my pocket and found the gun. She became angry. She started yelling at me and calling me all sorts of names. Harry was trying to pull me out of there before her father came downstairs and called the police. Finally I had sense enough to leave. We caught the train back to Chicago. Harry had no more advice for me except to give the gun back that night if possible. Give Helen time to calm down and make up some sort of story. Get a girl friend closer to home. It didn't have to be the prettiest girl in the whole damn state. Forget this Joe Chicago shit. No matter how tough you are there is always someone tougher.

I tried to call Helen a couple of times but she never came to the phone. I wrote her a letter and lied. I told her it wasn't my gun, it didn't have any bullets in it, and I was just trying to help a guy out. I loved her and I always would. She never answered. It was almost October by now and I started concentrating on my job. I began writing to Susan Mae in Nashville. Harry was right. Your girlfriend didn't have to be the prettiest girl in town. If you marry an ugly girl at least no one will try to take her away from you. I thought about asking Ann at the office out but it still felt like a bad idea. I would give my right arm for a night with Jackie but she was totally out of my league. I could always go to a whore house but it wasn't fun anymore. It had become somewhat degrading and a little too desperate. My problem was more than shyness, I just didn't understand women, and I was a little bit afraid of them. Somehow I knew I couldn't do without sex. I enjoyed it too much. Who was I kidding? I was still a virgin in my own mind. I wish I could find a woman that would show me what it is all about, even an ugly woman. Be careful what you wish for.

I was doing great at work. I was given more responsibility and the work seemed easier as I learned what I was doing. Co workers came to me for advice and I gained a measure of respect. I got a raise. What I especially liked and appreciated was that this was a company that really worked to protect their members. The Motor Club enjoyed an excellent reputation and it was a great place to work. These people really cared about doing things right. Ann especially seemed proud of me. I was gaining a confidence that I never had before in my life. I felt like I belonged and was making a difference. I even managed to save a little money ahead. I spent too much on my clothes but I always wanted to look good. I may have drank a little too much on my weekends off but I was young and I could handle it. It never interfered on the job.

A new major reform to our auto insurance policy was being considered. I was one of the underwriting people to be invited to a business lunch to discuss and analyze the proposal. I had carefully read the changes and thought I noticed a flaw in the coverage. As all the big shots were there, I kept quiet and listened. After three martinis I had to speak. I rose to my feet and was brilliant. I was completely correct. I caught something that the Legal Department had missed. It left us open to liability and I saved the day. I was a hero and made my boss proud. Even the beautiful Jackie looked at me with new found respect. I became the young man that was going places. The Sales Department wanted to lure me away from Underwriting. I had it made in the shade.

It was close to Christmas and we all drew one name to buy a gift for the office party. I drew Jackie's name. The limit was $10 but I bought her a custom jeweled pin shaped like an arrow to wear on her fabulous sweaters. It was obviously expensive and it embarrassed her. She thanked me sweetly and pinned it on. She wore it almost every day. Ann had drawn my name and had bought me two Scotch plaid ties like I favored. I was really touched. She blushed when I thanked her. I loved those ties.

I was the fair haired boy. It went to my head. I started thinking about going to college again. I felt that there would be no stopping me once I got a degree. To hell with my father and his family, I would make it on my own. Look how far I've come starting with nothing. I was feeling pretty good about myself. Without telling anyone I applied at Teachers Normal College in Chicago. It was tuition free and close to my friends. I planned on going there for two years and then on to a big college like Notre Dame. I had to tell them I wanted to be a teacher which really wasn't a bad career choice for me as I liked children. I gave notice at work.

To my surprise, everyone was happy for me. They threw a big party for me, gave me presents, and wished me luck. They made me promise to keep in touch and come back to work for them. There would always be a place for me. Some of the girls had misty eyes. I felt on top of the world. I said my farewells and left. Then disaster! Even though college was tuition free, they wanted money for all sort of things, and they wanted it now. I just had not saved enough. I didn't have it. I had to pass. I was too embarrassed to tell them at the Motor Club. I did not have a fall back plan. I couldn't believe my bad luck. I decided to join the Army. I was 17 and might be drafted at anytime soon. I thought myself smart enough to get into officers school. I would make a career out of the service and retire in 20 years. If there is another war they will probably blow up the whole world, me included. It was 1954.

My buddies threw a big all night party for me and I drank way too much. I was still drunk when I reported for the draft board physical. It seemed to take forever as we stood naked in one line after another to be examined by what seemed to be a hundred different doctors. About 11AM the liquor seemed to wear off and I had the mother of all hangovers. I didn't have any sleep the previous night. I was tired, miserable, and cold when it came to an end. There were four recruitment tables for each of the services at the end of the examination room.

There was a rumor that if you joined the Navy, you would do your basic training in California. It was the closest table. I staggered over and with my last once of strength I enlisted for 6 years in the US Navy. Now the bad news, they weren't drafting into the Navy then and there was a waiting period. I was expecting to leave that day. Go home and they would notify me in about six weeks. The way I felt, I would probably be dead in two weeks. At least my luck was consistent, all bad and worse. I didn't have enough money for six weeks. I would have to find a job.

Chapter 5

Sherwin-Williams paint factory hired me. My job was to hand truck drums of paint as they came off the assembly line to the railway cars to be loaded for shipment. It was hard heavy physical work requiring no brains but it paid well. I took a room at the YMCA which was close to work. My former roommate, Harry Cohen, had given up our apartment, disappeared, and ran off with Karl Rheinhardt's little sister Helga. Karl swore he would track them down and kill the Jewish crippled son of a bitch. I received a letter from Harry forwarded to me that gave me his new address in Oklahoma City. He and Helga eloped, and were expecting a baby. I never told Karl. He was a friend but I did not like him much anymore. I made excuses not to see him.

I basically kept to myself, worked 12 hour shifts, and drank too much. I met women in bars but I couldn't take them to my room at the YMCA. I was uncomfortable going to their place and too cheap to rent a hotel room. I did without sex and felt it was good practice for when I was called to do my six weeks basic training. I had just turned 17 that summer but I felt like an adult. I was determined to be an officer. For once in my life I was confident that I was going to succeed at something. Hell, I just might end up a God damn hero. Nothing could stop me now.

I was given three days notice to report for basic training at the Great Lakes training station. I quit my job and reported for duty. On April 2nd, 1954, I was sworn in and to my surprise, I had to take another physical. I had passed the draft board physical but the US Navy was more thorough. It seemed they wanted their men to do more than fog a mirror. I felt that I was in the best physical shape of my life. I even showed up without a hangover, a good night's sleep, and a huge breakfast of steak and eggs. They caught a slight heart murmur, curvature of the spine, and 2nd degree flat feet. I was assigned to the induction center until it could be arranged for me to appear before the Physical Evaluation Board. Because of my previous military training I was made Acting Chief Petty Officer in charge of processing men thru the induction center.

After a couple of days my boss and superior officer had enough confidence in me so that he would check in, leave me in complete charge, and disappear for the day. For almost two months I was in total charge of processing several hundred young men before they were assigned to basic training units. This involved testing, taking indoctrination classes, physical training, and discipline for the recruits. I had to take these shaved head civilian monkeys and ready them for Navy life. Once my hair grew out a little, I acquired confidence, wore a tailored uniform, and had my ACPO insignia sewed on my sleeves, you couldn't tell me from regular Navy. When I yelled "Jump" the men moved. I was King Shit and I loved it. I'd be happy to have stayed there the rest of my life.

Once I acquired the "look" I was able to move freely around the base. No one questioned me. I took to going to the base Petty Officers Club. Back then all they served was beer. There were two women bartenders and I was dating one of them. There were very few places where we could be alone but I had my share of grass stains on my dress whites. I didn't have private quarters so over night sex was not an option. I started eating at the regular navy mess hall where the food was better than in the processing section. Suddenly I was ordered to join the next basic training company. My boss promised to put in the word so I would be made a company commander. Just my luck, the powers in charge had a relative that was made company commander. I went from ACPO to seaman recruit in less than three minutes. To make matters worse the appointed acting CO was a Southern boy who hated Yankees and especially my arrogant Chicago attitude.

I made the mistake of raising my hand when they asked if anyone played a musical instrument. I was assigned to play the tuba for the base Navy Band. I not only hated the tuba but I wasn't a very good musician. It got me out of some guard duty assignments but I still had to complete all of my six week basic training. It was during exercise training that I came to heads with my Rebel CO. The curvature in my spine made it physically impossible for me to touch my toes. The CO thought I was malingering and had two of his ape men try to force me to bend. It didn't happen. I had sense enough not to slug the son of a bitch but evidently the look in my eyes scared him. The next morning I didn't get out of bed. They tried to force me but I stood fast. I stayed in bed for about two hours when the Shore Patrol came and took me away. It was time for the Physical Evaluation Board.

Not obeying a direct order is a serious infraction that you don't want on your personal record. I was hoping for a chance to explain or I could kiss Officer's School goodbye. No one questioned me or seemed concerned. Two days later I appeared at the PE Board. Standing before the board of regular Navy officers, they read my medical report out loud. The head officer spoke "We have decided that in combat that your defective heart might fail when other men are depending on you. Do you have anything to add Seaman Recruit Joseph John Kennedy the Third?"

"No, Sir, except in the heat of combat I might get shot too."

"The Navy wants only the best odds. You will be informed of our decision. You are dismissed."

My discharge was rushed through before I had 90 days active service which would have entitled me to benefits. On June 18, 1954, with exactly 2 months, 18 days, of Navy service I was given a General Discharge under Honorable Conditions for medical reasons. It took all of two days to release me. As I had mailed all my civilian clothes to my mother when I enlisted, they stripped me of all my military clothing including my tailored dress uniforms, and gave me the ugliest civilian clothes I ever saw. Combat boots, purple pants, yellow long sleeved dress shirt, flowered tie, sick green sports coat, and a black broad brim hat with a purple feather. I looked like a poor man's pimp. I was made to wear the outfit until I left the base. I immediately threw the hat, ugly tie, and sports jacket in the nearest public trash can and caught a bus to down town where I was going to buy the biggest steak dinner to be had. I was a civilian again with a difference. Now I would not be drafted. I could get on with my life. Screw the Navy. It was their loss.

I got off the bus in downtown Chicago and went into the finest restaurant I could find. I looked like an A-1 Jerk with my combat boots and purple slacks. The waiters wore tuxedoes and white gloves. I had about $400 dollars in cash and a $100 mustering out Government check. For a moment I thought that they were not going to let me in but they did. I ordered a double gin martini on the rocks and I was handed the menu. I wanted the biggest steak they had but I was not familiar with the various cuts. I ordered the most expensive steak on the list hoping it would be the largest. The wine steward brought me the wine menu. Not knowing a thing about wines, I just pointed out one. Well, the steak was fillet Mignon, thick but small, and the wine was terrible. I picked out a nice desert from the cart and it was the best part of my lunch. For the money it cost me, it was close to being the most disappointing meal I ever had. I tried not to show it and left a large tip and got the hell out of there. I caught a bus to my mother's house on the South side. The last she had heard from me was that I was in the Navy.

I arrived at my mother's house to find my step-dad Rod there alone. He seemed genuinely happy to see me. Mom was out visiting someone. Rod insisted I go out with him for some ribs. I was still full from my steak dinner. I didn't want to hurt his feelings, so I went with him. While I tried to force ribs down with cold beer we talked. He asked me what my plans were. I told him I was going down to Nashville, Tennessee to see my girlfriend Susan Mae. I stopped writing her when I joined the Navy but now I was ready to settle down. Hell, I might even get married and have some kids. Susan Mae would make the perfect wife and mother. She was almost 16 and I was going to be 18 in July. Rod didn't think much of the idea. I didn't tell him about the money I still had left and I had two hundred dollars mustering out pay coming.

I spent the night at home. The next morning Rod drove me to the station and I took the train to Nashville. I checked into the YMCA and phoned Susan Mae. She did not seem to happy to hear from me but she invited me over for dinner with her family. After dinner we went out on the front porch where she told me the truth. When I joined the Navy and she didn't hear from me, she thought that I didn't care for her anymore. She had moved on with her life and had a new boyfriend Randy Joe Baker and well, they were practically engaged. I tried every trick in the book to change her mind. I could sense that she still loved me but out of loyalty to this Randy jerk, she would not let me kiss her. This only made her more desirable. I was from Chicago. I could beat any country boy's line any day of the week. I was a man. I've been around. How could any woman resist me? I agreed to meet with this Randy if she could arrange it and I went back to the YMCA with a good feeling.

Randy Joe phoned me and I had him meet me at a club. They didn't have bars back then. They were all private bottle clubs. You paid a buck or two to be a guest member and brought your own bottle. You paid for the ice and the mix and they kept your bottle behind the bar. I was drinking Jack Daniels and soda when Randy Joe came in. What a wimp! I couldn't believe it. He was a small little boy compared to me. He didn't even drink. He's nobody's competition. What in the hell did Susan see in this guy. It was beyond me. Within three minutes after sitting down tears were flowing from his eyes.

He told me that he was in the Tennessee National Guard and he was leaving the next day for two weeks training exercise. He loved Susan Mae and was afraid that I was going to steal her away from him. I actually felt sorry for this jerk. I told him that before I joined the Navy that I too was in the Guard. As a fellow comrade in arms, so to speak, I promised him that I wouldn't see or speak with Susan until he returned. Then she could decide. I thought he was going to kiss my hand he was so grateful. He left and I got drunk.

True to my word I did not see or call Susan. In retrospect it was probably the most stupid thing I ever did. The next two weeks I spent getting drunk, playing big shot, and spending my money. It was on a Tuesday morning, suffering the hangover from hell, that one of my drinking buddies brought me the news. Randy Joe returning from his two weeks training eloped with Susan. They were married. This was the last straw. Everything I ever wanted in life turned to shit. The people who were suppose to love me tried to kill me and have me locked up. I was tired of fighting, my money was almost gone, and I didn't have a job. I decided to kill myself. I didn't tell anyone. I was just going to do it.

I bought a bottle of Jack Daniels and started drinking. It was strange. I was just numb and I couldn't get drunk. The day passed slowly as I drank whiskey and washed it down with tap water in my small room. When it started getting dark I bought another pint bottle and headed down a quiet deserted road until I reached a bridge over three rail road tracks. My plan was simple. I was going to jump off the bridge in front of the next train. As I waited I started cursing God. I swore that when I got to Heaven I was going to kick His ass. I shook my clenched fist at the sky and ranted like a crazy man. Then a calm came over me. I turned my face to the heavens and told God I would put myself in His hands. If the train came down the middle track, I would kill myself. If not, I would try one more time. The head light of a train shown in the distance. I prepared to jump. If it came down the middle, I was done for. It was now in God's hands. If anyone should ask why I killed myself, I'd say "I wanted to see God". Everything was all right. I was prepared to die... The train came closer, ever, so slowly.

"Jump, jump, jump" I kept shouting loudly to drown out my thinking. The die was cast. I was ready. The damn train came down the right side. I finished the bottle, smashed it on the bridge, and climbed down. I would try one more time. God had saved my life. For what? I didn't know. Maybe, He wasn't through screwing with me yet. I went back to my room to sleep it off. I was hoping that I would never wake up. I had drunk enough to kill an elephant. I should have used a gun. The next morning it felt like an elephant was sitting on my head. It took me three days in bed to get well enough to get up. Finally I was my bad ass self again. I went out and got a job on the very first try. Good thing too as I was down to my last ten dollars.

I no sooner got my job when my last $100 check from the Navy came. I was now employed as an assistant medical laboratory technician at Vanderbilt University. From the bulletin board I got a lead on a boarding house where I got a private room and board for the princely sum of $10 a week. I got a huge breakfast, brown bag lunch, and dinner every day but Saturday and Sunday. Saturday we had breakfast but on Sunday we were on our own. It was close enough to walk to work, the family who owned the house was nice, and they had a beautiful daughter

19 years old, Sandi. Except for the short money, things were looking up.

My job was simple but important. I had to promise that I would stay at least 6 months. I was to take care of sixty rhesus monkeys, 45 who were just babies to be used in two experiments. One was a study on how Atomic radiation affected the digestive system, the other involved a vitamin C deficiency. Being an animal lover I made the mistake of naming each monkey. I raised them, fed them. and cleaned their individual cages. As I was the only one they saw for days at a time I became the only parent they knew. It took a while for the older 15 monkeys to trust me but the young ones took to me at once. I hated that I had to kill them.

The older monkeys that were exposed to radiation who didn't die immediately were examined periodically, blood tests, x-rays, death, and autopsies. Half the young monkeys were fed a complete balanced diet, the rest the same food minus vitamin C. The ones without the vitamin C were examined periodically, given blood tests, x-rays, some killed, and autopsied. Vitamin C deficiency results in a very painful disease called Rickets in humans. Some of my little friends as they got sick, no longer could eat. They just sat there in terrible pain, arms crossed, with silent tears flowing down their agonized faces. I suffered with them, more so, because I knew that if I just gave them a vitamin C pill they would get well.

I will never forget their screams of horror, or how desperately they clung to me as I took them to get their tests. Unless tests were scheduled during the weekdays, the only one they ever saw was me. I saw them twice a day to feed them. To get to my monkey room I had to walk thru a long large room of dog cages filled with approximately 100 or more dogs at any given time. Like my monkeys these dogs didn't get to see very many people. They barked. If you never heard over 100 dogs bark at the same time, you don't know what noise really is. Try it with a hangover and you will get an idea of what Hell must be like.

The University was known for turning out some of our finest surgeons. These doctors did not learn their skills practicing on humans. They used dogs. I got to see butchered, bandaged, bloody, and legless dogs enough to last me a life time. The helplessness of not being able to change this private animal Hell was really getting to me. I was not getting paid enough but I had given my word to see it thru to the end of the experiments. It was here that I learned the principle of sacrificing the few for the good of the many. You can rationalize almost anything from the right perspective.

From the Radiation experiment it was learned that in an Atomic war that those who were not immediately killed could recover from their compromised digestive system. Fifteen monkeys sacrificed their lives for this. The monkeys that died to prove that we need vitamin C in our diet was a waste of lives, research, and money as I am sure someone must have known this already. To be fair, the research was to discover how little vitamin C was needed to perfect an inexpensive but lifesaving diet for the extreme poverty stricken people of India. I know the reasons but I will never forget the screams and the tears of my captive monkey family. Was it all worth it? I'll never know.

Aside from the job, my life was better and in many ways enjoyable. Nashville is a beautiful city and the people warm and friendly. I was living on short money but then things didn't cost very much in the mid 50's. Mr. Ernie Brown and his wife Lilly owned the boarding house where I was living. They were devoted church going people who didn't believe in drinking alcohol. Mr. Brown owned a small café that sold beer. His wife was constantly yelling that he was going to hell for selling the devil's brew. He was a nice man who ran the café by himself and was never in a hurry to go home. I would eat there on Saturdays, they were closed Sundays, and I would often stop by for a beer. He sold it by the quart only and you had to drink it there. Ernie confided in me. He loved his wife, he believed in the church, but if he didn't sell beer, the café wouldn't make any money. He never drank himself and never asked me not to. I brought my friends there and he appreciated the business.

It was at the boarding house that I met Franklin Delano Roosevelt O'Hara who was two months my senior. Frank was a good old country farm boy who never wore a pair of shoes until he enlisted in the Air Force. He had a nervous breakdown when they tried to train him to be a radio man. Like me they gave him a medical discharge before he got his 90 days active service in. Frank loved the city life and took to Nashville and women like a duck to water. He was never going home again except to visit. He never told his folks that he was discharged. He survived by working as a dance instructor for Arthur Murray Dance Studios and posing nude part time for art classes. He was not a particularly handsome man but he was tall, easy going, and had a great sense of humor. Women liked him as a big brother. I liked him because he knew one hell of a lot of beautiful women and all the fun places to go. We became best friends.

Where ever there were women, drinking, and dancing you would find me and Frank. Usually we would also find Doctor Kisrah Misrah from India who was one of my bosses at Vanderbilt University. Dr. Kisrah was here on a work visa heading up the vitamin C deficiency studies. He did not want anyone to know his business away from the university and swore me to secrecy. This was cool because he always shared his liquor with us. He particularly liked young blond women with huge breasts. The women considered him relatively harmless, laughed at him behind his back, but were more than happy to drink his liquor and help him spend his money. I didn't blame them as Frank and I were just like them. Women hung around us mostly because Frank was a good dancer. I made a mental note to learn to dance better. I had some great times, met a lot of beautiful women, but no sex. I was too shy and inexperienced.

Seemingly out of nowhere, the medical photographer at Vanderbildt became our half-ass buddy. Johnny Crunch was a weird little dude who had an annoying habit of always being a little too close to you. He seemed particularly fascinated by Frank but he was free with his money. Women tended to avoid us when he was with us but after enough drinks, everyone got along fine. Then Frank laid the bomb on me. Johnny was making porn films and wanted Frank and me to make one. He would supply two women and pay us $150 each for an hour's work. All we had to do was to have sex with these beautiful women under stage lights while being filmed.

Frank was willing but he would not do it unless I did it too. I needed the money, I was always horny, and the idea of being a porn star sort of appealed to me. I was basically a shy and private person but something like this would give me the confidence with women that I dreamed of having. Yet, I turned it down. I told Frank that I had seen plenty of these stag films when I was in the National Guard and you never knew where they might turn up. Someday I might be a lawyer, a judge, or run for office and the film might turn up. I didn't want to take the chance. What if his mother ever saw it? Or mine? Frank saw it my way but Johnny became a real pain. He kept pleading with us and offering more money. I told Frank that Johnny had to be queer. We both avoided him and there went my movie career!

It seemed as if every third person in Nashville played a musical instrument, sang, or wrote songs. Eddie Gephardt stepped into my life. Eddie had a great talent for playing guitar. Unknown to me at the time Eddie not only had a drinking problem, he was also into drugs. I got talking with Eddie at one of the drinking clubs where he was more than happy to drink my liquor as long as I was paying. I always talk too much when I'm drinking. I mentioned that in high school that I had written a little poetry and that I had always dreamed of being a writer. Eddie insisted on seeing my poems. Most of my poems were short where the first letter of the first word of each line spelled out a girl's name. I used to sell these for a dollar to boys to give to their girlfriends as their own. It was one of the many ways I made eating money when I was broke.

I bought a bottle and we went to Eddie's room. He slowly read my batch of my scribbling. ‘Man, you really have a way with words. I’d give my right arm to have your talent. Have you ever tried writing songs?”

“Not Really.”

“Well, you’re going to write a song right now.”

Eddie with his guitar and me, high on good old Jack Daniels, wrote a song “I Tried So Hard to Tell You”. Eddie swore it was the best song ever since sliced white bread. I didn’t think it was so good. I told him about the song lyrics I wrote one night for Helen Rock. He had me recite it and he put a tune to my phrasing. I had always thought of it as a possible song for Nat King Cole but Eddie put Western music to it. Now this was really good! We were on a roll. Eddie told me about an idea he had, and we knocked out a song “Please Tell Me That You Love Me.” Then things got a little silly as I got drunker. Somehow I made it home but the seed was planted. I was a God damn song writer, maybe, the best ever.

The next day on a coffee break, hung over, I wrote “I Still Love You”. It took me ten minutes. There was no stopping me. I wrote over 25 songs in three weeks. I was going to be rich. That night I wrote a long letter to Helen. She never answered me, the Hell with her. When you are rich you can buy all the women that you will ever need. Of course, I didn’t know a thing about music, song writing, or marketing. But I was on my way up, where ever that was. “Climbing on a bar stool seems like up to me....” Am I good or what?

My new friend Eddie got busted on narcotic possession. Frank showed me the article in the paper. It seems that Eddie was a con man. He sold stolen lyrics to people who wrote music and stolen tunes to lyric writers. Some of my lyrics may have been sold without my knowledge. The music to "Please Tell Me That You Love Me" may have been composed by someone else. I made copies of all my lyrics and mailed them to myself for protection. I told Frank that I didn't care if anyone should steal my songs, it just proves how good I am, and I can always write another one. I never saw or heard from Eddie again. Getting girls up to my place to hear my songs sure beat the tired old saw about seeing my etchings.

I started hanging around the Grand Old Opery Club across the alley from the stage. All the great Western performers came in there and I made it a point to meet as many of them as I could. Frank wouldn't come with me as he didn't care for Western music. I was awed by all the legendary talents and did not mention my song writing efforts at first. I was basically nobody, and was mostly ignored. It was a tight circle of friends. Most of them just stopped in for a quick drink and rushed back to perform. Two exceptions were Hank Williams' widow, Audrey Rose, and Johnny Cash. Audrey Rose, a very gracious lady, let me buy her a drink and we talked a little. Johnny Cash and I got drunk together one time. It was before he married June Carter. Johnny was probably the wildest man I ever drank with. He wanted to go somewhere else to drink and we left together. We took his car. He drove like a crazy person. The sign said slow down, curve ahead. He just floored it. I thought I was a dead man drinking.

Johnny Cash was interested in my song "I Guess Maybe" but I was not ready to sell it as a Western song. I wanted Nat King Cole to sing it. Johnny got mad and left me sitting in the club and took off. Many years later I tried to contact him as I changed my mind about the song but he never returned my call. By that time he didn't need me. He probably never did. Chances are he didn't remember me. Years later, I met Earl Bostic and his wife in a night club in Long Beach, California. He invited me to sit at his table during intermission and was interested in my song "I Guess Maybe". He gave me his address and made me promise to mail a demo to him. I did and he never got back to me. I never did sell that song and in my opinion it was the best one I ever wrote.

Chapter 6

I walked into Acuff & Rose Publishing, who published more western songs than anyone in the world. I told the receptionist that I wanted to see the head man. The office was empty except for her and one other man. The man overheard me, came over, shook my hand, and introduced himself. He invited me into his office. It was Fred Rose, himself. I told him I was a song writer and handed him my note book of about 80 songs I had written. We must have talked for over an hour. He was a very gracious and interesting man. He had, of course, known Hank Williams as well as all the great song writers and entertainers. He finally got up and took me to a huge storeroom just overfilled with shelves of papers.

"Son, these are songs I paid for and never published. What makes you think your songs are any better? I got some Hank Williams songs here. Not every song he wrote was a hit. Most were, but not all of them."

It was like wanting to be a book writer and going to the library and seeing all your competition at one time. There were thousands of songs sitting on those shelves. I realized that it takes more than talent to make it, luck and timing is what it is all about. I got some great advice from Fred Rose but he sure took the wind from my sails. I thanked him, shook his hand, and got the hell out of there. A song writer, my Irish ass, song writers are a dime a dozen. I did learn that most artists write their own songs and why not? I couldn't play an instrument or sing. I almost never wrote another song.

I had my first blackout from drinking. It was scary. I just could not remember anything from the previous night but bits and pieces. As time went on and blackouts became more frequent, I accepted them as being a normal result of drinking. I always had vivid, disturbing dreams and soon the line between reality, dreams, and blackouts blurred. I no longer could tell what was real. I mostly acted all right when I was drinking according to my friends. As I didn't have a car, I didn't drive. I didn't force my attentions on women or behave badly. I accepted the situation and tried not to worry too much. I knew I had a terrible temper but I stayed out of trouble. I wasn't fighting at the time.

I had an open invitation to go to church with my landlords, the Browns. Ernie, in spite of selling beer in his café, was a deacon of the church. I knew I couldn't put it off forever. I agreed to go. I figured I would score major points with Sandy who was really starting to look good to me. We all went to church where I was introduced to Pat Boone. He had heard that I wrote some pretty good songs from Ernie and said that he would like to see them. He invited me to dinner with his family the following Sunday. Who in the hell was Pat Boone? I had never heard of him. He had some radio show and sang. I was from Chicago and I wasn't going to give my songs to some nobody. I didn't take to this man. He smiled too much and was too clean and nice. I put him off with an excuse. I never did show him my songs. I would have bet Pat Boone never took a drink in his life. How could he ever understand what I wrote?

One night when I was drinking too much and going from club to club, someone invited me to a house party. I was looking for the toilet and was told it was upstairs. On the second floor I passed an open door to an office. It was like a dream in slow motion. There on a desk glowing in the moonlight was a beautiful typewriter. I had always wanted a typewriter but could not afford one. It was like a gift from heaven. This belonged to me. I went to the open window behind the desk. I tried to get the rope from the drapes to tie it to the typewriter to lower it down out the window. I couldn't get the rope loose and I had nothing to cut it with. I remember recently reading an article about a baby that fell out of a five story window and wasn't hurt. I figured if a baby could do it, why not a typewriter? Even if it got damaged, it would cost less to fix than to buy a new one. I threw it out the window.

I hurried downstairs, pushed thru the guests, and went out the back door to retrieve the typewriter. Ii looked pretty busted up. I suddenly remembered that I still had to take a piss. I walked to some bushes by the back door. I was relieving myself when a police car came. They were shining a searchlight on the broken typewriter. It was probably hard to see what it was.

"What is it we have here, Sir?"

"Gentlemen, I don't know. Why don't you see for yourself?"

I zipped up my pants walked thru the back door, pushed thru the crowd, walked thru the front door, and ran like hell. I hadn't the faintest idea where I was. I heard the police sirens and dived behind some bushes. They went speeding by. I waited until it was quiet and started running again. Another siren, I hid again. This went on for a while, sirens, police cars, and me hiding every time. I evaded them. I finally realized where I was. I had to get home. I couldn't let them catch me. Somebody at the party could probably recognize me. I was so drunk that I could hardly think straight. I stayed in the brush for what seemed like a long time. Finally it quieted down. I took a chance and started walking quickly towards home. There was a large hospital between me and home, about three long well lighted blocks to travel.

It was quiet. I took a deep breath and started walking. There was a siren and a squad car screeched around the corner. I was about half way down the street, I turned quickly, ran up a flight of steps, and entered the hospital. Walking quickly, trying to look like I belonged there, I found some stairs, and walked down to the next floor just as the police came into the lobby.

"Did you see where he went?"

The corridor was deserted. I could hear them coming down the steps. I was trying doors. They were locked. Just before the police reached the bottom of the stairs, I found an unlocked door. I quickly entered and shut the door behind me. It was totally dark and I was alone. I felt my way along the wall and came to a closet. I went inside and closed the door. It was a clothes closet. I tried to hide the best I could and keep quiet. I could hear the police outside in the corridor. They never came into the room. Finally it was quiet. I waited at least an hour before I dared to move. I couldn't stay there forever.

I put on a jacket and pants that I found in the closet over my suit in the dark. I opened the door a crack. The corridor was deserted. At the end there was an emergency door on the side of the hospital closest to my home. I gathered my wits about me and started walking towards the exit. I almost made it when I heard a shout.

"Who in the hell are you?"

For the first time I noticed what I was wearing. The pants were too big in the waist and about 8 inches too short exposing my trousers. The white Jacket was way too small. I gathered the waist and made a dash for the exit. I made it. I flung it open. The emergency alarm sounded. It was loud. Several police cars raced down the street. It was walk, duck, and hide all the way home but I made it. The next morning I woke up and realized that it all was a dream. Then on the floor next to the bed was a pair of grey hospital pants. No, it was all too real.

I was scared out of my mind. I called in sick. They would have to get someone else to feed my monkeys. I wasn't going to leave the room. I had no intention of going to jail if I could help it. Frank brought me a newspaper. There was nothing in it relating to me. So far, so good. I didn't leave the house for six days. The papers had nothing.

As I hung around with an older drinking crowd I met mostly women older than myself. I got laid fairly regularly but it was always when I was drunk. I didn't know how to talk to or seduce women when I was sober. Basically, I felt there were two kinds of women. Whores for pleasure and nice girls you didn't touch until you were married. Saints or whores with not many in betweens. Girls my own age bored me. I felt they were unsophisticated and didn't know anything about sex. Sandy came into my room when I was pretending to be sick. We engaged in some heavy petting but she would not take her pants off. I did not know how far to push the issue. I liked her and I was afraid that she might think I was some sort of an animal if I pursued it. It was hell being so insecure. I felt that I would never understand women. I sure as hell was doing something right when I was drunk but I never knew what it was. It seems to be true that our Lord looks out for drunks, fools, and Irishmen.

I decided to get out of town. I called up and quit my job, had Frank find me someone who would drive me out of town where I could hitch a ride back to Chicago. In those days people would pick up a hitchhiker. Goodbye, Nashville, goodbye, Sandy. Chicago, here I come, right back where I started from.

I hitchhiked to Chicago from Nashville. I arrived home to find my mother Linda sitting in the kitchen smoking a cigarette and drinking a Budweiser. No one else was home except my half brother Chaz and half sister Teresa. "Hi Mom, how are you doing?"

"My God, Joe. You've grown even bigger. Are you here to stay a while?"

"Not long. I'm thinking of going down to New Orleans for the Mardi Gras. If I'm ever going to be a writer, I have to see New Orleans."

"I hate to see you give up on college." She got me a cold beer.

"I was lucky to have made it through high school. You wouldn't believe how expensive college is these days and for every hour of class room they want two hours of study. I'd have to work and there just wouldn't be enough time."

"Your father should have given you the money. He's a no good cheap bastard."

"Forget it, Mom. I'm going to be rich on my own. I've written over a hundred songs and I've been told I'm really good. One of the reasons I'm going to New Orleans is to learn Jazz and the blues. All I've written so far is Western and it really isn't my favorite kind of music."

"Your father owes you. His family put him through school. He should give you and Shaun money for college."

"Well, he didn't, he won't, and that's that. As far as he's concerned, I don't exist. He'll probably leave me some money when he dies."

"Don't count on it."

"Why not? I was his first born son. I think he must feel guilty about the way I was brought up."

"That son of a bitch has the first penny he ever made. He'll figure out some way to take it with him or leave it all to that whore he married. You or your brother will never see a dime of it."

"Are you drunk? I've never heard you talk like this."

"You can't get drunk drinking beer."

"Who in the hell who ever told you that?"

"Don't swear in front of your mother. It's a fact. I read it."

"How's Rod doing these days?"

"Working hard as usual. He's racing at Soldiers Field this weekend. Are you going to stay around?"

"I wouldn't miss it. What's he racing, Mod's or Stocks."

"Midgets. He's been doing pretty good at it. He's got top points in the United Auto Racing Association this year so far and he's only competed in about a third of the sanctioned races. This time it isn't a dirt track. It should be faster."

"Has he got a good car?"

"The best, Rod always get the best, because he is the best."

"Being foreman of a mob owned garage, the largest on the South side, doesn't hurt much either."

"We don't talk about that. Do you want another beer? Help yourself."

"Aren't you afraid that I might get drunk?"

"You can't get drunk on just beer."

Rod came home straight from work. He seemed glad to see me. The fight we had seemed to be forgotten. I think he was proud that I stood up to him. Tom his real son who was bigger than me was still afraid of him. While Rod wasn't a huge man, he was stocky and muscular. It was his eyes that were scary. He had the look of a killer. It was rumored that Avalon Auto Rebuilders where he worked was owned by the mob and that he got his job by making a problem go away permanently. It was said that the man who caused the problem slept with the fishes in a pair of custom cement boots.

Their entire fleet of tow trucks were equipped with police scanners and two way radios. Most times the tow trucks were at accidents before the regular police. The marks were offered free towing or a ticket for obstructing traffic if not moved in five minutes. The towing was free only to Avalon Auto Rebuilders and if the car was repaired there. The cops got $20 each for their trouble and the garage got most of the business. Insurance appraisers were paid under the table for high estimates, used parts were used, and charged as new. Nothing wrong here, just the way business was conducted on the South side of Chicago. Rod always received a large Christmas bonus, a generous salary, and always had the best cars to race.

Car #24 was no exception. Because the car was new or because the tract was faster than what Rod was use to, his qualifying time only got him into the semi-finals. I suspected that he held back in order to have a chance at winning first place in the semi-final than taking a chance of placing less in the final. Rod loved to win.

It was a hot summer Saturday at Soldiers Stadium. This was the first auto race ever held there on a cement tract and the stadium was sold out. Many of the big name auto racers from Indianapolis Speedway were there to compete with the local talent. Our whole family was there in the stands with matching racing jackets. Only my step-brother Tom was down with the pit crew. Like his father he had a talent for auto mechanics. The semi-finals were to be held Saturday with the final race held on Sunday, It was almost four o'clock when they lined up for the semi-final and last race of the day. Rod D'Angelo was in 4th place pole position. They circled the track twice in tight formation.

The green flag dropped and the race was on. The car in 2nd position pole pulled out wide on the first turn and lost control. He bounced off the cement bank, hit a straw bale blocking an entrance to the parking lot, tore a hole in a canvas curtain, and drove off the track into the crowded lot. Somehow he missed the parked cars, but a wire cable hanging between two cement posts caught him under the chin and killed him. The papers next day ran the headline "DEAD MAN WALKS". The track ambulance had followed him out the hole. The car had stopped, the driver got out, reached in his pocket and took out his keys. A doctor had a stethoscope to his heart. It stopped beating. The man took three steps and dropped dead.

They had dropped the yellow flag and stopped the race for about 20 minutes. An announcement was made. The man had died. There was a three minute pause of silent prayer and the race resumed. Rod D'Angelo moved into the empty position and the other drivers moved up one. They circled the track. The green flag was dropped. The exact same thing happened. Rod swung out wide, hit the wall, lost control, hit the same bale of straw, and drove out the same hole. As one, the crowd came to their feet. There wasn't a sound among the hundreds of fans. My mother's face turned white. Nobody knew if they had removed that wire that had killed the other driver. Rod reclaimed control of the car, made a u-turn, tore another hole in the canvas, and drove back on the track. He was back in the race. He won! The crowd went wild.

That night at home my mom made Rod promise to never race again. She was scared to death that he might be killed and who would take care of the family? Race car drivers couldn't get life insurance and Chaz would need medical help for the rest of his life. If nothing else Rod was a strong family man and could understand her concerns. He might cheat on her but deep inside he loved her. He could see that the whole family had been terrified when he hit the same wall that killed the other driver. He promised to quit racing.

That night my step-sister Toni crawled in bed with me. She was trembling. I held her tight. Before I knew it, we were having hot passionate sex. My God, she was only 14 years old. What kind of perverted animal was I? There is no question that I was half drunk but my own sister? Rod would kill me. What if she got pregnant? When I realized what I had done, I made her get up and go back to her own bed. I got dressed, went down stairs, and drank some of Rod's whisky. I had to get out of there or I was a dead man. There was no doubt in my mind that if Rod didn't kill me, God would.

Ever since I had my first blackout from drinking, I was terrified that I would kill someone when I was drinking and not even know it. I had nightmares about this that were so real, I would wake up in a cold sweat. I managed to get a complete set of false identification, a packed suitcase, and $100 stashed under my bed for such an emergency. When it happened, I could disappear at a moment's notice. Every large city seemed to have a skid row and that is where I would go.

This seemed like the perfect time to get the hell out but then again it would draw attention to what happened. I couldn't think straight. Toni couldn't tell. She would be scared too. Christ, I didn't rape her. She climbed in bed with me. I didn't ask her. She was my step-sister not my real sister. It was obvious that she had done this before. She sure the hell wasn't a virgin. It made no difference. If Rod found out, he would kill me, plain and simple. If I got Toni to run away with me, maybe we could make it. A 14 year old, what was I thinking? That doctor was wrong. I was crazy... I took another drink.

I had to do something, even if it was wrong. I could kill Rod in his sleep. It would most definitely be a case of self defense. That wouldn't work. Who would take care of the family? Mom would never forgive me. I had better quit drinking whisky. I got a cold beer. You can't get drunk drinking beer. What a joke. You can get drunk drinking water if you put enough whisky in it. I started laughing. Suddenly I was cold sober. I thought of Toni. I hadn't noticed it before but she was changing into a beautiful woman. I was getting a hard on just thinking of her. I was a snake, a stiff one, but a snake. I started to laugh again. It wasn't really funny but I would die with a laugh in the air, a song in my heart, and a smile on my lips. I was a genuine certified head case but I was all I got and what I deserved, the rest of my life stuck with being me...

Rod got up first. "Couldn't sleep either?"

"I just wanted to get an early start. Are you quitting racing?"

"For now, I promised your mother. I have to go down to the track and straighten out a few things. The finals are today. I don't suppose you will be there."

"I'm leaving today. I don't want to miss the Mardi Gras."

"Are you coming back?"

"I don't think so."

"Well. I'll say goodbye then. Good luck in whatever you decide to do. You're a good kid, you'll make it. Take care. You're always welcome here. Keep in touch with your mother and I'll see you sometime." He finished his cup of coffee and left. I waited for Mom to get up.

My mother got up and joined me at the breakfast table with a cold bottle of beer. It seems that she had given up on having a morning cup of coffee first. I told her I was leaving and she acted like she expected it, even relieved. I realized for the first time how much we had grown apart. She was growing old and worn out. She was Irish and still pretty in a wan sort of way but she looked as if life had drained her dry. Then Toni came in. She was absolutely glowing, She came over and kissed me on my cheek. Until last night she had never kissed me before. It was if she had changed from a little girl into a woman overnight. I was uncomfortable but my mother didn't seem to notice anything out of the ordinary. If the house was on fire my mother probably would not have noticed it. Toni stared into my eyes and smiled. I had to get out of there. I was falling in love with my sister.

As I was packing my clothes, Shaun came in and said he wanted to come with me. I loved my brother but he was only 15 at the time. I had a hard time taking care of myself. I told him no. For the first time in my life ever I saw him cry. He said he was afraid that he would never see me again. I told him he wasn't that lucky and that I would send for him later when he was older and graduated from high school. It was only about two more years. I made him promise me that he would finish school. A man was screwed without a high school diploma. Life was tough enough, without an education it was impossible. I left with my sea bag to hitchhike to the Mardi Gras. I was tough, Irish, and I was going to make it big. Doing what? I didn't know it then but it would be big...

Chapter 7

I rode a bus to the end of the line in South Chicago. I stuck out my thumb. I was on my way again. My plan was to swing down to Nashville, Tennessee and see if Frank wanted to join me for a trip to New Orleans. It didn't take me long to get to the Brown's house in Nashville. I walked in and caught Frank and Sandy making out on the living room couch. They both were embarrassed. I stuck out my hand. "I just stopped by to say goodbye. I'm heading down to New Orleans and I'll probably never get back this way."

Frank got up red faced and shook my hand. "Good luck, Joe. Let me know where you land."

"Yeah, right!" I turned on my heel and left. The hell with both of them. Frank was too dumb to ever be anyone and there are always more women to appreciate this big Irishman. I didn't need friends anyway. They just slow you down. I took a bottle of Jack Daniels out of my sea bag, took a couple of slugs, stuck out my thumb, and I was moving and grooving.

People picked me up for short hauls, I kept drinking Jack Daniels, and got drunk. I didn't have an idea of where I was. A man stopped and picked me up. "Where you heading?"

"I'm going to New Orleans for the Mardi Gras."

"Fellow, you sure as hell are on the wrong highway. I'm going to Texarkana."

"Great! I've never been there either." I climbed in his pickup truck and offered him a drink from my bottle. He took a long drink and we moved out. I fell asleep in the seat. He stopped, woke me up, and asked me if I wanted something to eat. We went into this truck stop café and he bought me a chili and a cold beer. His name was Ted and he was driving thru to San Antonio, Texas. I decided to go with him. I offered to buy another bottle but he refused and said he had better stick with beer. He bought a case of Budweiser and we hit the road.

It was hours later and midmorning when he dropped me off in San Antonio. It was stifling hot. I saw a sign at the Greyhound bus station that said Travelers Aid. Well, I was a traveler, hung over, unshaven, broke, and needed aid. Acting on a hunch, I approached the little old lady at the counter. "Excuse me, Lady. Do you know where I might get some work? I'm broke and need something to eat." I gave her my best little boy lost smile.

"Here's a voucher for a free meal. Go see Pete at the Post House Café. He might have something for you." I thanked her. The café was in the bus station. I walked over and asked the man at the cash register if I could talk to Pete. "I'm Pete Vella. What can I do for you?"

"Well, Sir. I just got into town and the lady at Travelers Aid says you might know someone who can help me get a job. I'm broke and need to get back on my feet."

"Can you bus tables and wash dishes?"

"I washed dishes the last three years of high school and had KP duty in the Navy. I can hand peel 100 pounds of potatoes in less than an hour."

"Can you start at 6 o'clock tonight?"

"Yes, Sir."

"Do you have a place to stay?"

"Not yet, but I'll be all right."

"Go over to the YMCA and see the manager, Sam Munster. Tell him you work for me and he'll give you a room on credit. Be back here ready to work at 6 PM, and shave."

"Yes, Sir. Thank you Sir, I appreciate it."

"Get going and don't call me Sir. My name is Pete Vella. I'm not a damn officer. Now get..."

"Right." I made my way to the YMCA, got a room on credit for $5.00 a week, took a shower and shaved, and lay down to get some much needed rest before I went to work. I really hated washing dishes but a job was a job. At least I would be eating until I got my first paycheck. I fell into an uneasy sleep. What the Hell was I doing in Texas?"

I reported to work early. The work was easy as it wasn't a very busy place but they didn't have a dishwashing machine. Everything had to be hand washed. No air conditioning in the kitchen, just a fan, and it was blazing hot. I was scheduled to work rotating shifts, alternating between busboy one shift, dishwasher the next. Two day shifts, two swing shifts, and then two graveyard shifts. I didn't ask about payday as I was just happy to be working.

The next morning I got up early and checked out the town. San Antonio was actually a small city, with a lot of history, and a very unique small river running thru the center of town lined with little stores, cafes, and bars. I found an eight cent hot dog, a five cent glass of beer, and telephone calls were only a nickel. Except for the tourists and Air Force Personnel, the people were mostly Spanish. If it wasn't for the blistering heat, I could have loved the place. I went back to the YMCA where I made a few friends and managed to borrow some money based on the fact that I had a job.

Lackland Air Force base was close by and this is where the men took their basic training. At the time it was considered a service mans town. Fast turnover of recruits, huge air force payroll attracted the women. It was not a level playing field as I was basically broke. I was not use to not having money and was looking forward to my first payday. After 12 days it finally arrived. My first check was for 12 dollars and some change. I asked Pete if the pay period ended the day I started and he told me that was for the week.

"Just how much are you paying me?"

"Thirty-five cents an hour."

"You're kidding me?"

"Hey, you said you wanted a job. I can get a dozen Mexicans to work for that. This ain't Dallas."

I felt like hitting him but I didn't. I owed two weeks rent, which was $10, but the worst part was then I had borrowed about $20 from various friends It looked like I was going to be stuck in this hell the rest of my life. I never felt so helpless before. It wasn't all bad. The Post House Café was cafeteria style and on my bus boy shifts when I carried the food trays for little old ladies, I would sometimes get a tip, usually a nickel. Once I got a quarter. It didn't get any better than that.

Sadie Stillworthy burst into my life like a Texas whirlwind. Sadie struck up a conversation with me at the Post House when I carried her food tray to her table. She was dressed in old fashioned elegance, a petite woman of about 70, with boundless energy and bright silver hair. Sparkling dark eyes shining from her beautiful satin crème face and her impressive tight figure showcased a women of charm, wit, and grace. She said she would like to meet me after work, buy me a coffee, and we could talk. What did I have to lose? I met her at a café along the river bank. We talked for hours. She was impressed that I wanted to be a writer and that I had written several songs. She invited me to her home for dinner. It seemed harmless enough so I went with her.

Here's the thing. She drove a 1915 Hupmobile, lived in an old huge mansion, and claimed she was once a movie star in silent movies. She had photos and a scrap book to prove it. I never heard of her but she seemed authentic. She had this player piano that I immediately fell in love with. I didn't spot it at the time but she wanted my young firm body. Up to now I had never had sex with a women over 30 that I was aware of and this Sadie could have been 90 or so. To be honest she looked good but she was really a relic from the past. She started rubbing me, unbuttoned my pants, and went down on me. I didn't try to stop her. I was uncomfortable at first but it had been a long time since I had been with a woman. And, Hey, she was a movie star of sorts. She didn't offer me any money but she did ask me if I wanted to move into one of the spare bedrooms. I declined gracefully and so as not to hurt her feelings I did her again. It was pretty good. I was going to have to look into this old lady thing.

For the next week Sadie and I spent time together. We got to be pretty good friends and she was a fun person to be with. She let me drive her Hupmobile and there was always plenty to drink at her place. I didn't know any men close to her age but I introduced her to some of my friends at the YMCA who were all invited to her house. Everyone just loved this old lady and she adored the attention. It seemed that once she had sex with me, she was good for a while. I was attempting to get a little space and time between us. It was about this time that a drinking buddy took me over to Maria and Marla's house, two young Mexican sisters who liked nothing better than sex and drinking Tequila. They never held out for money. They would ask, but if you brought over a pint you got laid. You were always welcome. They just asked that you called first.

Maria and Marla were in their early twenties. They were a little on the chunky side but had beautiful skin, hair, and deep dark eyes. They both had beautiful full, huge breasts that was their best feature. They were full of humor, warm, loving, and were wild cats in bed. I leaned towards the eldest Marla and spent several enjoyable nights with her. I had never met a women who enjoyed sex so much before and we would have sex several times in one night. Then came the night when I wanted sex for the third time and she rejected me. Drunk, I left her and crawled in bed with her sister Maria.

Maria opened her eyes and said "I was just dreaming about you." I climbed on top of her. Amazingly was neither sister was the least bit jealous of the other, or angry at me for doing both of them. This was my third week in San Antonio and I was learning about women like never before. All good things come in threes and if you count the two sisters as one, Kay Mendosa was the second event.

Kay approached me at the Post House as I was finishing my shift. She was a pale slender lady in her forties. Not a beauty but attractive in a sexy sort of way. At this time I would hit on any woman who was warm to the touch. Kay came right to the point. She was broke and wanted a man to take care of her. I bought her dinner and took her to Sadie's house. She put her up for the night but made it clear it was a onetime deal. I stayed the night, got up early, and sneaked into Kay's bedroom. She didn't want to have sex with me but after some persistent foreplay she gave in. At breakfast Sadie was annoyed with me. We had words. Kay and I left and it was made clear that we weren't invited back. Hell, there went my Hupmobile. I really liked that car.

I didn't know what to do with Kay. I didn't have the money or means to take care of her. I felt sorry for her. I went to the YMCA and put the word out that I had a nice woman who was looking for a man to help her out... One of my friends said he might know of someone. I introduced them and they went off together. He came back. I never saw Kay again.

As the flying fickle finger of fate would have it and at probably the worst time of my life, I fell head over heels in love. Mary Stone was probably the most beautiful girl I had ever seen. She was a customer eating alone around lunch time at the Post House where I was ending my shift as busboy. With the stupid paper hat I had to wear I felt like a real dork butt. She smiled at me as she caught me staring at her. The whole world seemed to be a better place. I had to meet this gorgeous woman or I would die on the spot. I went over to her table.

"Hi, I get off work in about 15 minutes. Could I meet you somewhere for a drink or something. I feel like I know you from somewhere."

"I think I'd like that. Where do you want me to meet you?"

"There's a little bar called "Turks" along the river. Do you know it?"

"I'll find it."

"I'll see you in 20 minutes or less."

"I'll be there." She left and left a dollar tip. I never considered myself to be a handsome man, just pretty average. I was tall and lanky, Irish with reddish brown hair, and hazel eyes. Unless I had a few drinks in me, I was usually shy around women. I didn't for the life of me know what women liked about me. I just considered myself lucky and felt it was about time. There had to be something better in life than the way my life was going.

I met Mary at Turk's Bar after work and it seemed we talked for hours. Mary was a year older than me and married to Jimmy, who was doing his basic training at Lackland. Mary came from a very wealthy family in Orange County California. Her father, Joe Miller, owned several real estate companies and was a self-made millionaire. To spite her father, Mary married a local boy who was crazy about her and, whom her father didn't like. Jerry, her new husband didn't have a dime and very little chance of being somebody. Not being able to provide the type of lifestyle Mary was accustomed to, they soon were fighting. Daddy refused to help and told Mary she had made her own bed now she had to lie in it. Jerry, who couldn't take it anymore, ran away and joined the Air Force. She was ordered by her father, under threat of being disowned by the family, to try and save her marriage. She followed Jerry to San Antonio and now she met me.

The physical attraction between us was intense. We had to make love or die. The desire was that strong. I could not take her to my room at the YMCA and Sadie's house was out of the question. Mary had a room on the third floor of a local hotel and we headed there. The desk clerk tried to give us a hassle.

"You can't go upstairs unless you are a registered guest."

"I rented the room for me and my husband." said Mary without hesitation.

"Are you her husband?" The jerk asked me directly.

"Why not?" I answered staring him down. He gave me a dirty look but he handed me the room key. Mary and I went upstairs.

This was not my finest hour. I almost never dated married women especially wives of servicemen. It just wasn't right but I could resist only so much. Mary was a Goddess and I was just a mere mortal caught in her magic spell. She took her clothes off and lay naked on the bed. As long as I live I would never find a woman as breathtakingly beautiful as this one. I tore off my clothes and climbed in bed with her. I almost passed out from the intense desire. We kissed and clung to each other, our naked bodies pressed hard against each other. Then she pulled away.

"Joe, we're going to have to wait. Jerry is going to call and I have to answer. I don't want to have to stop in the middle of anything."

Waiting was the last thing in the world I wanted and I believe the hardest thing I ever had to endure. It was actual torture to lie naked next to this beautiful woman and not possess her. Marry assured me, "You'll see, it will be even better for the waiting."

"When is he going to call? I can't last much longer."

"Sure you can. Do you want me to rub it with an ice cube?"

"You're kidding?" Then the phone rang.

"Hello, baby. I'm lying here naked just aching for you. How much longer am I going to have to wait?"

This was the first lesson I learned about the nature of women. This poor slob of a husband had no idea from the tone of her voice that his wife was lying naked in bed with another man, while flirting with him, the husband. I just couldn't believe what I was hearing. My desire cooled rapidly. Suddenly the call ended. Mary bent over and kissed me deeply. "I got plans for you."

We didn't make love. We had wild unbridled raw lustful sex for several hours. We talked. We bonded together if we were meant for each other. As San Antonio was a service man's town we came up with a plausible story in case any of her husband's friends saw us together. I was to be an ex-boyfriend that she formerly dated before she met Jerry, but I had left town. We met accidentally and as she was a stranger in town I was showing her around and protecting her from the local low life's. She still had fond feelings for me but she was a proper married woman now and she wanted to make their marriage work. I was uncomfortable staying the entire night so I went back to the YMCA.

After seeing Mary every available moment for the next four days, I was hopelessly in love, but afraid that we were going to get caught by her husband. We were just too obvious. I talked the situation over with my good friend Harry at the YMCA. Harry Lewis was an older man who felt I was destined for better things. He had read some of the things I had written and encouraged me to make something out of myself. He felt I had a lot of talent. His best advice was to get out of town for a while. He showed me an ad looking for insurance agents trainees. If they hired me, I would spend a week at a sales training camp. I went to see the man.

It was an impressive office but the man behind the desk was more so. He introduced himself and asked me why did I think I would make a good salesman? I told him the story about my first year in high school when I sold ice cream bars out of a three wheel bicycle. Each day there was an award for the top salesman and I won it 35 days straight. I wore red and white striped pants, a straw box hat, and played a ukulele. The children knew me as Uncle Joe but the secret of my success was that I hung around the parks where they played. I couldn't play well but I strummed my uke. and made up silly songs. I was a success until one of my testicles swelled up and I had to quit.

The man seemed rather unimpressed. “if you’re such a hot shot salesman sell me this pencil.” He handed me one from the desk. I don’t recall what I said but the man made me mad. I was inspired. I riffed off an impressive presentation of the pencil. If I was really selling pencils he would probably have bought a truck load. I was hired. I left the next day for a 10 day sales training camp and was to be paid the grand sum of $150.00 upon completion. I quit my job at the Post House, kept my room at the YMCA, and spent the entire night with Mary. Of course, she would wait for me and be true blue.

The camp was a joke. I was the youngest one there. The company was serious in its goals but the agents in training refused to take anything seriously. The classes were technical, boring, and not very motivational. We went to school five hours a day. We were housed in a barracks, ate like royalty, and had a lot of free time. There was an abundance of free liquor and it was all quality stuff. There was a swimming pool, tennis courts, and a nine hole golf course. We even had riding horses. I was never treated so well. The problem was that I didn’t really learn anything worthwhile. It was probably all the liquor I was drinking. Like I said, it was a joke.

Camp ended and they handed me my check along with a manual of rates, sales, and promotional materials. I was to be assigned a sales territory within the next few days. My problem was that I lied to them about having a car. Without one, you could not very well work your territory. I went back to the YMCA where Harry was glad to see me. He offered to buy an insurance policy from me as my first client but when I couldn’t explain the product he refused. “Hell, they didn’t teach you anything. You’ll never make it in this business. You better quit." I never did go back or return any of their calls.

Mary was next on my list. We met for lunch at the Post House. It was decided for me to go to Long Beach, California and get a room at a boarding house that her father owned. She would leave Jerry, come to California, we would meet accidently, and start dating. After the divorce, we would get married and I could work for her father selling real estate. As soon as I got to Long Beach I was to start real estate school. It sounded like a good plan. Suddenly two Air Force Military Police flanked by two regular policeman approached our table and demanded to see my ID. Once they determined that I was a civilian, the MPs backed down and the policemen took over. They had me go outside while they questioned me and Mary separately.

I never did particularly like police. These two oversized steely-eyed monsters scared the hell out of me. They wore their guns low on their hips like old time gunslingers, and looked as if they would rather shoot me than talk. They had the idea that I was some punk gangster from Chicago trying to run whores in their beautiful squeaky clean moral city. They thought I was trying to recruit Mary to prostitute for me. They knew about me sending Air Force men to the Mexican sisters for sex. They knew about Kay and hinted that I might have had her killed and hid the body. It would have been funny but these guys were dead serious. Luckily I had told Mary about everything and she stuck to the story we had made up. The bottom line was they were going to call her husband Jerry. If he didn't know me, I was going to jail.

They called the base. Jerry was on guard duty. It would take a while before he could come to the phone. The police brought us back inside the Post House, handcuffed me, and had us sit at separate tables until Jerry came to the phone. I had never met Jerry, I didn't really know what he had heard or knew, and knew only what Mary said she had told him about us. Sadie came in, had a cup of tea, sat at a nearby table and stared at me. I swear she was gloating. Finally they got Jerry on the line. He said he knew about me and I was an ex-friend of his wife from California. He said there must be some sort of mistake as I had an excellent reputation and my father was a well respected attorney in Chicago. The police let me go with a warning. "We know what you're up to. Don't leave town. We're going to nail your ass. You're not as smart as you think."

Chapter 8

It was time to kiss off San Antonio. Fortunately, Harry had found another job for me which I was considering, a substitute railroad clerk on the line to Corpus Christi, Texas. I was to substitute for clerks during their vacations. There was an immediate opening the next day in some small jerk water nowhere town and I grabbed the chance. I paid off every dime I borrowed and treated my friends to a last night on the town. I kissed Mary goodbye but did not think it advisable to go to her room. The rail road gave me a free pass and I left the next morning. I was 20 years old with a little more than a hundred dollars to my name. To hell with the police, I was gone and no forwarding address.

I got off the train with a trunk, sea bag, and my portable typewriter in this whistle stop town in the middle of nowhere. The town was so small it only had one bar combined with a general store and small café. No school or church. It had one dirt road running thru the center of about 12 rundown weather beaten houses. It was hot. Who would live in this hell of a desert. It was a railroad town where men could rest between runs. I went into the one room rail station and introduced myself. The clerk whom I was to replace took all of 10 minutes to explain the job to me.

Basically, my job was to flag the train down when the train arrived. I was to get the relief men to go on duty. I had a telephone but it seemed to be the only one in town. When I asked him how I was to find the men going on duty, he said "Just ask anyone." They'll either be at the bar or home sleeping. There was no other place. I could bunk on the cot at the station house and get my meals at the café. I could just run a tab and the railroad would take care of it. They had a strong union and a decent pay scale. He wished me luck and told me he would be back in two weeks. He was catching the next train to San Antonio.

I asked if there were any women in town. Just one married one at the café. There wasn't a whore in the whole town. I couldn't believe it. All these men making good money and not one prostitute. I gave the phone number of the two Mexican sisters to the clerk and told him to look them up. His train came and off he went on his yearly vacation. The job was boring. The phone had an automatic answering device but I was required to not leave the station for over two hours at a time. I went down to the bar. It had a juke box and one pool table. There wasn't a soul there. There was a cigar box to put your money in. The prices were posted on the wall and you just helped yourself. I took a drink and drank for three days. I managed somehow to find and notify the men when their trains came in, but I was bored out of my skull. All there was to do was to read or drink. I needed a woman. This job sucked.

I boarded the next train heading to Corpus Christi. My rail pass was still valid and wasn't questioned. I didn't say anything to anyone. I just left. I never asked for the pay I had coming. As if God answered my prayers, there was a lovely girl about my age on the train traveling alone. I asked her if I could sit by her and she said sure. Her name was Darlene Kennedy from Chicago and I swear if I had a twin sister, it would have been her. I felt an attraction to this woman like nothing I ever experienced before. It wasn't sex. It was something entirely else. We were soul mates. She was beautiful, tall, intelligent, never married, exciting, talented. All those qualities a man desired in a woman. I knew that having sex with this woman would be as natural as breathing. I never wanted to leave this beauty but she was getting off before me. I was tempted to give up all my plans, take a chance and go with her. For a moment I was sorely tempted, but common sense overwhelmed desire and we parted, never to meet again. I often think of her and what might have been.

I got off the train at Corpus Christi, put my gear in a Greyhound station locker, and headed for the nearest bar. I found a ten dollar whore and had my way with her. As I slept, she stole my money, and left. Luckily, she missed a 20 dollar bill I had hidden under my boot insert, just in case. It was time to head for Long Beach and start my new life. From looking at the map, I could tell I would have to make my way to El Paso (God, I was tired of Texas), to Phoenix, and basically across to Long Beach. I got my stuff and hit the road. It looked like a long way to go on 20 dollars but the lack of money never bothered me. Something always turned up and I could always find a job. I wasn't lazy and I was getting all this great experience for when I wrote my book. At the end of the rainbow there was Mary. I'd be a somebody yet.

Many interesting people picked me up, some bought me dinner and drinks. On the road I stuck to eating chili and beans and drinking beer. The trip was long and the weather was hot in Arizona, Texas, and New Mexico. Sometimes I had a long wait between rides. I'll never forget how I felt when I finally reached California, crossed the mountain range and first experienced the ocean's cooling breeze. I passed miles and miles of unfenced orange groves where one just could just pick an orange right off the tree. Finally, I arrived at my destination. It was 1955. I was 20 years old, and had 37 cents to my name.

Long Beach California was a Navy town. Downtown West of American Ave along Ocean Blvd were rows of bars next to one another. The streets were busy and there were a lot of pretty women wearing very little clothing, all looking healthy and full of fun. I spotted a dollar bill on the street and picked it up. Within five minutes of arriving, I had increased my net worth over 300 percent. I stopped in a small café and asked the owner if he had any work I might do. He let me take out some trash and mop the floors. He fixed me a hamburger and two fried eggs. I didn't have the heart to tell him that I especially hated fried eggs from being forced to eat them cold when I was in boarding school. I ate, choked them down, and asked him if I could store my stuff for a few hours in his store room. He said yes and gave me two dollars. I left to get a much needed cold beer.

The first bar I stopped at was called the Saratoga. It was packed. I got two free beers while I was there as two customers bought the house a drink. The women were friendly enough but it was obvious that they were looking for someone to buy them drinks. I left and thought I had better scout out the town and get my bearings. I would need a place to sleep and a job pretty quickly. South of Ocean Blvd was an Amusement Park called the Pike. I was watching the roller coaster when some young boy stood up, got his head cracked open on a beam, and fell to the pavement dead. After the excitement died down I went up to Ocean Blvd and started hitting cafes asking for work. One thing I had learned about restaurant work, you always ate good, there was usually a high turnover of help, and most bosses would give you an advance on your pay.

The first café I went into said that their dishwasher hadn't shown up. If he didn't show up in the next 30 minutes, I could have his job. He gave me a cup of coffee while we waited. The man did not show or phone. I started washing dishes, pots, and pans by hand. Didn't these people ever hear of automatic dishwashing machines? Their regular dishwasher finally showed up with some story and the boss bought it. He let me finish the shift. He told me if I still needed a job tomorrow to check with him. He paid me in cash, six dollars and change. The bastard took out withholding on eight dollars. I'm sure, seeing he paid me cash that the government would never see the withheld taxes. Everyone has a scam going. I felt like hitting him but I was too tired. It was a busy night and I worked hard. I thanked him and left to get my gear.

I had enough money to rent a locker at the Greyhound station to stow my stuff until I found a safe place to stay. The trick was to keep clean, get enough to eat, don't get arrested, and don't call attention to yourself. It was getting late and I decided to go back to the Saratoga and have another beer. It was only thirty five cents. It seemed that the bars closed at Two AM and it was a little after one. I hadn't the faintest idea where I was going to sleep that night. I spotted an all night movie, 3 features for $.35 a block off Ocean Blvd on Pine Ave. That might work. The bar was closing. I left tired and sober.

As I was walking down the street I noticed a woman in high heels limping going in my same direction. I quickened my pace and caught up with her. “Excuse me, Lady, It looks like you could use some help”

“I seemed to have twisted my ankle. If I can hold on to your shoulder until I get home I would be grateful.”

“Sure thing, glad to help.” She put her hand on my shoulder and I put my arm around her waist to steady her.

“It’s just a couple of blocks. My name’s Iris.”

“And I’m Joe Kennedy from Chicago. I’m new to this town.”

“Do you mind sitting on this park bench for a moment? I’m really beat.”

“Sure, take all the time you need. I’ve got no place to go.” We sat on the bench and Iris offered me a cigarette. I declined as I didn’t smoke and looked her over. She wasn’t beautiful but she was attractive and sexy. Her low cut short dress was a little too tight and she wore too much makeup. She looked like a hooker. “What does Joe Kennedy from Chicago do, besides rescuing damsels in distress?”

“Right now, It’s the only thing on my plate. I just got into town and I don’t have a job yet. I’m a song writer and hope to be a writer someday. All I need is a break.”

"Do you have a place to stay?"

"No. I was going to check out that all night movie house."

"If you don't mind sleeping on the couch, you can stay at my place a couple of days if that will help you."

"Are you sure?"

"You seem like a nice boy. Not too many people help each other these days. Just don't steal any of my things. I haven't got much but I want to keep what I've got." Iris got up and we continued on to her place. I thought she might be joking about the couch but she gave no indication that she wanted sex so I didn't try anything. Her foot was probably hurting her. I slept on the coach. It was one room with a Murphy bed, a small kitchenette along one wall and a tiny bathroom with a shower. It was small but clean. She had no problem taking her dress off in front of me but she crawled into bed in her underwear and that was that. I fell into a deep sleep.

The next morning before she left for school, I got the Iris story. She was going to barber college on very little money. She wasn't a professional but she would bring the occasional man home. She had a small list of regulars who gave her extra money. She said that she appreciated my help but I would have to get my own place soon. With me there her regulars wouldn't be coming around. I told her that I understood and that I would move out as soon as I could or whenever she wanted me out. I told her I was sorry that I didn't have any money to give her but when I got a job I'd like to be one of her regulars. She gave me a long look and said that would be nice. She gave me a key to her apartment and left for school.

I took a shower, shaved, and left. I headed for the boarding house where Mary and I were to meet accidently when she left her husband and came to California. They didn't have a vacancy. I'd better find a job fast. My current housing situation did not look to promising and one of Iris regulars just might try to beat me up. I wasn't particularly scared but I wanted to stay out of trouble. I had a habit of getting into more trouble accidently than most people did on purpose.

I checked the phone book for the dishwashers union and went to see them. They sent me to Hof's Hut downtown Long Beach. I was hired as a dishwasher on the swing shift starting immediately for the princely sum of $1.25 an hour. After working three shifts I was able to get an advance of $20. I went to the YMCA but they didn't have rooms available. I found a room off the Pike for $8 a week and was glad to get it. Iris was getting a little peeved that I was still there. I was getting horny but I wouldn't spend my hard earned money on her. We stayed friends and I let her cut my hair at barber college rates of $.15. Back in those days I wore a flat top hair cut and fit right in with the off duty Navy personnel.

I heard of an opening for a busboy at the Talk of the Town in Belmont Shore. I thought that you had to be 21 to work in a dinner house and I lied about my age. I was hired and I quit Hof's Hut. The owner Mr. Mum, took a liking to me. When I was finished with the dinner crowd, he would let me work behind the bar training to be a bartender. I loved working behind the bar but I was not of legal age to be serving drinks. After a couple of weeks I quit. I liked the man too much to jeopardize his liquor license. I never told him why I quit.

I lived on Ada Street. There were two rows of small apartments downstairs and single rooms on the second floor that shared a common bathroom. The area was south of Ocean Blvd and just west of the Pike. It was called "The Jungle" and with good reason. It was cheap housing where the Carney's, Navy personnel, merchant seamen, bikers, working women, and assorted bad characters lived. There were three bars in the Jungle and I hung out mostly at the Sea King close to my room.

It was a tough bar and if there weren't three fights a shift, it was a slow day. My turn came and I had to show some asshole that it doesn't pay to mess with the kid from South Chicago. The owner was there. "Kennedy, I like the way you handle yourself. How would you like to work here?"

Mac the day bartender was always drunk, had money in his pocket, three beautiful girlfriends, and a wife somewhere. It looked to me like the perfect life. Hell, I took the job. Why not? The bar opened at 6AM, closed at 2 AM, and I started working relief shifts. I started at $18 a shift, plus drinks, and tips, no meals. Directly across the way from us was the bar the "Tops Neptune", Their day bartender was a retired Navy Chaplain by the name of Stu Newman who had worked there almost 20 years. Stu was a gay man but a real nice person. The gay crowd tended to stay away from our bar as we were considered rough trade and frequented the Neptune. We used to joke that Stu was the only ordained bartender in town and he probably was.

After a few paychecks I moved into a furnished apartment downstairs on Ada Street and my sex life started picking up like a runaway train. I checked a few times to see if Mary had called or left me a message but nothing. I wasn't too particular about women and quantity aced quality. If you're drunk enough they're all beautiful. All women seemed to love bartenders. Life was good.

One day when I got my paycheck I noticed I had been paid for 4 days that I didn't remember working. "You're drinking too much" I said to myself. I never seemed to feel drunk, just high and maintaining it. However, every time I took a drink I marked it down. I was drinking a quart of whisky a shift, straight shots washed down with tap beer, and then sitting at the bar and drinking even more. At this rate I was going to kill myself. I decided that if I was going to be a bartender, which I loved, it would have to be in a better place, one where you are not required to drink behind the bar.

I enrolled in the local bartending school and paid cash for my tuition. The Sea King was a shot and a beer toilet. I had to learn the fancy cocktails and proper glassware. I aced the course in two days. I already knew how to handle customers and work a cash register. The instructor took an immediate dislike to me and said I had a bad attitude. I told him he could shove his fake school with its colored water. We got off on the wrong foot when he told me to use clear nail polish. It would be a cold day in hell before Joe Kennedy would wear nail polish. All in all I did learn enough to be dangerous and get the better jobs. I got a bartending job in a nice neighborhood working class bar called the Wade Inn. I lasted all of one week. I got drunk on my first paycheck and didn't make it back to work.

I needed a break. I decided to hitch hike to Chicago to see my mother and my brother Shaun. I took Route 66 the entire way and it took me three days. Everyone was fine and glad to see me. Chicago had changed as much as I had. Most of my old friends were gone in the service, jail, moved on, or dead. I did manage to find Billy Thornton, my friend from Fenger High School. He was working at Great American Screw Corporation where his step-father was a general plant manager. He said he could get me a job. I wasn't too thrilled about living with my step father, Rod. So I signed on.

I was a machine operator running a threader machine. Twelve hour shifts, six & seven days a week. The money was great, the loud noise was unbearable, the work was hard, tiring, and not enough time to rest and recover. I took a cheap room in a small hotel close to work where some idiot tested outboard engines under my window during weekdays when I was trying to sleep. I had to drink myself to sleep. I didn't have the time or strength for women and was usually too tired to care but I was making good money.

A job opened up on the blast furnaces in the Heat Treating Department. I called Frank O'Hara in Nashville. The job paid $12.00 an hour straight time. Frank had never made over sixty cents an hour in his life except for his short stint in the Air Force. He jumped at the chance. I wired him bus fare and he came. He lasted exactly two days on the job. He was afraid of fire and couldn't get close enough to the furnaces to work them and he was fired. He was furious because he felt that he had let me down.

Billy was fed up with his step father trying to run his life and telling him what to do. Billy was afraid that he would kill the son of a bitch. I was bone tired of the dead end job, and Frank didn't know what the hell to do. I suggested that we all go to Long Beach. Over several rounds of cold beer it was decided that we go. Billy had a car but he owed way too much money on it. His step father had co-signed the loan on it. We decided to hitch hike and leave the car behind.

Frank had a small bag of clothes, Billy had two suitcases mostly filled with expensive shirts he was accustomed to wearing, and I show up with a footlocker, Navy sea bag, and my portable typewriter. It would take at least a small truck to pick up all three of us with the stuff we had. We decided to split up. Frank and Billy would stay together and I would go it alone. We made arrangements to meet at the Sea King when we got there. We separated and they got the first ride. Occasionally we would see each other on the road and once we were actually at the same café at the same time.

Frank and Billy actually got to Long Beach almost a full day before I did. They got a single room at a small inexpensive hotel downtown. They found the Sea King and were drinking there when I showed up having put my gear in a locker at the Greyhound station. Frank had actually found a job of sorts as a dance instructor for the Arthur Murray Dance Studios. It was commission only but it was something. We shared our road stories and before we got too drunk, I rented a room on Ada St where I used to live. They didn't have a vacant apartment. The next day I went to see Mr. Mum at the Talk of the Town. All he had was a dishwashing job that I took. None of us were good at saving money and together we didn't have much. I wasn't worried about myself but I was concerned for my friends. I had talked them into coming out here.

I had two good meals every night at work and the cook fixed me two sandwiches to take home that I gave to Frank and Billy. I got off work at two in the morning and walked home along the beach to downtown Long Beach, from Belmont Shores, a good 45 minute walk. One night the night bartender left the liquor storeroom unlocked. I saw my chance and I took it. I took two bottles of whisky and hid them in the garbage pail until I could stash them outside. It was chilly along the beach that night and I sipped on the whisky to keep warm. The beach was usually deserted that time of night. Suddenly the beach was covered with squirming, flipping, silver tiny fishes, thousands of them.

It was Grunion coming to spawn. I had heard of Grunion but I thought people were putting me on. I didn't believe they were real. I had enough to drink so that I couldn't believe my eyes. I was actually scared. I drank some more and got the hell out of there. The rest of the walk was deserted, quiet, and restful. I arrived at Billy and Frank's hotel. I pounded loudly on the door yelling "Here's your God damn sandwiches." When Frank opened the door I pushed passed him, threw the sandwiches on the bed, and promptly vomited on the floor. They were evicted the next morning. I don't remember how I managed to get home that night.

They had run out of money. Frank was able to get the manager of the dance studio to let them crash there at night, but it was temporary at best. I wasn't making enough money for the three of us and frankly I was a little tired of being the only one working. Billy couldn't find a job and Frank couldn't close a deal on a dance lesson contract. I decided to take my job back as bartender at the Sea King and Billy went to work as a dishwasher at the Talk of the Town, my old job.

Billy was a good looking boy who always got the best looking women with almost no effort. He hooked up with a beautiful cocktail waitress, Rudy, that he met at the Stroller's Club and moved in with her in her one bedroom apartment. She never asked him for a dime towards rent and gave him most of her tips for his spending money. Billy, like me was 20, while Rudy was 27. She could have any man she wanted but she loved Billy.

Billy was rather indifferent towards women. He liked them but he never showed any affection in public. He never was jealous and was confident that another woman one would come along and they always did. In High School he was never without a girl friend and they were always the best lookers in the whole school.

Frank, on the other hand knew a lot of beautiful girls, but in all the years I knew him, he never had a steady girlfriend. Somehow, it did not seem to bother him. Nothing bothered Frank. I never saw him lose his temper or get in a fight. Whatever life threw at him, Frank accepted and soldiered on. He was the ultimate hippy before they came on the scene. Frank seemed to mix with the younger college crowd, Billy blended in with the young upward-mobile professional working group, while I tended towards the rough, bad-ass, hard-drinking, trouble making group. We were different but we were good friends and partied together often. Life was good.

Chapter 9

I was drinking too much. I was maintaining my bartending job at the Sea King but blackouts were more frequent. I had my own apartment again on Ada St. I was waking up with women I didn't remember. A few I knew but most were total strangers. I don't know what line I used when I was drunk but it obviously worked. I had more women in one week than many men had in their entire lifetime. It was 1956 and I just turned 21, the legal age to drink. Party on and on, there was no tomorrow, just today, and we were all going to live forever. Live fast, die young, and have a good looking corpse. We couldn't die young and live forever, so, we had to live each day as long as possible.

Shaun Robert Kennedy, my little brother, showed up unannounced on my doorstep. He ran away from home just three months before graduating from High School and hitched to Long Beach.. He was fed up with Rod D'Angelo, our stepfather mistreating our mother. He was 16 years old. I didn't know what to do with him It was obvious that he wasn't going back home. I got him fake ID that was good enough to get him into a bar but I couldn't find him a job. He stayed with me and eagerly joined the party life.

Shaun, like I was at his age was shy around women, and he was a virgin. He started drinking in excess and was drunk most of the time. I didn't know what to do with him nor could I control him. His original plan was to join the Marines when he turned 17 which was the coming December 17, 1956. To do this he had to have written permission from our mother. I called her but she refused to sign the papers, claiming he was too young. I told her that Shaun was running wild, I couldn't take care of him on the money that I was making, and he definitely was not going to come home. The Marine Corp would give him a chance to grow up and make a man out of him. The way was going he would probably end him up in jail or be hurt from fighting. She finally agreed to sign the papers. I was relieved but it was two months before he turned 17.

Shaun was a tough kid and in great physical shape from weight lifting. But he was not able to handle the older, heavier, more experienced men he tended to get into fights with, most of whom could hold their liquor better. Shaun was the hardest headed person I'd ever met. The kid would never give up. Even when he was a small child, you would have to beat him to death to get him to do something that he didn't want to do. I let him drink in the Sea King when I was working so I could look out for him, but it was a tough crowd.

I had earned some respect and had some good friends but Shaun had a wise mouth like me and was always getting into trouble. One day my boss said to me "Your brother looks too young to be in here".

"Do you think I would jeopardize your license by serving a minor? Check his ID. Everyone in our family looks younger than they are. You should see our mother." This is how I answered him remembering how I was only 20 myself when I had worked for him. Shaun at 16 no way looked like an adult except that he was big. The boss believed me. I was all right unless the Vice Squad came in and checked Shaun's ID. It sure wasn't that good. Between me and Billy Thorton we managed to keep my brother from getting himself killed, but even Billy was getting tired of fighting Shaun's fights.

Finally the day came and Shaun joined the Marines Corp. We threw him a big party, sobered him up the next day, and put him on the bus. We collectively kept our fingers crossed that one he would pass the tough physical and two that he could get thru basic training without slugging someone. He made it on both counts. I was proud of him but I also missed the little runt.

It was about this time that I hit a cop and got in deep shit with the Long Beach Police Department. It wasn't just any cop, it was Captain Harvey Johnston of the Vice Squad. I was at a motorcycle party in the Jungle, drunk as usual, sitting on a couch with each arm around a girl, when this buffoon bumps into me and my drink spills over onto one of the girls. I felt that the jerk did it on purpose. I got up and hit him in the jaw with everything I had. He didn't even blink. It was like hitting a brick wall. "How would you like to finish this outside, punk?"

I had a sober moment. The man was a giant, his arms were the size of my legs. There were a lot of my biker friends at the party. I thought that they would stop this guy from really hurting me if I couldn't handle it. I was called out. Nobody calls Joe Kennedy a punk and gets away with it. I had to fight. I went to the door. His partner was outside, hand cuffed me, put me in a choke hold, knuckles in my back stretching my stomach. "Hey, I didn't know you guys were cops"

"Sorry, punk." The giant hit me hard in the stomach. They dragged me to an unmarked squad car, threw me in the back seat, and one of them got in with me and began hitting me. They parked somewhere and beat me unconscious. I came to in a solitary confinement cell. My chest hurt so bad I could hardly breathe or move. I screamed until a guard came and got me a doctor.

"I heard that you fell down a flight of stairs?" said the doctor.

"Do I look like I fell down a flight of stairs?" He just shook his head. They took me on a gurney to the local hospital for x-rays and returned me to my cell. My ribs weren't broken but the cartilage was separated. The doctor gave me pain pills and bandaged my ribs. It was the last I saw him.

They held me for 72 hours before they charged me with drunk & disorderly. I was beaten so badly that they wouldn't even let a trustee see me. It was always a uniformed cop who brought me my meals and they kept the one little metal window closed so no one could see me. I wasn't allowed a phone call. Finally they had to take me to court. When the Judge called my name I couldn't come to my feet by myself and two prisoners had to help me up. When the charge was read and I had to plead, I said "I'll plead guilty, your Honor, with an explanation. I didn't know these men were policemen, they were in plain clothes, and did not identify themselves. I have sense enough to not ever hit a policeman."

"Mr. Kennedy, I'm giving you 5 days for the drunk charge and 10 days for disorderly. Maybe, by then you will feel better." That was that. Fifteen days in jail and I did heal slowly and painfully.

I got my job back at the Sea King. Billy had disappeared somewhere and I had a problem. The Vice Squad began coming into the Sea King rousting the customers. The boss couldn't have this so he had to let me go. Many of my customers worked at the local oil refineries and talked me into giving it a try. Back in those days we didn't have a union hiring hall. We gathered at the gate before each shift and the foreman would pick the men he needed, usually from one to ten men, or everyone, when the plant had what they called a shutdown.

It was obvious who got picked first. It was the ones who were kicking back to the foreman. The word was put in for me and I was hired as a laborer. The work was hard, dangerous, and dirty but it paid well. I was always a good worker and in a matter of a few weeks I was made a helper. I refused to kick back to the foreman so I didn't get to work regular except for the shutdowns. Between six local refineries and unemployment insurance between jobs, one could make a fairly decent living.

Shaun finished his basic training and came to Long Beach. I had just been laid off at Texaco . The timing was perfect. Shaun had a 10 day leave, we both had money in our pockets, and he wanted to go to Tijuana. Why not? Along with two friends we drove down to Sin City across the border. One of our friends spoke Spanish and was going to show us around and keep us out of trouble.

I couldn't believe my brother. He had become a man. I don't know what the Marines did to him, but he could have been a poster boy for them. For the first time in my life I was a little afraid of him. I was in awe. And how he could drink! It seemed he couldn't get drunk. He had a tight control of himself. And the women! The first bar we went to we all had a whore. After the first one Shaun had another, and then a third. I couldn't believe it. In one day he had sex with seven different women. He beat my all time record by four women and this was my little virgin brother! Why in the hell didn't I join the Marines?

Shaun's leave was over and he left to be stationed in San Francisco for special training. Back in Long Beach, broke, I nailed a bartender job at a nice restaurant and bar named the Crows Nest. Nice customers, good tips, and great people to work for. It took only a week before the Vice Squad found me and started frequenting the bar. It got so when the Police stopped me for a traffic violation it was "Yes, Sir, No Sir" until they ran me. They must have had a code that disclosed I was a cop beater for then they ceased being nice. I would get slammed against the car, arms twisted up behind my back, and usually handcuffed as tightly as they could force them.

It was rumored that the cops use to stop the elevator between floors and beat on their prisoners in the old jail house in Long Beach. I knew it to be true for often I was the one beaten. I was getting picked up every time I turned my back for whatever they could dream up. It was definitely time to get out of town. I guessed it would take about a year before they would forget me.

Billy had shown up. He was working as a dishwasher for the Copper Skillet, a small coffee house. He was no longer living with the barmaid and he really hated not being able to find a better job. There was no way he wanted to go back to Chicago. Frank was starting to make a little money as a dance instructor, was dating a lot of beautiful women, and hanging out with a college crowd. He was happy and didn't want to make a change. I said my goodbyes and started back to Chicago hitchhiking. It was one wild ride.

Once I made highway 66 it was a straight shot to Chicago. My first ride was Ted Marsh and he was in a hurry. Seems he had been out of work and he and his new wife weren't getting along because of lack of money. He finally got a job, hurried home to tell his wife the good news, even borrowed money so they could have a celebration in a nice restaurant, only to find that she had left him. Her father had wired her money and she caught a Greyhound bus back home to Oklahoma. Ted put the medal to the pedal and floored his old car to the max. He was determined to catch up with the bus, get his wife back, and make it back to California to start his new job in the morning. He drove like a mad man. She had a three and a half hour head start on him.

Police would stop him for speeding. He just stuffed the ticket in his pocket, gritted his teeth, and soon as the cop was out of view, he would floor it again. He drove me over a 1,000 miles at top speed before he let me off, and sped off. I often wondered if he ever caught up with his wife. As luck would have it, my next ride was an off-duty ambulance driver who, like Ted, was in a hurry.

Tommy was the emergency standby for the Budweiser Clydesdale horse parades that were held all over the United States. He had three days off and he was driving to Chicago to spend a night with his girlfriend. He was going to make it or die trying. I guess he picked me up to talk to and keep him awake. That ambulance would do an easy 120 miles per hour and that is how Tommy drove . He would slow down a little as he approached a town, turned on the siren, and drove flat out. He brought me right to my Mother's front door, siren blazing, and drove off peeling rubber. Needless to say, it was my personal record for hitchhiking to Chicago from Long Beach which I did a total of seven times.

I stayed at my mother's house a couple of days until I grabbed a job. This time I was a soda jerk at Melody Lanes, a drive-inn that specialized in ice cream specialty creations. Similar to a bartender the girls played up to me to get a little extra, but it was a kid's job. I just had to do better. I remember my first office job with the Motor Club that I obtained thru a free placement service. I went downtown to see them. I was offered and accepted a job at Lerner Shops as an Assistant Department Head at a fairly good starting salary. It was a Jewish owned business.

I knew nothing about Jews except for a girl I dated briefly in high school named Renee Levy. Her father was from the old country and I could tell that he wasn't too happy with me seeing his daughter, but he always treated me well and with respect. I never understood the bigotry against Jews and I figured here was an opportunity to learn why. At my young age I sensed most people were jealous because they were mostly successful and kept to themselves. I knew of course what happened to them in World War Two and it was beyond my comprehension. I was determined to find out the secret of their financial success. It was said that they controlled the world's wealth. I went to work for the Jews.

I worked for Lerner Shops for six months. At the time it was the longest I'd worked for anyone. It was hard work but I liked it and it paid extremely well. Basically, we were a distribution center. New York would ship us goods and it was our job to ship them to the various 37 stores Lerner retail stores in the Mid West. Lerner Shops sold medium priced women and children clothing and accessories. This was the age before computers. All information was stored on IBM pin punched data cards. I worked in an open office with my immediate boss and 47 to 50 women, two of whom were my personal secretaries. Our office was responsible for the entire women's' line.

The business plan was basic and fairly simple. We tracked sales for three classes of stores, A, B, & C A stores being the largest and with the most retail sales. Our job was to keep them supplied with merchandise with the minimum shipping costs. Detail, accurate records, and timing were everything. As long as everything went smoothly, everyone was happy and I was pretty much left alone to do my job. As when I was in the Navy I basically ran the whole department. I was the youngest executive in the entire organization and quickly got a raise.

Everything went smoothly. I worked had, never took a coffee break, and ate lunch at my desk. I was always a hard worker regardless of the job. I felt that you make your own good luck. I learned early that the only one that was going to take care of me was me. I almost quit drinking and when I did drink, it was very little. I was on my way up.

It took me an hour to get to work and an hour to get back home on the South Side to the small apartment I had rented. Recalling the many beautiful women my friend Frank O'Hara met thru dancing, I applied for a part time job as a dance instructor after work with the Fred Astaire dance studio just three blocks from Lerner Shops downtown. I would get off work at 4:30, grab a quick dinner, and learn ball room dancing from 6 to 9PM five nights a week. In our class there were always 25 to 40 absolutely beautiful women instructor trainees. After classes I would take as many as 12 to 15 of these gorgeous women out to the best night clubs in downtown Chicago. They always paid for their own drinks when men weren't buying us a round. What a trip, walking into a nightclub with all these women and being the only male escort. I never made out with any one of them. I was just too tired and didn't have enough time.

I had two main rules about women that I tried to live by. Don't date married women or women you work with. There were many beautiful young women that worked with me in the office and one of my well-developed young personal secretaries showed a obvious liking for me. I didn't know it but the office women had a betting pool on which one I would date first. It seems there is something about women which prohibits them from allowing men to stay single and happy.

It was someone's birthday or something. As usual I was too busy to pay attention when May, my secretary, asked me if I wanted some. I looked up from my desk to face those beautiful full breasts in a tight pink sweater staring at me inches from my face. I couldn't think. I was speechless. I blushed bright red. I looked down and saw she was offering me some chocolates from a candy box. "Oh, you mean candy?" I stammered. The girls in the office laughed so loud that the big boss opened his door to check out what was happening. I was so embarrassed I started choking. It just made it worse.

May was 18, short, beautiful, and well endowed. She asked me out to a family function. Against my better judgment I went out with her. I made a pass, she rejected me, and from then on, I could never get a decent days work out of her. She would pretend that she didn't hear me. I was afraid to fire her as the other women would think I did it out of spite. I didn't have the faintest idea what to do. I just soldiered on the best I could and worked without her help. It put more work on my other secretary but she never complained.

I was invited to several business functions, dinners, seminars, and sometimes I joined some of the higher executives at a bar after work. I found Jewish men to be very warm, generous, and intelligent. They seemed to keep their personal lives to themselves but they had a good sense of humor. I was made to feel a part of the crew and treated with dignity and respect. The only secret I found out about them was that they always did business with their own people. They would drive a mile out of their way to buy a loaf of bread from a Jewish owned store rather than the corner store. I personally thought it was a smart thing to do and could see how keeping your money within your own group maximized profits.

The downside was I was the highest paid non Jewish executive in the entire organization and there was little or no chance for advancement. I loved them anyway. I probably didn't have a discriminating thought in my body except for stupid, lazy & mean persons. I played the cards I was dealt in life and felt privileged to sit in the game. Of course, I was young and naive then.

It was about a month before Christmas when New York shipped us 10,000 little fur muffs. As this was a new item without any previous sales history, I went to the warehouse to personally inspect them. They were the cutest things I had ever seen. They were made to look like animals, rabbits, cats, dogs, etc. Little girls would love them. I just knew this was going to be a big seller and I expected future shipments. As timing is everything, I shipped them all out immediately. Within a week the A stores were ordering more of these muffs. I didn't have any more. I checked the warehouse daily but New York didn't ship anymore. The A stores sold out and went over my head to my boss. He called me into his office.

"What the hell is the matter with you Kennedy. Ship these stores their muffs. What are you waiting for, the after Christmas sale? They're calling me personally. I don't need this grief."

"I haven't got anymore."

"The invoice showed they shipped 10,000."

"I shipped them all out."

"You did WHAT?"

"I shipped them all. I expected more."

"You shipped $10,000 worth of untested merchandize without authorization from me?"

"I checked them out personally. I knew they would sell." I believed that he was going to have a heart attack right in front of me. He couldn't speak for a moment. "Ship them from the B & C stores now."

"I can't. They're asking for more too. Get on New York. They're not returning my calls."

"Get back to work and never do anything like this again without checking with me. This is gambling with company money. It is not business." I didn't try to argue. I left. All 10,000 muffs sold except for two returns for being defective. I was proved right but I was still wrong. This hurt.

There was one other young man who worked for Lerner Shops at our location. Bob Caswell was his name. He had a lesser job than I did basically doing the same thing on a much smaller scale in the children's clothing line. Bob was Polish, non Jewish, one year younger than I was, and came from a poor family. For someone who was raised with five sisters, he was completely naive about women. His father had passed away and Bob had to work to help out. He had never finished high school.

We became pretty good friends and he admired the stories of my wicked life. He especially liked it when I took him with me to one of the night clubs with the all the dance instructors. He lived on the South side of Chicago and I introduced him to all the few friends I still had. I felt sorry for him but I liked him. He was a good guy but nothing like me. He was 20 years old and still a virgin! I believed he was going to die one he was so shy.

Suddenly without notice Franklin DeLano Roesevelt O'Hara showed up from Long Beach, California, to see me. I put him up at my apartment. It was great to see him and he looked good with a California tan. As usual he didn't have much money with him. Seemed he hitched to Nashville to visit his family and decided on a whim to come to Chicago to see how I was doing. Frank, Bob, and I hit the bars and had a blast. I had to quit the dance studio to spend time with Frank. I was drinking too much and really not getting enough rest. Frank wanted me to come back to Long Beach with him. He had arranged to drive someone's brand new car to Long Beach with all expenses paid.

"Are you crazy, Buddy? I got it made here. Good job, good salary, lots of women, my own pad, Why would I leave this?"

"Joe, I know you. You would be happier washing dishes in California than fighting this cold weather, snow, and ice here in Chicago. And the women are friendlier in Long Beach from what I've seen her. You're working way too hard."

"No way, Frank. Good jobs are too hard to find these days with only a high school education. I'm staying here. Christ, I've got 50 women working under me."

"You wish."

"You know what I mean. Quit asking me. I'm staying."

The next day as I got off the elevated to walk the two blocks to work along the icy streets in downtown Chicago, I looked up at the sky. I realized it was the first time I had looked at the sky in five months. Frank was right. I've been working too hard. It was Monday morning and with my hangover the day wasn't starting out too well. May was pulling her usual routine pretending that I didn't exist, my boss was upset over something I didn't get finished last week, and suddenly I was just plain tired of the whole mess. Frank stopped by to say goodbye and I told him "Let's go get a cup of coffee."

It was the first coffee break I ever took while I worked there. "Frank. Let's go pick up my stuff. I've changed my mind. I'm going with you." I never said a word nor did I ever go back. Again I was on my way to Long Beach and, as luck would have it, my first job was washing dishes at Pierpoint Restaurant on Terminal Island.

Chapter 10

On the way back we stopped off to visit with my old roommate Harry Coen who was living in Oklahoma City with his wife, Karl Rhienhardt's little sister. They had a little baby and were doing just fine. He had no contact with his wife's family whatsoever. We all went out to dinner. Harry put us up for the night and the next morning we left. I never saw or heard from him again.

Wayne Brodski owned Pierpoint Restaurant and he was a first class idiot, disliked but tolerated by most. True, I was only a dishwasher but he had a bar and I was hoping to be his bartender, but he treated me like I would never be anything but a lowly dishwasher. It seemed he was a no class jerk that had the good fortune to marry into a rich family who bought him the restaurant. He had a God complex and felt he was better than everyone. I couldn't see how his wife stood him. She looked like she had some class. I did my usual great job and was soon promoted to busboy. For some reason Wayne seemed to like me. Not enough to be his equal, but he let me live in his world.

Outside the restaurant was a huge outdoor sea water tank with live sea lions which was the attraction that brought people to the restaurant. The food was good, prices were fair, and the place was clean. In spite of Wayne it did a good business. I behaved myself and kept a low profile. I didn't know if the Long Beach Police Department had forgotten me yet. Frank hadn't seen Billy for some time and I was determined to find him. It took me a while.

Meanwhile, I got a job as a vault teller for the Bank of America on Pine Ave in Long Beach. The salary was $1 an hour. The job basically was working in a basement room next to the vault, counting armored car deposits and making change for the regular tellers as they needed it. I handled between $100,000 to $250,000 cash per day. Then, after the bank was closed to the public we would go into the vault and verify each other's and the tellers cash deposits. The vault held no less than two and a half million dollars in cash every day.

I always thought of myself as an honest person. For example, I took pride in the fact that I never stole so much as a dime when I was a bartender. This was totally different. Cash mistakes were made both by the tellers and the merchants in their deposits. I could have taken advantage of this and no one could prove otherwise. I was the verifier. Money no longer held a true value for me. I handled so much cash that it seemed like play money. It wasn't mine so I didn't take any but I devised a plan to rob the vault.

The plan was real, simple, and completely doable without anyone getting hurt. With three more men we could make off with all the money we could carry. I talked it over with Frank, Billy, and a new friend Bobby Dubbs from the East coast. After two weeks of examining and questioning the plan from every angle over beers, we decided to do it. Billy was a gangster at heart, Bobby would just as soon kill a man as look at him, and Frank would go along with anything. Bobby wanted to have a gun just in case. I had planned everything down to the last detail without the use of any weapons except chloroform.

I was starting to get uncomfortable. Then I had a thought. I wanted to be a writer. Why not write a book about the caper, they would make a movie out of it, and I would make as much money as stealing it. I called it off but it was too real. I quit my job. The bank liked me and begged me to stay, even offering me a raise, but I refused. The temptations too great. It would have been too easy. I never did write that book. It was a great plan though.

I decided to go back to the Oil Refineries where I could make eight times what I was paid at the bank. I had met Bobby Dubbs or Bobby D as he preferred to be called, thru a pool hustler I met at the Sea King, a Bostonian named Kenny DeSilva. Little Kenny was a small man who was the best pool shooter I ever saw. It was rumored that he was born on a pool table in the back room of a Boston bar. He was the most unintentional funniest person I ever met. We became best of friends. Bobby D was his childhood friend who was visiting from Boston. I was a little scared of Bobby D, everyone was.

Little Kenny worked as a machine operator in a union can factory that manufactured beer cans. The work was seasonal. When he worked, there was a lot of overtime, and he made good money. When he was laid off, he collected unemployment insurance, supplemented by union insurance, and mostly played the horses. He always bragged that he won consistently. For extra money he shot money pool and he always knew he had a job when they started making more beer cans. And he drank, we all did then.

Kenny taught me how to shoot pool. I was a little better than average but I was never in Kenny's league. He being small, needed a large man to partner with for protection when he gambled. It didn't matter how good I was as he could always run the table when he wanted to. He knew the tricks of the trade and I was expert at keeping the suckers to make the bets. The more I drank, the worse I shot,. The more I shot off my big mouth, the more they wanted to beat us.

"You guys just ain't ready for us yet" was my taunt that got us into the money games. The only problem was that you couldn't tell when Kenny got drunk, he would never admit it, but his game would suffer. Nobody wins all the time but we did pretty good. So good in fact, that when we were both out of work, we took two months off and hustled pool games from Long Beach to Baja, Mexico. We made enough for expenses, drinking, and wild women.

There was no question that Kenny carried me in shooting pool, but I did my part raising the bets, keeping him out of trouble, and attracting the women. The more we spent, the more women we got. We ate good, stayed mostly at cheap motels and frequented local bars. We had to keep moving as the local talent didn't take to being hustled. It was a strange life but it had its charm. Me I was drunk or hung over most of the time. Good thing I was young, healthy, and tough. I was gathering a lot of great stories for when I wrote my book.

Back in Long Beach, Big Bob, a true giant of a man, who owned the Circus Room bar on American Ave, got a hard on for me and wanted to play me a game of pool. He was a top pool player and he thought I was a big phony. He wouldn't play partners with me and Kenny. He wanted one on one with me. I kept turning him down as I knew that I didn't stand a chance to beat him but I knew the day would come. The pressure kept mounting. I could have just stayed out of the bar but the word was out. It was going to happen.

I went in the Circus Room alone. I was more than a little drunk. Big Bob spied me and came over. "Are you ready for a game now or do you have another lame excuse. Your hot shot buddy's not here to hold your hand."

"Listen, Bob. I'm tired of you ragging on me. I told you that you just are not ready for me yet. I don't want to make you look bad in front of your friends but if you insist, I'll tell you what I'll do. I'll play you one game, and one game only, win or lose, for $100." And I shut up. $100 was a lot of money in those days.

"You're on." We both laid our money on the bar and flipped a coin. I won. I elected to break and he racked the balls. The word spread fast and a crowd was gathering around the table. I was going to get beaten badly. Bob was the best. I got up, grabbed a cue stick from the wall rack without looking, and went to the table. Big Bob was standing there with his custom cue stick ready to run the table. Barely aiming I hit the cue and broke the rack. With a sound like a rifle shot I made the eight ball on the break. Acting like I did it every day of my life, I said "Any questions?" I walked to the bar, picked up the money, gulped my drink, and got the hell out of there. It was the only time in my life that I ever made the eight ball on the break.

Bobby D had a close resemblance to Bobby Darin, the singer. A bunch of us were at the Wilton Hotel Sky Room hustling some tourists for drinks. They thought Bobby D was actually Bobby Darrin, the singer. The funny thing was that Bobby D did fancy himself a great singer and pulled it off. Mel Torme was the headliner that night and accidently we were sitting next to his table of friends. Two of the girls with his party overheard us and they also thought Bobby was Bobby Darin and invited us to join their party. The waiter moved our tables together and we had a grand old time until Mel Torme took his break and joined us. He, of course, knew Bobby wasn't Bobby Darrin but no one believed him. They thought he was joking. Bobby D was pestering him to sing a song on stage.

Mel was getting hot as he wasn't getting any attention and out of meanness let Bobby D sing on the next set. He introduced him as Bobby D and to our surprise Bobby sang "You Don't Know Me" like a real professional. The applause was better than Mel Torme had gotten all night. After the next set Mel jumped all over me in the men's room. He tried to sucker punch me but his bodyguard stopped him. It seemed Mel's girlfriends were paying more attention to us than to him. I thought we better get out of there and we did taking the tourists with us. They even took pictures of them with the famous Bobby D back home with them. I think I'm also in the photos with my big Irish mug. Bobby D went back to Boston.

At the time in California women weren't allowed to serve hard liqueur unless they had their name on the owners' license. Bars hired what was called "B" girls to serve drinks and attract the male crowd. Many of these women would share their favors with their bartenders. The "bikers" had their mamas, we had our bar girls. It was only natural that I hit on the new bar girl who was getting off shift at the Sea King.

I was drunk and the new girl was sexually attractive. She came and sat next to me at the bar and I bought her a drink. Things were just getting hot and promising when a friend of mine said he wanted to talk to me. I got up and promised to be right back. My friend laid it on me.

"I guess no one told you Kennedy, but that's no girl. It's a man."

"You're joking, that's one sweet woman."

"Take a closer look"

"It still looks like a woman to me."

"Damn it, Joe. I'm your buddy. It's a man!"

I went back to the bar to get a closer look. It still looked like a sexy woman but my friend wouldn't lie to me. As I was checking things out, in came lover boy Billy.

"Hi, buddy, who is this beautiful creature you have uncovered here in this den of savages?" He elbowed his way between us. I was going to tell him the story but Billy had taken too many girls away from me before. I just introduced them and left them together and went across the street to the Tops Neptune.

The next morning I was having a drink at the Sea King when Billy came in and sat next to me. "Kennedy. You really are a son of a bitch, aren't you?"

I didn't say anything, quickly finished my drink, and left. I never learned what happened. Billy would never tell me but they left the bar together to go home. That was the last girl he ever tried to take from me.

Sally Marshal was a legend in the jungle. A very beautiful woman of 24 with a body to die for, deep sparkling black eyes, and long lustrous black hair down to her waist. Sally made a very good income selling her body in an area where most women were giving it away. Everyone loved her if they slept with her or not.

It was 6am and I had just opened the Sea King bar when Sally came in and asked if she could have a drink on credit. I poured her a shot of brandy into a cup of black steaming fresh coffee. "Rough night, Sally? You don't look so hot." I had never seen her look less than picture perfect before.

"Do you remember when I left the bar last night? I took a short cut home through the alley and a guy pulled me into the parking lot behind Weston's laundry. He put a knife to my throat and raped me, the son of a bitch!"

"God, that's terrible, Sally." "Yeah, all he had to do was ask." And that was the Jungle. The city of Long Beach eventually tore it all down along with the Pike.

Like many horse players, Little Kenny never talked about his losses but he would always brag about his big winnings. We all got a little tired of hearing about his easy money. One day I told him the next time that he had a sure thing to be sure to let me know. I had hoped it would slow down his endless bragging for he couldn't possibly win all the time. I was getting a hair cut in the shop next to Sylvia's Bar on Anaheim street when Little Kenny comes in and hands me an envelope.

"What's this for?"

"Your horse came in."

"What Horse?"

"Damn it, Kennedy. The horse you bet on yesterday when we were in the New Yorker. Don't you remember?"

"I don't remember yesterday, let alone the New Yorker."

"Well, you gave me $20 to bet. You won." There was $400 in the envelope. I bought the drinks at Sylvia's.

Now that was the first horse I had ever bet on. With this kind of luck I just had to go to the track with Kenny. Frank, Billy, and I gave Kenny $150 to bet for us and off we went. He lost all our money plus his own. I never bet another horse again.

I managed to get Billy on a shutdown at Texaco but he quit after two days. I couldn't believe it. He couldn't stand getting dirty. My friend was vain. He was a handsome man that women always fell for and most men were jealous of him. Back in Chicago he was one of the toughest kids on the block. He always was a sharp dresser and wore expensive fancy shirts but this was a side of him I never suspected. Pretty boy had feet of clay. I felt justified for all the pretty women he managed to get by just a snap of his fingers. Let him be a dishwasher the rest of his life.

Billy feeling like he had let me down disappeared for a couple of months. Little Kenny was hustling pool in Sylvia's Bar one night without me, won big, and on his way home was robbed and beat up pretty badly. His right eye was partly paralyzed and it forever affected his pool game. He would never admit it but he could never play with the skill he had before the beating. He started feeling depressed and kept pretty much to himself. He started drinking too much and feeling sorry for himself. He wouldn't listen to anyone.

Frank pretty much drifted away from the Jungle scene and hung with a college crowd at the Hofbrau Club in the old Robinson Hotel a half block South of Ocean Blvd. In the same hotel was the Saddle & Spurs nightclub that had dancing where Frank could really shine. The Lido ball room on the Pike closed at twelve midnight and a lot of the older crowd made their way to the Hofbrau Club just three blocks away. They had an accordion bar where they passed the microphone around and everyone sang over huge pictures of cold draft beer. Frank had a good memory, a fair voice, and sang many risqué humorous songs. He was King Frog in a small pond. Everyone knew and liked Frank.

My Brother Shaun showed up on his first leave from the Marine Corp with his great plan for us to have a drink in every bar in Long Beach. He wanted to bet me fifty dollars that he could out drink me. I told him we had better save our money. There were one hell of a lot of bars in Long Beach but we could give it a try. I insisted that we stick to beer as I didn't want a drunk driving arrest. We started at the Sea King at 6 AM. My plan was to hit all the bars in walking distance so I would not have to drive. How many beers could one person drink?

We had a beer at the Sea King, Tops Neptune, and the Palm room. On to the Pike, Ocean Blvd, and any joint open, the Nut Shell, Rainbow Club, Hollywood on the

Pike, the Checkerboard, the Saratoga, Midway, The Cruiser, New Yorker, Alibi, The Silver Dollar, Stroller's Club, Circus Room, Helen's Haven, Apple Valley Steak House, Clancys, the Pink Elephant, Old Mexico, V-Room, Press Club, Turf Club, Chili's Don's, Brownies Annex, Spuds, the Hung Jury. Then up to Anaheim street: to Davenports, Sylvias', the Blue Room. I really don't remember the rest, I don't know how my brother got back to duty, and I don't know who won the bet. Somewhere we got separated and I came to in my own bed. I'll never try it again.

My close friends gone, I stayed pretty much to myself, drinking too much, and going from job to job telling myself I was getting material to be a writer. The police seemed to have forgotten about my hitting one of them. But I was getting arrested often for drinking and fighting. I usually had money enough to forfeit bail and avoid actual jail time longer than over night. I often thought about Mary but there was never any word from her and I didn't know how to contact her.

One day when I was between jobs and drinking at the Sea King, Billy walks in. He was broke, out of work, and up against it. He was living with some queer and was getting real tired of fighting the guy off. I told him that he didn't have to live with a queer and that he could move into my apartment if he didn't mind sleeping on the couch. I phoned Wayne at Pierpoint Landing. As luck would have it, he needed a dishwasher. On my recommendation Billy could start the next afternoon. We had a couple of drinks together and he stayed with me that night.

Billy went to work the next day and planned to go over to the homosexual's apartment when he was not there to get his things. He had his own key with "My Billy Boy" inscribed on it. Billy wanted me to go with him but I refused and waited for him at the Sea King. Billy went to get his stuff and came back with a TV set for me. He took it because I didn't have one and he liked to watch the Friday night fights. He also trashed the man's apartment and broke all of his precious rare record collection.

Billy was to work the swing shift. The cook at Pierpoint Restaurant phoned me and told me that Billy better not come in. The police were there asking about him. He didn't give them my address. Billy panicked. He didn't know what to do. I told him I had a little money. Let's get out of Dodge. It would probably blow over after awhile. The Police Department wasn't too fond of homosexuals and they would probably just go thru the motions. He agreed with me. I looked up Little Kenny to say goodbye and he wanted to come with us. Frank thought we were all crazy and wished us luck.

Off the three of us went in my car to Orange County one county over and stopped in Costa Mesa where I had just enough money to rent a one bed room house behind a larger house that the landlord and his wife lived in. The old man was hesitant renting to three young single men, but he evidently needed the income. I turned on my Irish charm. We were all clean, dressed well, and fairly sober. We had a home. Now we needed jobs. Our only income was my unemployment checks. Kenny had been disqualified for getting caught working under the table and Billy didn't want his real name on anything.

We settled in. I got the bed room, Billy the couch, and Kenny slept on the floor having lost the coin toss. None of us could find work. To pay the next month's rent I sold my old ford. I had paid $100 for it and I sold it for $125. Bus transportation was sparse in that area which made it more difficult to search for jobs. I tried all the local bars for a bartenders job but no luck. Billy was afraid to look for work and Kenny was on a daily drunk spree. He was on a one year suspension from his beer can factory job, for being drunk on the job and he really wasn't trained for anything else. He had left home young and never finished grammar school. He survived in Boston by cleaning up bars and a little pool hustling.

One thing Kenny was good at was house painting. I made up some flyers for him and we covered the neighborhood. No luck. We talked the landlord into painting our rental home for a month's free rent and he bought it. Kenny sobered up enough to do the job but just barely. My car money was gone and we were getting low on food money. We subscribed to a home delivery dairy service that we paid once a month and they extended a little credit. We ordered and lived off milk, cheese, eggs, and any other food products they had. When I couldn't pay the monthly bill in full for the third month in a row, the delivery man got worried. He didn't cut us off though as he was afraid that we wouldn't pay period.

Things were getting desperate when I couldn't pay the rent. We owed everyone we could borrow from. Jobs were nonexistent in the small town of Costa Mesa and times were slow for everyone. Money was tight. We promised everyone that we would soon be working but even we didn't believe it. We were stuck in nowhere hell. I was getting a little tired of carrying the load for all three of us. Kenny was drunk most of the time and Billy was the sloppiest person I've ever met. While he was always personally clean, he would leave his dirty clothes anywhere, and he never cleaned any part of the house. These guys just weren't pulling their weight but they were my buddies. I was the one that brought them here.

Just when things were at their lowest point, I got a job in nearby Santa Ana about six weeks before Christmas 1957. I was hired to work as a sales clerk for minimum wage plus commission for Buffum's Department Store. I was to work in the Menswear Department and start three day paid training course immediately. I barely had the bus fare to get there. Luckily I had a decent wardrobe for Buffum's was a high class fashion store. The down side was I wouldn't get my first paycheck for two weeks and they had a policy of no payroll advances. How the three of us were going to make it for three weeks on little money was scary but at least I was working. We put in a large order with the milk man. I thought he was going to have a heart attack but he delivered.

I went to the three day training sessions. We used incomplete previously used sales order books to practice on. Each order book was consecutively numbered. When we went on the sales floor we would be assigned and be responsible for each new book. During coffee break I stayed behind and tore several pages out of every book and saved them for possible use. The training was predictable, boring, but thorough. I couldn't wait until I got into actual sales. The commission was 10%, their prices were high, and I was a good salesman. I was going to sell more than any temporary salesperson they ever hired. They would have to keep me on after Christmas.

The first setback was not only did they pay every two weeks but they held back a week. It would be three weeks before I got my first check. There would be only about 10 day's commission bonus paid and it was before the Christmas season really started. Knowing the exact date I would get paid I was able to tell everyone that we owed money to just when I could pay them. Everyone seemed satisfied except our milkman. He still looked like he would have a heart attack. I didn't care. I had my own worries, having enough money for the three of us to survive until my payday. I would lose my unemployment insurance checks when I started working. It was only $35 a week at the time but it was something. Now it would be two weeks with no income. I would make it somehow. I always had.

Chapter 11

Now I've always had a little larceny in my heart. I've been honest for two very basic reasons, I didn't want to go to jail and I pretty much believed in the Golden Rule. I also didn't believe in stealing chump change but for a big enough score, I might chance it. If I could take down the big guys and rationalize it, I would do it. Buffum's was the big guys who charged too much, paid little wages, and believed that they had a fool proof security system. I was going to find a flaw in their system just because they acted so superior. If I could get away with anything to equalize my low pay and not get caught, I was going to do it. I found the flaw the first day of work and it was a beaut. We were going to survive and in style.

They did not have enough cash registers for all us new hires. There were as many as seven sales clerks using the same register each punching in their private code to record their sales. I could have Kenny or Billy come in as a customer, write up a large order on one of the sales slips not registered to me and which I lifted from the training room, and then punch up the wrong number on the register. My friends would have a receipt and there was no way it could be traced back to me. Even better, was a cash sale. I would write it up on the unregistered sales slip, ring the wrong code number, and put the money in the cash drawer. Later I would take out money to get change from the main cashier and on the way pocket the extra money of the cash sale. My first day on the sales floor a lady bought a $75 sweater and paid cash that ended up in my pocket. Steak dinners and drinks for everyone that night to celebrate.

My favorite trick, which was a little risky, was to be the first one on the floor. Before the others arrived I had a new wallet, belt, cuff links, money clip, tie, and silk square. I put on the belt and tie in the store room on the pretense of doing stock work. I always was careful to remove the price tags. I wasn't all bad. I did become their top salesman of all new hires.

I did it by looking for little old ladies who had lists of gifts to buy and suggestive selling. I made it my business to know the merchandise. If they bought a sweater, I would suggest a matching shirt, pair of socks, a tie, and so on. I was fast on my feet, polite, aggressive, and fast with the required paper work. I did not socialize with other help during floor time, never took breaks, and avoided answering the phones when possible.

The week before Christmas was the busiest time I decided that was the best time to have my friends work for their Christmas presents and build up my personal wardrobe. Neither one wanted to chance it but I talked them into it. Billy came first and walked out of Buffums with over $300 in merchandise with a valid receipt in case he was stopped. He wasn't. It was Little Kenny's turn. He was scared silly and arrived half liquored up. I was going to call it off but it worked out great with Billy and I was more than a little pissed off at Kenny at the time. As I piled more and more merchandise on the counter Kenny started to sweat. He started to shake. He looked guilty as hell. I finished up as quickly as possible and gave him two large bags to carry. He practically ran out of the store. No one stopped or questioned him. It was fine. We did it. Christmas came and went and I was laid off. I made a commission of a little over $1200.

My landlord had been hovering over me like a vulture. He suspected I was getting money from somewhere. I told him I would pay him everything I owed when I got my check. The milk man had given up on us and probably resorted to praying. I know it wasn't the right thing to do but we decided to leave town without paying anyone. I had worked too hard for that money and we were going to need it now more than ever. The night I cashed my paycheck, we packed, caught the last bus to Pacific Coast Highway, and caught the Greyhound to Long Beach. I often thought of going back someday and paying that nice old trusting man who was our landlord but I never did. I had crossed the line. I was no longer a nice person.

Billy Thorton, my tough friend from Chicago, had had it. He decided to join the Air Force. I took the bus with him to Los Angeles where he was to muster for basic training. I lent him $100 for spending money. As I was walking back to the station to catch the bus back to Long Beach a woman called my name. It was Linda, 2300 miles from Chicago, a girl I had gone to Fenger High school with a million years ago. She seemed excited to see me. She was working and living in Los Angeles now. She told me that she had had a mad crush on me in high school.

"Why didn't you say something?" I asked. "I probably didn't have a girlfriend then."

"I was too shy. Maybe we can go out sometime?" She wrote down her phone number and gave it to me. I slipped it in my pocket, said goodbye, and walked away. I never did call her. All I could think of was that I lost my buddy and I might never see him again. We shared a lot of good times together. I caught the bus to Long Beach where Kenny and I shared a room on Ada street in the Jungle. At least the police never caught Billy.

I looked up Frank in the Hofbrau Club. He was still a regular there. He had grown a wild red beard and wore square granny glasses. I correctly guessed that he wasn't teaching dancing anymore. He looked like a hippy freak. He had a job on the Long Beach State Campus as a lab tech assistant, like I used to be. It didn't pay much but Frank never needed much. He was happy to see me. He confessed that he was now no longer a virgin and if I would buy a beer he would tell me all about it. I went one better and bought us two of their famous $1.25 steak dinners, plus all the beer we could drink. Frank had a thin girl friend named Georgia and I met her sexy girlfriend Violet. We had grand old time together and we all ended up at Violet's house for a party with about a third of the bar customers.

I remember writing a song when I was in Nashville; "Women just are trouble. Women are all the same. They all tell different stories but it all ends up the same." Violet had her story and it was really something. She was married and her husband was in jail for unpaid traffic tickets. Their religion didn't allow their women to wear any makeup, sexy clothes, or high heels. They were forbidden to touch, hold hands, or kiss anyone other than their spouse. And here was Violet looking like a high class hooker. Bright red lipstick, tight low cut short silver dress, with what looked liked high heeled glass slippers. Her husband was in jail and she was out to make up for lost time. She looked like Jane Russell with the body to match. She had beautiful long black hair and deep violet eyes. She took me like Grant took Richmond. I didn't have a chance. It was the wildest night of sex I ever had up to then.

The affair with Violet lasted a week and then her husband was released. I missed her but I really needed a much earned rest. I saw her on the street a few days later without any makeup and almost didn't recognize her. She was so plain looking that you would not have looked at her twice. When I had her she was the most beautiful sexy warm woman I had ever known. It was unbelievable. I'm still half in love with her memory. It was a week to remember a lifetime, now a wonderful dream to try to forget.

His probation served, Kenny was called back to work at the can factory. He moved into his own room down the hall. Each room had a sink but we shared a bathroom. We had to eat our meals out. I was collecting unemployment insurance again but my money was running low. It was time to look for another job. I liked to party, drink, and the ladies. Bartending gave me the chance to have all three. I picked up several jobs working parties at the Lafayette Hotel and made a good friend with the boss. I was a good bartender when I was sober and not hung over. Being tall, young, and Irish gave me an edge. Most people liked me.

My worst fault was talking too much when I drank, being sarcastic instead of funny, and too quick to temper. I didn't look for trouble but I didn't run from it either. I'd get in more trouble accidentally than most people did on purpose. I would be the first one to defend a woman, little child, or an animal that I thought was being abused. Smaller men would pick a fight with me and I would have to defend myself. My reputation was going South and my arrest record was adding up violations. This showed a bad attitude towards society. There were times I didn't like myself.

I received a letter from Bob Caswell from Chicago. When I left Lerner Shops without notice they promoted Bob to my job, but he could not handle it. His sisters were now old enough to help out the family and he wanted to join me in sunny California. I was glad to hear from him and told him to come ahead and hitch hike out. I'd help him anyway I could. I should have known better. Bob flew down and I met him at the Los Angeles airport. By then I had my old apartment back in the Jungle and he could stay with me until he found something. Bob was different from all my other friends. The man never had more than three drinks at one time in his life. He was a virgin at 22, never been to jail, or been in a fist fight. This was the first time he had ever been away from home. I thought of him as a little brother. I never knew what he thought of me nor did I care. I liked the man. You could trust him to be himself and he was a good person.

I took Bob around to show him the town and introduce him to all my friends. Frank welcomed him with a big bear hug that I thought would have broken every bone in his small body but he survived nicely. He especially took to Little Kenny and they quickly became fast friends, but the people at the Sea King less so. He would have a drink with us but I never saw him drunk the entire time we lived in the Jungle. He seemed fascinated by the lifestyle but kept a respectable distance like it might rub off on him. I heard of a bus boy job at the Reef, a fine restaurant on the waterfront, that was in walking distance if you didn't mind a 30 minute walk both ways. I coached him on his duties and what to say. He got the job. He was probably the best bus boy they ever had.

For three months Bob worked as a bus boy and never once complained. He was always on time and wore a clean ironed shirt every shift. He was careful with his money and soon had his own apartment in the same building as I. It was during this time that I got caught driving drunk and had to do 30 days in jail. I did my time in Wayward Honor farm just outside of Long Beach proper. It was here that I met E. Moran Salazar Woodworth the 4th who was serving six months for public intoxication. He had the bed next to me and the only one there I felt I could talk to. He was fascinating.

He was a small man who had been everywhere, knew a lot about everything, had delicate good manners, and was a gourmet cook. He was well read and played a good game of chess. The man was polite, clean, and interesting. I didn't know it at the time but he was also a homosexual.

I knew very little about homosexuals. There was Percy Malone Smith, the gifted piano player in high school and Ted Beck who picked me up once when I was hitch-hiking to Long Beach. Ted was an English teacher in a small town who gave me a ride supposedly to the next town. We got talking and drinking blackberry wine. He ended up taking me about 500 miles. The more he drank it became apparent that he was gay. Claiming that he needed a short nap before he drove back home, he stopped and rented a room at a motel. He offered me the room for the night and bought me a new bottle of wine. He lie down on the bed with his clothes on. I sat in a chair sipping wine.

"Why don't you come and lie down with me and rest for a few minutes?" he asked pleadingly patting the bed.

I mustered up my most menacing look. Actually I thought it was pretty funny. "I think you better get out of here right NOW!" I growled. You never saw a man move so fast in your life. He was out of there in 3 seconds. I had a good night's restful sleep, got up, showered, and hit the highway early the next morning.

I knew a few gay men with the Tops Neptune being next to the Sea King bar. They all seemed like good people, better dressed, more educated, interesting, and talented than the regular crew I hung with. They knew I was straight, liked women, and mostly left me alone. Not having any as close friends I actually knew very little about them. I knew some men hated them, my brother Shaun was one, and enjoyed taunting or hurting them. Like I said, I didn't spot Moran Salazar as being one. He had been in Europe and I thought his somewhat feminine gestures were continental. What did I know?

Three days before I was released from the honor farm Moran approached me. "Joe, I'm scared. I'm going to be released next week. I'm broke, I don't have any friends here on the Coast, and I don't know what to do?"

'Don't sweat it. Look me up when you get out. I have an apartment. You can stay with me for a while until you get back on your feet." I gave him a few dollars and my address on Ada Street. I should have known that anyone serving six months for just drinking must have had a problem. I liked the man. He was different and interesting. I just didn't know how different.

I'd been home about four days when Moran knocked on my door around 9AM. We were still celebrating my freedom and all of us were slightly drunk. I invited him in, handed Moran a drink, and told him the couch was his as long as he wanted it. I introduced him all around. The man completely took over my life.

It was a 24/7 party of all times with my apartment as the hub. Seven people ended up living there. I had the bed, Moran shared the couch with his current gay friend, someone slept in the bathtub, one on the closet floor, one on the dining room table, and one person under it. It was a basic unit of six men and one female and there was always someone passed out who couldn't make it home. The bars closed at 2AM and we were the after-hours party. The high-fi played constantly and everyone was high, and not only on liquor.

When the bars reopened at 6AM, Moran basically got all the guests to leave. He was a genius at getting a little money from everyone for food and liquor. Almost all guests brought liquor with them. Once a day, Moran would cook an elaborate seven-course dinner for everyone. Each course was served with a different wine.

He was a great cook. Of course there was a buffet breakfast at 2AM for our guests. At 3AM Moran would go out and steal flowers in the neighborhood so we would always have fresh flowers. He also managed to keep the apartment sparkling clean.

Moran was a wife any man would be lucky to have if he was a woman. He never bothered me and what he did was his own personal business as far as I was concerned. Most other people knew he was gay the moment they met him, most didn't care. Women just loved Moran. He did their hair, makeup, and helped them with fashion. They paid more attention to him than to me and I was jealous. I just didn't understand it. I guess they felt safe around him.

The party continued for about four months. Never once did the Police interfere. There were a few complaints about the flowers but no one would squeal on Moran. At first, people thought that I was gay too when Moran moved in. The rumor bothered me for a while. But I knew who I was and had enough confidence in myself so the hell with what anyone else thought. My friends knew that I was straight and that is all that really mattered. I really didn't know that Moran was gay until I caught him on the couch unexpectedly with another male. I was so drunk at the time it didn't matter. As long as he didn't mess with me, I didn't give a damn.

Laura was a working girl who had four rented rooms she used to bring her tricks to. When her rooms were occupied she would often come over to the apartment and climb in bed with me to get some rest. We never had sex as she was always too tired, but I had a rain check. It took me three years to cash in. She was still beautiful but slightly shop worn by then. During the four months Moran lived there I had very little sex. I was too drunk for most of the time and there just wasn't any privacy. Other couples would engage in sex practically in the open but I was too shy, embarrassed, or private. I was careful to keep clothed around Moran. One never knew.

What really surprised me was that Bob Caswell and Moran became best friends. Bob had an apartment in the same building and was a frequent visitor. He would take a drink but I never saw him drunk. He was still a virgin as far as I knew but he certainly wasn't gay. My usual crowd was too rough for him. In Moran he found a man of quiet refinement that he evidently appreciated. We could usually expect Bob for dinner with us and like everyone else he would chip in a few dollars. How Moran could possibly fix such wonderful meals on such little money was beyond me. I suspected he shoplifted. Later I discovered that he talked one of the girls, a supermarket cashier, to scam for him. He would pick up a $6 pot roast and she would ring it up as six cents. Her Navy boyfriend was one of our regular party guests.

I heard of a cashier job available at Bank of America where I used to work as a vault teller. I thought it would be a perfect fit for Bob Coswell and I told him to apply. A high school diploma was a requirement but Bob never finished school. Bob didn't lie and wouldn't apply. I kept after him. "Do you want to be a bus boy the rest of your life? You're 22 years old. Go for it. Tell them you graduated. What's the worst that can happen? You get the job, they find out, and they fire you. So what? You didn't have the job in the first place. On the other hand, they may never find out and if they do, they might like you well enough to keep you. Damn it, go for it."

Moran agreed with me. Bob applied for the job and was hired. They never checked his school record. It was a perfect fit. He kept the job almost a year before he disappeared from my life. Bob's whole personality changed for the better. He seemed happy for once and started to enjoy life more. Sue, a Navy wife who lived in one of the apartments, had a lot more to do with it than the bank job. Sue was the ultimate unobtainable wet dream. Every man lusted after Sue but she was married and ignored us all. She and her hulk Navy husband attended our parties but under the watchful eye of her jealous husband, no one dared to make a pass at her. Then her husband went overseas.

Sue stayed away from our apartment for quite a while. Then she had a small party at her place. Sue always had a tendency to drink a little too much and that night was no exception. To my surprise she came on to me strongly. He husband's best friend was there to watch her and kicked us all out when Sue had too much to drink. I took the liberty of secretly unlocking her back door. I waited a decent time after the chaperone left and entered her apartment. She was asleep in her bed. I took off my clothes, climbed in with her, and held her in my arms. She woke up slowly, snuggled her hot body to mine, and kissed me. We had hot sex all night long. It had been a long time for me and Sue was like a wild womanI sneaked out the back door, before dawn, locking it behind me, and joined the winding down party at my place. Sue never said anything about that night to me. I later wondered if she even knew it was me. It was some of the hottest wildest sex I ever had.

A month later the rumor was that beautiful sexy Sue was going to leave her husband for Bob Coswell. We started seeing them together holding hands and gazing lovingly into each other's eyes. This was definitely the wrong woman for my buddy. I tried to talk to him. He wouldn't listen. He was in love. I tried to tell him that when her husband came back, he would kill him. That caught his attention. He was already feeling guilty about being with a married women. He was raised a Catholic. Finally, I lost my temper and told him flat out that if he didn't quit seeing that slut I would beat the shit out of him myself and send his dead broken body back home to Chicago. He had never seen me mad before. He gave up his apartment and disappeared to somewhere. He still worked at the bank but I never went to see him.

I couldn't believe it. Bob had his own key to Sue's apartment. He was one lucky son of a bitch. My good buddy was no longer a virgin, and his first sex partner was the best. I pitied the poor girlfriend that would have to live up to what Bob lucked into. Little Kenny saw him frequently and I kept track of him thru Kenny. Sue gave up her apartment and disappeared. No one I knew ever saw her again. Kenny told me that Bob Coswell had a new girlfriend but was afraid to bring her around as we might steal her from him. He trusted Kenny and he needed Kenny's car for dating as he didn't have a car of his own. A few months later Bob, disappeared completely. No one knew what happened to him.

Chapter 12

I had grown tired of Moran never working. I was collecting unemployment insurance. He claimed that he couldn't find a job. I asked him, "If I found him a job would he take it?"

"Anything, Joe. Nobody wants to hire me." I took him at his word and called Wayne at Pierpoint Restaurant again. He needed a dishwasher. I put Moran on the phone and he was hired. He lasted all of a week. When he left he managed to steal 45 pounds of frozen jumbo shrimp. All our friends were invited to the famous shrimp feast at my apartment. Seven courses, seven different wines, of course, and an artistic flower arrangement for the table. Moran was like a wife without having the sex. From what I had heard maybe he/she was exactly like a wife after one had been married awhile. Who cared? I had plenty of willing women for sex but where could I find a good cook and housekeeper like Moran? And there were those fresh flowers every day.

Tony Mendoza, was a brother of two older Mexican sisters who owned and operated Weston's Laundry in the Jungle. Their business was located next to the sea wall between the Sea King bar and our apartment building. For 15 cents a pound Weston's would wash and fluff dry our laundry. I knew little Tony from the Sea King and he considered me his friend. I once pulled two men off him who were beating on him in the alley behind the laundry. Tony had some pretty shady friends and I more or less avoided getting too personally involved with him. The Mexicans as a rule pretty much stuck to their own.

One night around midnight Tony came over to my apartment and wanted to borrow my car for a couple of hours. Moran who was holding my car keys told him "No". Tony said he would not ask me if it wasn't really important. I was starting a new job the next morning and I couldn't take the chance of not having my car. Tony pleaded almost with tears in his eyes. I compromised and told him I'd drive him to wherever if he promised it would only be two hours or less. Tony said he would have to ask his cousin Pedro and would be right back. He didn't look too happy.

Tony came back alone and said "Let's go."

Moran said "No way, Joe's had too much to drink."

"Give me the God Damn keys. It's my car. It will be a cold day in hell before you're ever big enough to tell me what to do." Moran gave me my keys and I left with Tony.

Cousin Pedro was waiting outside. I was introduced and we shook hands. It seemed that Pedro had been fired from his job that day and wanted to go back and clean out his locker. He had some money, pot, and a gun in there he didn't want discovered. He would pay me $50 for driving him out to Harbor City to get his belongings. Away we went. They had to show me the way as I was pretty drunk but insisted on driving.

When we stopped at our destination, it was pitch dark. There were very few lights on in the factory. It was obviously closed. Tony and Pedro climbed out of the car. "Wait here." They climbed over the fence. Something was wrong. They were after something more important than a clothes locker. What the hell have I gotten myself into?

A Police car pulled up behind me. Two cops got out and checked my ID. They made me turn my lights out and they went dark. I sobered up fast. “Where are your two friends?”

“I’m alone. I don’t know what you’re talking about.”

“What are you doing out here?”

“I don’t know. I’m lost. I stopped to take a piss. I haven’t the faintest idea where I am. Could you tell me how to get to Long Beach from here?”

“How did you get here in the first place?”

I had a date with a girl in Harbor City. I must have taken a wrong turn somewhere coming home. I got turned around somehow.”

“Get over here behind your car” We waited. I was expecting Tony and Pedro to come running across the field and climbing over the fence. Nothing happened. After about ten minutes the cop spoke.

“Alright, Mr. Kennedy. You can get in your car and drive home. Drive straight about a mile until you come to an intersection. Take a left and go to the first stoplight. Take another left and drive till you hit American Ave. Turn right and you hit Long Beach. Get out of here and don’t let me catch you here again. Understood?”

“Yes Sir. Thank you Sir. I was really lost.”

“Yeah, right. Go now.” I drove away. I started shaking. I pulled over to stop. I couldn’t leave my friend Tony alone. He was in trouble. I waited a while. Then drove back. There were lights and police cars everywhere. I gave up and drove home. The party was still going. No one missed me. I had another drink.

It was 4AM that morning when the police came pounding on my door, got me out of bed, handcuffed me and took me in. The next day I was questioned by detectives. It was a while before I pieced the story together. It goes without saying that I lost the job.

It seemed Tony and Pedro set out to rob the cash at the factory credit union where Pedro had a job. When they attempted to break in they set off a silent burglar alarm. When they heard the two way police radio checking my ID, they stopped whatever they were doing. Other police came after I left and entered the grounds to search for intruders. When they were discovered they started running. They were ordered to stop and shots were fired. Pedro stopped immediately and was captured. Tony kept running and ran all the way back to Long Beach where he was arrested the next afternoon as he waited for the next bus to Mexico.

Pedro sang like a bird, Tony refused to say a word, the Police picked me up and there I was. I was finally set free after 72 hours because Pedro admitted that he had never met me until that night and it was the same story I told them. Pedro pled guilty and served six months. Tony pled not guilty and spent nine months in jail as he couldn't bail. His sisters refused to help him. I never saw Tony again.

A few days after I was released I was drinking in the Sea King when a woman attacked me from behind. I was knocked to floor and before I was bashed with a barstool, some friends restrained her. I had never seen this woman before. It was cousin Pedro's wife, Maria. She blamed me for getting her precious husband jailed. When she calmed down, she started to cry. She was broke, they had four small children, and no food. What was she to do?

I tried to tell her the truth but she wasn't buying it. Pedro was a good man and would never take a chance of hurting her or the children. It was me and Tony that led him astray. I was getting pissed. Tony could have cleared me if he had opened his mouth, Pedro should have shut up and not involved me in the first place, and I didn't know what they were planning. Now this bitch, Maria, blamed me! I gave her $4 and told her to come back in an hour and maybe I could help her.

Then I did the worst thing I ever did in my life. I introduced her to Larkin who ran a string of whores and dealt in hard drugs. Larkin gave her money and the promise of work. When big mouth Pedro got out of jail he didn't have a family anymore. The children were taken away by Welfare and his wife Maria was crack street whore. I heard Pedro that took his own life. If I ever needed an excuse to drink, I had one now. What kind of monster had I become?

I should have seen it coming. It was at my apartment after one of Moran's famous dinners, that he put his hand on my leg and looked into my eyes and said. "You know, Joe. I really love you."

I backhanded him so hard he flew across the living room and smashed into my hi-fi scratching my favorite record. I got up off the couch, pulled him up by his shirt, and hit him with my fist. It took three people to pull me off him. I stormed out and went down to the Sea King. Hours later I came home to find him sitting in a chair sewing his cut arm with needle and thread. He had a swollen face and a black eye.

"I'm sorry I hit you Moran, but our agreement was that you were never to touch me."

"I'm sorry too, I had a little too much wine. You know I'm fond of you."

"Right in front of my friends. Now, everyone will think I'm gay too. Don't ever do that again. I might really hurt you."

"I won't". Our Landlady came to the door.

"Joe Kennedy, I want you out of my apartment now. That was a terrible thing you did to poor Moran. Get out. I don't ever want to see you again."

"You got to be kidding. I'm the one who pays the rent here. He's my guest."

"Out now or I call the police."

"Can I get my stuff?"

"You have 20 minutes." I packed my gear and left. That night I slept in my car. It seemed by hitting Moran I lost almost every friend I had and I was the one who discovered him.

The next day I found Little Kenny, gave him my car and pink slip, and told him to sell it for me. I was going back to Chicago and didn't think the car would make it. Long Beach was bad news for me. It was time for a fresh start. We shook hands goodbye and I was gone.

One thing I could thank Moran for was that he helped me find Mary Stone. Every time I got depressed when drinking I'd talk about her. I knew her father's name and that he was a big time real estate broker with several offices in Orange County. Moran got one of the girls to phone claiming to be a girlfriend of Mary and got her address in Wichita Falls, Texas. Billy had finished his basic training and was also stationed there. It was a good sign. I was going there. I didn't know it but if there is a hell on earth, God put it in Wichita Falls, Texas

Hitchhiking to Wichita Falls was mostly uneventful except for one black man who picked me up. He was sucking on a gallon jug of wine, It seemed he just looked black. He was a Hawaiian who married a Southern white woman. Her relatives believing him to be a no good lying black man persuaded her to leaving him. He was driving up to Arkansas to try to get her back. He loved her and couldn't live without her. Tears flowed from his eyes as he talked about his love and as he drank. I honestly couldn't tell what race he was and I could care less. With his permission I crawled in the back seat to sleep.

With a terrible screeching of brakes, the car skidded and spun around a few times before it came to a stop. The driver peered over the seat. It was the drunkest face I had ever seen. He slurred what sounded like, "You drive for a while."

As I got out the back door he somehow climbed over the front seat into the back and passed out. It was pitch black with no moon. I took a few deep breaths to clear my head and climbed into the driver's seat. The keys were in the ignition. I turned on the head lights. Nothing. I got out of the car. We were about six inches from driving off a mountain cliff which I couldn't see the bottom of and a good forty feet off the highway. I started shaking badly. I had just missed death by inches. What could I do? I drove on.

Several rides later I arrived at the small town of Wichita Falls, Texas, wearing a big white Texan hat. I got a hotel room. It was blistering hot. After unpacking I went out to get lunch and a beer. I made my way to the air force base and asked for Billy Thorton. He came to the gate.

Billy looked the best I had ever seen him. He was a Corporal and as I was soon to learn he practically ran the entire base under the radar screen. Billy took me in to be photographed for a permanent civilian pass that gave me access to enter or leave the base at any hour. He took me to his barracks, gave me a bed to use, a locker, and three sets of fatigues. He said I could eat free in any mess hall on the base except the Officer's Club. He did not know Mary but her husband Jerry was in his platoon. We left the base and had a few beers in a bar across from a beauty parlor where Mary was working as a hairdresser.

"When did you start wearing a cowboy hat?" asked Billy. "You look like a jerk."

A man who gave me a ride bought it for me. I liked it and he said everyone in Texas should wear a good Western hat. It keeps the sun off your face. I think it looks cool."

"Whatever, take it off when you're with me. I got a reputation in this hole."

"As what, a gangster?"

Billy pulled out a hand gun and laid it on the table. "What else? I'm from Chicago. It's a big deal out here. I run all the girls and the gambling. I say 'Jump', they ask 'How high'. What do you want to do about this Mary?"

"Hell, I don't know. It's been over a year since I've seen her. She might have forgotten me by now. I would like to know why she never came to California."

"Do you want me to talk to her husband or something? I could have him restricted to base for a few days."

"Don't do anything yet. I want to talk to her first alone. I'll catch her when she finishes work."

"It's your call, good buddy. I got to go. I'll see you at the base later." He picked up his gun and left. I sat there drinking beer for about two hours watching the beauty shop. Finally, Mary came out.

"Mary! Mary Stone" I called out. She stopped and looked my way. She was still tall and as beautiful as I remembered.

"My God, is that you Joe Kennedy? What are you doing here?"

"You never came to Long Beach so I had to find you."

"Come walk with me. I have to get straight home."

"Are you still with your husband Jerry?"

"I'm afraid so. We have a baby now. I can't leave him. My father would kill me."

"Is the baby why you never made it to Long Beach?"

"After you left San Antonio I found out I was pregnant. I couldn't leave then. I tried to contact you but all my letters came back. You're not much on leaving a forwarding address."

"Is the baby mine?"

"I don't really know. It could be. What do you want here?"

"What do you want?"

"Joe, I missed you and thought of you often. It's not what I want but I have a life with Jerry and the baby. I really don't know you. We were together less than a week and that was a long time ago. I don't know what I want".

"Do you love me?"

"That's unfair. I don't know anymore. I did. Maybe, I still do. I'm just not sure."

"Well that's honest. Where do we go from here?"

"Come home with me for dinner and meet Jerry and the baby. Jerry knows all about you. Well, not everything."

"Just what exactly?"

"Well, he knows that we once loved each other and were going to get married. You disappeared then we met accidently in San Antonio and you disappeared again. He really wants to meet you."

"What the hell for?"

"I don't know. Are you coming to dinner or not? You don't have to be afraid of Jerry."

"I'm not afraid of anyone, ever." I lied "I want to see the baby." We went to Mary's apartment to wait for her husband to come home. The baby looked like me.

Jerry was a surprise. He greeted me warmly and said he was glad to finally meet me. He was obviously insanely in love with his family. He asked what I was doing in Wichita Falls. I told him I had come to see my buddy, Billy Thorton, who was stationed there, and accidently saw Mary in town. I told him Mary and I kept bumping into each other every couple of years. It was hard to keep a straight face.

Jerry was a small man, shorter than Mary. I found myself liking him and feeling sorry for him at the same time. After an excellent dinner, Jerry suggested that he and I take a walk together. I agreed. He knew a lot more about us than Mary led me to believe. He thought that we loved each other and that I had come to take her away from him. With tears flowing down his face he told me that he was willing to give her and the baby up for her happiness. He would not stand in our way if I would promise to take care of them and treat them right. He warned me that Mary was a rich man's little girl and she was spoiled rotten. He could never give her the kind of life she deserved.

It was like a dash of icy water in my face. I didn't have a job or any money. I wasn't ready for the responsibility of a wife and child. Hell, half the time I couldn't take care of myself. I told Jerry that I wouldn't come between a man and his family. I could tell that he loved them and that they belonged together. I would be leaving town the next day for Chicago and chances were I would not ever see them again. I wished him the best of luck, gave him my hat, and told him to tell Mary goodbye for me. True to my word I left town the next morning. I never saw Mary or heard from her again.

My third ride to Chicago was a very sad woman. Her divorced husband took their son to his small home town in Texas and refused to give the boy up. The law was useless as he had powerful local influence and wealthy parents. She was tearfully driving back home and had to talk to someone. I no doubt took advantage of her and we had sad miserable sex. I was beginning to believe that I was a sex addict. I'd screw any woman warm to the touch.

I reached Chicago to find that my step-dad had lost his job. A pending Senate Crime investigation scared the owners. They closed shop and disappeared. Rod had just bought a cocktail bar he named "The Gear Grinders". He spotlighted a midget race car in the front window. All his racing trophies and photos were behind the bar. He served pizza and beer and catered to the racing crowd. His father was the day bartender while Rod worked nights. I was there just in time to take over relief shifts.

There were several basic things wrong for this bar to be a success. First off, it was on one of two of the only diagonal streets in Chicago. Most people couldn't find it. Rod and his father never were bartenders and did not know anything about it. "We sell beer and whiskey. If you want a beer or a straight shot, we got it. If you want those fancy ass drinks, go drink somewhere else."

This didn't sit well with everyone. The biggest mistake was they gave the drinks away. Anyone who called Rod by his first name couldn't buy a drink. Their money was no good. Rod had to play big shot. It didn't take long for Rod to go thru all his savings. Rod listened to me, agreed with me, but never changed a thing. He soon lost the bar.

I convinced them to move to California. Rod sold the house and we all came out to Long Beach. My mother took a dislike to Long Beach almost immediately and they moved up the coast to Malibu to a motel. I stayed behind in Long Beach. They eventually put a down payment on a four bedroom house in Van Nuys. From the freezing cold of Chicago to the smog and heat of the valley, it was a bad trade. Rod didn't know anyone on the West Coast and more important, no one knew Rod D'Angelo.

I decided to stay away from the Jungle for a while and took a room on Third Street, off Magnolia, half a block from a beer bar named the "Wee Inn". The owner a big kind bear of a man was called Benny. He let me run a tab. As he had sandwiches as well as beer it came in handy when I was broke. My savings gone, I was surviving on unemployment insurance with short time employment at the refineries.

I was drinking too much again but mostly beer. Two things changed that really made things easier for me. Petroleum Maintenance, one of the many contractors at the oil refinery, let me work as a pipefitter. The Oil, Chemical, and Atomic Workers Union 1-128 started a hiring hall. Petroleum Maintenance wrote me an all important letter qualifying me with the union as a 1st class rigger, pipefitter, & Boilermaker. As most of the work was maintenance opposed to construction, I could handle it.

The Union hiring hall had a three color card system based on the number of hours worked. The best card was the white card. All the ass kissers, the ones who paid off the bosses, and also relatives of the chosen few started with white cards. White cards were hired first and they got the best and most jobs. It took me over two years to get a white card. The oldest layoff date had first hiring preference. Everyone worked during shutdowns. Between shutdowns work was scarce except for the few permanent jobs that were taken by white cards when they started the new system. Most work was temporary, paid good, and that's is how I liked it. Between jobs I partied, drank, tended bar, and let my work card age for the next time I really needed work. This basically was my life for the next 25 years.

From 1957-1962, I had 18 arrests for drinking related arrests. In 1975 that number had reached 32 arrests in Long Beach alone. During that time I also had worked exactly 32 bartending jobs in Long Beach. It was an interesting statistic but not one I was proud of. Not having a steady work prevented me from obtaining any sort of credit or the ability to improve my status. Then I had an idea. I started using the Union as my last job. They would affirm that I was a member and for how long but would never reveal any other information. No one could prove that I hadn't worked steady. It worked perfectly. I once had 18 major credit cards at one time.

By paying a few days early and always more than the minimum for a period of one year, I not only built up an excellent credit rating and higher credit limits but if I didn't pay after one year it was not a criminal offence. It was their fault for trusting me or not verifying my original information. This came in handy when in the future I had to use a different name.

Chapter 13

It was 1959 and I turned 24 years old. I was maintaining. Women, wine, and song were my life but it was more like cheap women, excessive drinking, and bar fights. I still had my dream of being a writer and a notebook of song lyrics that I wrote while in Nashville. I used my song notebook to entice women to my room. It worked better than that old saw "etchings'. Finally one day a drinking friend of mine introduced me to Harry who believed himself out to be a music agent. Harry showed up at my place with a tape recorder and two quarts of Jack Daniels. He wanted me to put all my songs on the tape recorder.

Whether I had a tune or not, record them the way I wrote them. I was broke and half drunk. I started drinking the Jack Daniels, Harry stayed sober. I sang every song I had written plus the ones I had started and never finished. I ran out of songs before the whiskey was gone. Desperately searching for anything to stall Harry and keep the whiskey there, I searched my pockets. I found a few cocktail napkins with some lyrics on them.

It seems that the night before, after the bars had closed I went to a café I tried to impress and pick up some woman who caught my fancy. I threw out my best line that I was a song writer. She challenged me to write her a song. With the jukebox blaring loudly in my ears, I composed the following on the back of cocktail napkins.

"Oh, oh, my Love, I love you oh so much. Oh, oh, my Love, how I want to touch your lips with mine and hold you close to me" by the time I had finished the song the girl had left without me.

I was so drunk when I found them in my jacket pocket that I recorded them as "My Love, Oh, Oh." on Harry's recorder. Harry left leaving me the whiskey. I was sick and hung over for two days. I picked up my unemployment check and I was back in business. I was drinking in the Saddle & Spurs when Harry came rushing out of nowhere. "Joe, Joe, Where the hell you've been? I got our song recorded." He dragged me to a telephone booth, dialed a record store, and told them to play our song. He gave me the receiver, and for the first time, I heard "My Love, Oh, Oh" recorded by the Long Beach Deville Sisters on a Spry Label.

I sent a telegram to my mother, bought $20 worth of records, and mailed them to everyone I knew. From working at the Sea King I knew the jukebox man and he promised to put my record on every jukebox in Long Beach. I got paid $750 in advance and that was the last I heard of Harry. I had met so many phonies since I came to California that I swore that I would never trust anyone with my songs again. Instead I would write a novel, they would make a movie out of it, and then I would get my songs in the movie. It was a great plan if I ever got around to writing a book. Eventually I got tired of hearing my song. It was without doubt the worst song I ever wrote.

The $750 I got for my song paid my bills and bought a lot of drinks. It also got me lucky with women. It was while hanging at the Wee Inn that I lucked into having sex with several different women in one day. I had always been in awe of my brother Shaun when he got leave from boot camp and made his record of having sex with seven different women in one day. I set out to break his record with one that he could never beat, even if I had to pay for it like he did. With a great start of five conquests, the aid of several friends who were betting on the results, and even a few women who were willing to see how much I could accomplish, I set a personal best with thirteen women, with only one of them twice. I became a local legend and for months I had all the sex a man could ever want.

It was during this period that I met Maxine. She was a married woman who had a face that looked like a gorilla and the shoulders and weight of a football linebacker. Her saving grace was her incredible melon shaped breasts and her insatiable sexual appetite. No one messed with me when I was with Maxine. Everyone was terrified of her. She always paid for my drinks. She was perfect for me. The more I drank the better she looked and I really had to drink a lot before I would bed her.

The main problem with Maxine was that she was possessive. She had some cute girlfriends but they were too afraid to talk to me and she drank to excess. She was the first woman that I'd ever met who could out drink a man. Her husband was a 20 year Navy man and stationed out at sea. Maxine had no fear and didn't worry about being seen with me.

The husband's ship came in. Being a prudent man by nature, I thought it best that we end the affair. I was drinking at the Wee Inn a few days later when Maxine came in with her neighbor, Gloria. She wanted me to come to her apartment for a party. At the risk of life and limb I refused. She insisted. It was to be a party of just the two of us. Again I said no.

"Harry brought home a case of Jack Daniels. We could have some. He's on duty at the Navy shipyard. Please, I've missed you." Never being the kind of man to turn down a woman who could probably kill me with one hand, and having a fondness for Jack Daniels, I went to her apartment.

There was no Jack Daniels. She wanted my body. She ripped off her clothes, grabbed me in a bear hug, and pulled me down on the Murphy bed. As she lay back she passed out and started this snoring. She was completely out of it. I managed to get out of her sweaty embrace and made haste to go. She had told me when we got there that her husband had hidden the case of liquor and she couldn't find it. It was a small messy efficiency apartment. If there was Jack Daniels there I would find it, and I did.

By going into the small closet, turning completely around, and looking up I found that her husband had built a shelf close to the ceiling. There was the case of Jack Daniels, green label, unopened. I managed to take it down and looked for some way to open the wood crate. I found a claw hammer and got it opened. I took six bottles in a paper shopping bag and got the hell out of there. I went to my room, hid five bottles in my dirty laundry bag, opened one, and drank it until I passed out.

The next thing I remember was Maxine and Gloria shaking me and trying to wake me up. I had neglected to lock my door. I was too incoherent to speak. The almost empty bottle of Jack Daniels was on my table so they knew I took it. They tore my room apart looking for the missing five bottles but didn't find them. They finally left and I went back to sleep. They did take the almost empty bottle. I thought that was a terrible thing to do. I had risked my life going home with Maxine. If her husband caught us, I would be dead. I never did meet the man but I heard later from people who knew him that he was a small mouse of a man.

I was at the bar with a few friends two days, later when Maxine walked in sober. She came directly up to me and without menace said quietly. "You owe me $80. I had to replace those bottles before Harry missed them. Do you know how hard it is to find green label Jack Daniels anywhere in Long Beach. I finally found some on the

Navy base but they all had the tax stamp on them. You better hope that Harry doesn't notice."

"You know I'm not working. I'm drinking on credit. I can't pay you until I get on at the refinery."

"I'll be here. Eighty dollars as soon as you get it."

"Right" She went to the other end of the bar and ordered a beer. I was feeling uncomfortable. If she continued to drink and got drunk she might do me some damage. I left and said in a loud voice that I'd be right back. I went to my room and came back with a tennis racket. I proceeded to tell Benny and my friends about how I had won some important national tournament and that this racket was my most prized procession. I left the racket sitting on the bar when I went to the men's room. Sure enough, when I came back, Maxine had my racket.

"I'll just hold this until you pay me, OK?"

"Yeah, fine. Just please take good care of it for me. It means a lot to me. It's priceless." With a smug satisfied look, she tucked it under her arm, finished her beer, and left. I never saw her again. I had bought the old racket at a thrift store for 25 cents and used it to hang my clip-on ties on. Not a bad trade for six quarts of Jack Daniels.

It was time to leave town, yet again, for my health. I packed my stuff and caught a bus to Van Nuys giving up my room and leaving no forwarding address. Everyone was glad to see me but the next morning as I left to look for work Rod caught me in the garage.

"Look Joe, I don't mind you coming to see your mother, but if you're looking for a job, don't bother coming back without one. I can't afford to raise you. You're a big boy now. I married your mother not you." Things had been rough for Rod since they moved to California. I understood where he was coming from but except for unemployment insurance, I was tapped out. I had better find a job or I'd have no place to sleep that night.

I hit everyplace within walking distance after I caught a bus to the business section. There were no jobs anywhere. It was late in the afternoon when I stopped in Gately's department store. They made me fill out a work application before they informed me that they had no openings. As I was leaving the store manager came by.

"Just a minute, young man, let me see that." He took my application. "I see that you have some experience selling men's wear. I need someone for three days before Father's day. It pays $1.25 an hour. Do you want it?"

"Yes, Sir."

"Can you start tomorrow?"

"Yes Sir. Thank you Sir."

"Susan here will get you fixed up. See you tomorrow morning at 9 AM sharp." He walked away. I had a job! When I got home Rod couldn't believe it. He had been out of work for over three months. I didn't tell him it was only for three days.

I started work the next morning. It was a small department. All the regular help was on salary with 10% commission. I made up my mind to be the best salesman they ever had. When the suit man or the shoe clerk went on a break, or went to lunch, I sold in their sections. I didn't take breaks or lunch. I used the skills I learned at Buffums and worked hard. At the end of three days, I had sold more than any salesperson in the store. If I had been on commission like the regulars, I would have made over three times what they paid me in salary.

My mother asked if I could do anything to help Rod find work. I checked the want ads and found that Earl Scheib's Auto Paint needed a shop manager. I told her to get Rod to apply. He would have to go to Los Angeles to apply. He didn't have gas money and he didn't have the clothes for an interview. I gave him money for gas and he called and made an appointment.

I went to work and when the suit man was out to lunch I pulled a new suit size 44 regular, off the rack and sent it down to the tailor for a rush job on alterations, making the cuffs. I had my step-sister Toni, who was only 12 years old at the time come in to pick it up. I had a bag consisting of two dress shirts, ties, belt, shoes, wallet, socks, underwear, cuff links, etc. made up and waiting in Will-Call for her. She almost couldn't carry all the stuff. She was nervous but she did it like a pro. Rod was now ready for his interview.

It was risky getting away with this much merchandise as the regular salesmen were always scoping out everyone's sales. I had to write everything up on a credit purchase to a non-existent person and not ring it on the cash register. By doing it ahead of point of purchase as if it were a phone order and putting it in Will-Call, I got away with it. Salesman did not have access to internal store records. I had enough total sales that it was covered. I felt it made up for not being paid a commission. Rod got the job in a shop in Panorama City and they gave him a company car. It was all good.

After working three days the manager handed me my pay envelope. The store paid in cash. "We're having our annual parking lot sale in three days. I don't suppose you would be interested in helping us set it up and working as cashier?"

"Yes Sir. I need the work. My step-dad's out of work right now and I have to help out."

"You got it, young man." For three hard hot days I helped set up for their big parking lot sale. I worked my ass off for $1.25 an hour. I was beginning to regret that I didn't rip off a new suit for myself. The set up was horse shoe shaped with one entrance and the cash register at the exit. I found the store manager.

"Mr. Brown, is there any chance of getting a commission. With only one salesman representing each department I would have the chance to sell a few things myself, especially when they're busy with a customer or off the floor on break."

He looked me right in the eye and with a straight face said. "Will you work for 5% only, no salary?" The old pirate got me mad.

"Yes sir." I was determined to best this situation. I studied the set-up. The only department that did not have an outside department salesman represented was the toy department. They had no salesmen that time of year, only an old man as manager. I went to him and asked him what is the most expensive item you have. It turned out he had plastic swimming pools. The biggest one was a 20 foot pool selling for $427.

I set up an above ground 20 foot Doughboy swimming pool filled with water next to the my cash register. I took the water filter pump and set it so it splashed water up into the air to fall back in the pool. A pool ladder in the center of the pool with a bikini clad manikin completed my display. I stacked assorted sized pools nearby, wore a broad brim straw hat, and I was ready. We had the hottest week on record. I sold an all time record for the store.

I told my mother I could get her a much needed area rug and she had a neighbor drive her to our sale. My mother was basically an honest woman and almost had a heart attack when I didn't stop with just the rug. I loaded the car with a new bike for my sister Toni, a wading pool for my little brother Chaz, new sheets and pillows. I could have gotten much more but my mother made me stop.

The sale ended, I was laid off, I was paid $842.67 for one weeks work.

Rod hadn't been paid yet on his new manager's job. I bought champagne, sirloin steaks, and groceries for a week to celebrate our good luck. I got drunk and stayed in bed the next day. I forgot to tell Rod that I was laid off. He thought I lost my job by not showing up and he blew his cool.

"You make more money in one week than I ever did and you blow off your job. You're a complete irresponsible idiot." The hell with him, I went back to Long Beach. Unless he reads this book he will never know that I was laid off. They just didn't have a place for me. If it wasn't for my creative help, he would probably still be out of work. Me, I could always get a job within three days if I wanted one.

I moved back down to the Jungle and what was left of the old gang was happy to see me. I had money in my pocket. Even my old manager on Ada Street relented and let me rent an apartment again. Moran couldn't pay the rent, of course, and was long gone. Maxine was gone along with my good friends Frank and Bob Caswell. Only little Kenny was left. I went down to the union hall and got a job as pipefitter for an emergency shutdown at Atlantic Richfield oil refinery.

I worked forty-eight straight days, twelve hour shifts, and even pulled a couple of doubles. For the first time in my life I took "bennys" to stay awake. I drank too much but I had always stayed away from any kind of drugs or smoking. I made a ton of money with overtime, time and a half, double time, shift work, and weekend incentive pay.

The withholding on my first paycheck was more than half of my pay. This had to stop. The government was getting far too much of my money. I worked too damn hard for it. I decided to start some kind of a business of my own so I could write off expenses like the oil companies did. I started with a line of jewelry. Now I had the tax write-offs and could keep most of my hard earned money in my own pocket. And the best part was that I had more money to drink with.

Between jobs, I would walk into a bar with three boxes of rings that I would sell for $10 each or three rings for $15. My cost was two to four dollars each for quality costume jewelry, many, with genuine stones that I bought wholesale. Barmaids would get men to buy them rings and necklaces. I was drinking free from the profits, and scoring new girl friends by giving away free sample merchandise. I had hit upon the perfect scheme, at least for me. It worked.

There were a couple of problems. The first was attempted theft. Customers would take 5 rings to examine at one time and return 4. I solved that problem by carrying pennies and when a ring was sold I would put a penny in the empty ring slot. That way I could tell if someone didn't put a ring back. Next, the unemployment insurance office. If you made a false statement you could lose your benefits and possibly go to jail. I wrote down part-time self-employed and when they insisted I tell them how much I made, we had a problem. I asked them if I should report gross or net sales. If I bought a pencil for 5 cents, sold it for 8 cents, and the cost of sale was 4 cents I actually was losing 1 cent.

They couldn't understand the concept of having a business that was losing money for the tax benefits. I thought of these government workers as having "A" minds. If you gave them a "B" problem they go to pieces. They said write it down and we will make a determination. I said write down what? I can't write down what I earned if you don't tell me how you determine earnings. Around and around we went. I was allowed to make $25 a week before they would deduct anything from my unemployment insurance check so I made sure to write down something under that. They stopped bothering me. Most of my business was under the table and not recorded. God forbid, if I showed a profit and had to pay taxes on it.

I found a wholesale source in Hawaii that was selling shell jewelry. Puka shell necklaces were a big fad at the time and were selling in the high end stores for as high as $100 a necklace. I bought them for 28 cents each in lots of 25 and sold them like hot cakes for $10 each. I was getting too successful and not staying under the radar. I had to get a California resale license and a peddler's license, or I was going to get in trouble. By going legitimate, I knew I had to keep and submit records. This was becoming a huge headache but the tax deductions were worth it. I kept more money in my pocket, drank almost free, seduced more women. Best of all, at this time unemployment insurance benefits were not taxable. Life was good.

When I left Lerner Shops in Chicago without notice and wrote for my last paycheck, it arrived without a letter. Lerner Shops, in their downtown Los Angeles offices, offered me a job. I caught the red car on American Ave and went to see them. It was an hour ride on the street car and I didn't like downtown Los Angeles. They understood why I had left Chicago in the middle of winter and insisted that their people take their lunch and coffee breaks. I was offered a similar job with more money. It was tempting but I turned it down.

I didn't like oil refinery work particularly. It was hard, dirty, and dangerous. It paid well, took little thought, and jobs didn't last forever. Best of all, when I was laid off, I didn't have to go back to work until I wanted to. At the time the Long Shore man's Union had the best pay and benefits. It was basically a closed shop. Each member was allowed to sponsor one person a life time. It was usually a family member. I found a single man who was willing to sponsor me for $1,000. I could get the money together but I turned it down for the main reason that they had a guaranteed minimum hour work week and I would be unable to collect unemployment insurance. Also, the men were mostly a rougher and tougher element of workers than our union members. I sometimes worked casual labor on the docks and drank with them in their local bars. These guys were too tough for me.

There was a street in Calumet City that ran between the Illinois and Indiana state line that had a reputation for being lawless, rough, and tough. And it was. Gambling, fighting, prostitution, you name it, they had it all. Bars lined both side of the street. The first time I drank there I was 17 years old. I was drugged, robbed, and came to in an alley. They took my shoes, wallet, money, ID, and belt. In San Pedro they had Beacon Street that was even worse. It had the reputation of being the toughest street in the world. You guessed it. I had to check it out.

Shanghai Red's and the Bank Café are the only two bars I remember. A man was killed in a knife fight in the Bank Café the first night I drank there. You could get laid for two dollars in the back seat of your car, by a black woman, as long as you didn't want to take your time. Colorful and interesting as it was, it was too dangerous for me. I did my drinking in Long Beach and nearby Wilmington. Even after I became a bartender, I did my drinking in rough joints. If I got drunk and made an ass out of myself, I fit in. It was a good thing I was young or life would have killed me.

Chapter 14

Life settled down to a routine of working, drinking, and screwing. There was a lot of what we called "Hamburger Girls". You buy them a hamburger, they would sleep with you. This was a lot cheaper than spending your hard earned money on a woman in a bar hoping to score. One did not always get quality, but one sure had quantity, if one was so inclined. Being Irish, by nature, I was always so inclined especially after a few drinks. Men like my brother Shaun, Bob Caswell, and Billy Thorton would not even talk with a woman unless she was perfect in every way let alone touch one. I wasn't so fussy. They just had to be warm to the touch. In truth, I could always find something beautiful about every woman I ever met with a few notable exceptions. The more I drank the better they looked, and drink I did. I often thought that women should be the ones buying the drinks for just that reason. It seemed to me that the men who demanded perfection missed out on a lot of fun, sex, and the pleasure of knowing a lot of interesting women.

In spite of my excessive drinking or because of it, I attracted a lot of women. I suspected it wasn't my looks or my sterling qualities. There is a kind of woman that gravitates towards bad boys and bartenders. I had a selfish rule at the time that if a woman didn't put out on the first date, she never got a second chance. I also never knowingly dated married women or those who wanted to get married. Being able to resist everything but temptation I broke my own rules and sometimes got in trouble. It was never my fault. It seemed I was always dating women who wanted to change me or have me support them. I didn't date many women twice. I preferred the safety in numbers. It was easier as long as there was availability. I'm ready, my place or yours?

Free love and casual sex... We were rushing into the 60ths. Frank and I were probably hippies before they coined the word. Except that I was always a hard worker and took life seriously. Frank never took anything serious, worried about anything, or cared about anyone including himself. When Frank disappeared from my life, he ended up in Berkeley, California. He was the perfect man, in the perfect place, for the times. While I never saw Moran again I heard he came back to Long Beach broke. He tried to get a job at Pierpoint Restaurant again. Wayne picked him up and threw him out. Never expecting that Moran would ever come back, I had told Wayne all about the shrimp feast that we enjoyed on him with the liberated shrimp. Poor Moran, he probably never knew why Wayne threw him out. As they say, crime doesn't pay. A shrimp shouldn't steal shrimp.

LSD and Thunderbird wine came on the scene at about the same time. It's hard to say which did the most damage. Cookie, a homosexual retired Navy cook who lived in the apartment next to me, was one of the first to experiment with LSD. It became his God and his chosen life to recruit every living thing to its wondrous benefits. Even pets were not safe around this disciple of better living thru chemistry. This old man's other goal in life was to seduce my young body.

Before he discovered LSD and his intentions weren't quite so obvious, I liked Cookie. He was an intelligent and interesting person. He would often invite me and my friends in for drinks and his delicious cooking. There was no one in the universe that could make fried chicken or pineapple up-side-down cake like this gifted man. He took an interest in my future. His mantra being that I should try everything at least once if I wanted to be a great writer. As I had no inclination towards being gay, nor was into drugs, I felt relatively safe as long as I didn't drink too much around him.

Then Cookie started getting too weird for comfort. LSD was truly affecting his mind. He would often stare vacantly at nonexistent matter and break out into hideous bouts of insane laughter. He became insistent that I try LSD. I was afraid that he would spike my food or drink with it without my knowledge, and. So I quit coming around. One day they came and got him. They carried him out in a straight jacket and he was laughing. He thought it was a coat of many colors. It was the last time I saw him. I never bothered to check on him nor did I know if he had any family. At least now, the dogs and cats in the neighborhood would be safe.

The Long Beach jail wasn't large enough to house all the drunks who passed out drunk the day that they introduced Thunderbird wine. Most wines at the time were dinner wines with an alcohol content of 11%. Thunderbird weighed in at 20%. The difference was more than most could handle. Consider this, at 211 degrees you have water, but at 212 degrees it becomes steam. One degree can power a locomotive. The difference in humans being the increased level of alcohol could topple a man. Thunderbird was introduced in a small but inexpensive bottle. It almost brought an entire city to a halt in only one day. It was soon followed by other designer fortified wines but by then tolerance levels were up. I thought Thunderbird tasted awful but I had to try it.

Kitty showed up in my life. She would crawl into bed when I was sleeping. She would be asleep in my bed when I came home. It seemed Kitty was always there with her hot body. Kitty enjoyed sex and I enjoyed her but she wasn't much of a looker. She wasn't unattractive but if she was a painting on the wall, I would have thrown it out after about a week. I didn't want her around all the time but I didn't want her to be not around. I couldn't figure out how she was getting into my apartment. I'd change the lock but she would still show up in my bed.

Many men would consider themselves lucky but I didn't. She never cost me anything except a little breakfast or a drink once in a while. She never asked me for money nor was she demanding in any way, except for sex. She was very aggressive and would not take tired for no. She even cleaned the apartment and washed my dishes when I wasn't there. It was like having a wife without the expense of a license but I soon longed for more variety. It was embarrassing to bring a girl home with me to find Kitty asleep in my bed. While many women liked a man who was popular, this was too much.

While I was trying to find a nice way to get rid of her without hurting her feelings, and going crazy trying to find out how she was getting into my apartment, she stopped coming around. The next time I saw her was a good three years later. I was walking on the Pike, hung over, horny, and almost broke. Suddenly, Kitty threw her arms around me from the back and kissed me. That day she looked good.

She insisted on going to her place where she claimed we could drink some beer. Who am I to turn down a free drink? Within minutes after shutting her door, she was naked, the bed was down, and she was eagerly pulling me onto the bed. There was a terrible pounding on the door. The whole room shook. "I know she's in there with someone and I'm going to kill them both."

"Who the hell is that?" I whispered.

"It's my husband.'

"You didn't tell me you were married."

"I'm married."

With every blow to the door it seemed as if it would break down. I looked around. We were on the third floor, in one room, without a back door. There was no way out of there except through the front door. I grabbed an iron, my clothes, and hid in the closet. If her husband broke in and found me, I was going to hit him with the iron and run like hell.

Her husband sounded like a giant with a loud deep drunken voice. He had a friend with him who was trying to calm him down. “Come on let’s go get a drink. She’s not home. We’re going to get arrested.”

“She’s there. Someone’s with her. I’ll kill them both.”

Thank God, the door held. The friend finally talked him down and it was quiet. After a while I came out of the closet with the iron in my hand. I was shaking badly. Kitty wanted me to come to bed with her. I just wanted to get out of there in one piece. I went to the door and listened. It was quiet. I dropped to the floor and looked under the door. There were no feet there. They could be hiding down the hall, waiting. I had to do something. Still holding the iron I opened the door a crack, blocking it with my foot. Nothing happened. I opened wider. I didn’t see anyone. I threw the iron on the bed and walked out slowly, backwards, as if I was coming in. They were gone. I got out of there and ran all the way home. Definitely, I was not going to date married women. I didn’t know. Kitty wasn’t wearing a ring. I never saw her again.

I sensed that I could not continue to live my life like this. I knew I could change and do better but there was a part of me that was enjoying this kind of life. I rationalized that I getting valuable experience for when I started writing. I knew college graduates that did not seem to have a brain in their heads. I had what I called “street smarts”. I was strong, a survivor, and in the end it would all turn out good. I was Irish, young, and had a sense of humor. While I couldn't beat every man in the world like the great John L. Sullivan, I could stand up to any man, and if need be, run like hell.

It was 1960 and Thanksgiving was around the corner. My mother invited me home for the annual feast. My brother Shaun was on leave and was going to be there. I decided to forego my usual holiday bar hopping and go my folks. It was a decision that changed my life forever. I met Medora, my mother's best friend at the time. She was the most beautiful, sexy, intoxicating woman that I had ever met in my life. She was with another man. When we were introduced, she smiled and looked at me. I knew I had to have this woman or I would be lost forever. I would have gladly killed the man she was with if I thought it wouldn't upset her. The touch of her hand was like a lightning bolt to my soul.

I don't recall the dinner or the ride back home. For days I was obsessed with the thought of Medora. I couldn't get her out of my thoughts. Other women didn't interest me and my indifference seemed to attract them like flies. I ignored them all except for a few regulars. I'm only human at best. But no woman could ever live up to the image I built up in my mind. This was ridiculous. I was 26 years old and behaving like a teenager. I came to my senses. So a woman got to me a little. So what? Nothing that drink and more women can't help me forget. I was tough.

Shaun got kicked out of the Marine Corp. The story was that he was in a bar fight, got grabbed from behind, turned and hit an officer without thinking. As it was a Marine officer and my brother broke his jaw, they took it badly and booted him out. I would have thought that this was the kind of men we needed to fight our wars but no one asked me. My brother was out but to the end of his life he would always be a Marine in his mind, heart, and soul. He was the toughest minded person I've ever met.

Shaun received high school credit, went to radio and electronic school before he was discharged and was determined to get an engineering degree. Nothing was going to get in his way. It took him seven years, studying every free moment, and going thru two wives before he made it. He went to school part time, full time between jobs, and took correspondence courses until he got his degree. He use to make fun of me for collecting unemployment insurance, calling it welfare, but when he needed it for his survival while going to school he took every dime he could from anywhere and everyone.

He became an engineer, remarried for the third time, and bought a home in Diamond Bar. While his previous two wives were beautiful they both were pretty much sluts. The second one tried to seduce me. The third one he lucked out with. She had beauty, brains, and a career. She also had three children of her own by a previous marriage. Her two older daughters were into witchcraft and impossible to control. He was making a grand salary but he was incredibly tight with his money. He was my brother and I loved him. That is probably why I didn't have sex with his second wife. A man has to draw the line someplace.

Long before Shaun's first marriage disaster, we spent some time together in the Jungle. He even stayed with us during the Moran visitation. He had exclusive rights to the closet floor. He fixed an inside lock on it as he didn't trust Moran, and couldn't stand homosexuals. This was a shame because they really liked him. I think Cookie and Moran both shared wet dreams about my brother. Shaun could have had almost any woman he wanted, including all of my girl friends, but he was basically shy and holding out for the right one. Luckily for him, Billy Thorton, and Bob Caswell, there is more than one perfect woman in the world. I, for one, wasn't waiting around for one. Life was too short.

Shaun drank too much and got into a few nasty bar fights. As a well trained ex-marine he came out alright. The Kennedy brothers were getting a tough reputation. There was no doubt that my brother was the better scrapper of us two. I hoped the day would never come when we had to square off against each other. The downside was that I was getting into more fights because of Shaun. The Master brothers were a good example. John and Roger Masters both worked the oil refineries and mostly drank at Spuds Bar, which Shaun and I frequented. They were two ass holes. They both were big, tough, mean and foul tempered. Usually high on drugs when not drunk, they had the nasty habit of picking on smaller people.

Shaun and Roger liked the same girl. Roger challenged my brother to a fight in the alley. When Shaun went outside to settle matters, brother John joined in, and it was two against one. I wasn't there and Shaun took a beating, but managed to get away. He warned me never to fight Roger as he fought dirty. From then on Roger was always trying to pick a fight with me. I made it a point to avoid him whenever possible. Then John Masters and I got into it.

It was early morning I was drinking in Spuds Bar when John stumbled in toting a long sharp sword. He was play acting as a pirate and swinging the sword around recklessly. He was high on something and totally out of it. When he came close to slicing a girl's head off, I sprang from my stool, and took his sword away. He swung at me, I easily ducked, he lost his balance, knocked over three bar stools, and fell to the floor. I handed the sword to the bartender and walked out the door. He followed me roaring to kill me with his bare hands. John was a giant bear of a man and strong from hard physical work most his life but he was slow witted. We started to fight. Suddenly he just stopped fighting and put his hands by his sides. I hit him several times as hard as I could. It didn't faze him. I tried kicking him in the knee to put him down. The man just wouldn't go down. My arms were getting tired. Suddenly he began to smile. I felt a cold chill and I was very much afraid. I stopped and walked away. He just stood there smiling. He did not come after me.

The word was out. Roger Masters was going to kill me for fighting his brother. Not much for avoiding a fight, this time I listened to Shaun's advice, and did my drinking elsewhere. The local odds were about even that I could win but I didn't need this fight to prove anything to anyone, least of all to myself. Months later, when the three of us were on the same job, on the same shift, it was never mentioned. It was forgotten. However, I was careful not to walk anywhere where the Master brothers were working overhead, just in case. This Irishman wasn't that dumb.

Before we got our Union Hiring Hall it was not a requirement to use union help during shutdowns or temporary hires. Most maintenance companies had two separate units, one being non-union, so as to be able to bid lower on work contracts. Most maintenance jobs were non-union while most construction work was union. Some trades like crane operators were always union. I believe it was all sorted out in back room deals where the rich got richer and the working man got shafted. So what else was new?

The union started to challenge the status quo. By calling a general strike they could effectively shut down daily activities of an oil refinery. Loyal union truckers would not cross a picket line. The powers that were quickly got a law passed that said the union could only picket the gates that members used. The refineries made all the non union workers use the one same gate. As all refineries had more than one gate, this effectively made a strike ineffective.

Manuel Mondoza was general foreman of PemCo, a non union branch of United Engineering Company. As such, he did most of the hiring at Texaco for their maintenance and emergency shutdowns. Before the hiring hall we were hired at the gate. As I was big, strong, and young, I was usually one of those men hired. I was a good hard worker and over the years we built up a good relationship. If I did not know something, I would ask. I refused to do a job unless it was done correctly and safely. I pretty much got all the work I wanted. Then came the hiring hall.

Now the union wanted to exert its influence and power, and expand. All jobs must be thru the union and only union members in good standing could go to work unless there weren't enough men to fill the job. Then non union help could be used but they must join after 30 days. Manuel Mondoza had a long time lucrative kick-back scam going that he wasn't about to give up for no damn union. Manuel was from Mexico and was hiring illegal's as laborers and making them pay him a percentage of their wages. In many cases he was getting sexual favors from the women. Manuel was both married and a family man. Nobody seemed to care but the union wanted their dues.

It was none of my business what was going on except I was vaguely worried that many of these workers didn't speak or understood English. Some of our work could be extremely dangerous and how could you depend on someone in an emergency who couldn't know what was going on thru lack of communication? I really didn't want to see these people hurt. The other business with Mendoza was on him. I didn't really know or care. I just knew the rumors.

The union called me aside and offered me the job of union steward for PemCo workers at Texaco. As such I would have to be the last person laid off. I would have job security, protection, and limited power. They told me what they knew about Manuel Mendoza and that it had to be stopped. For many years I believed in unions. I respected then, believed in them, and was a strong supporter. I had read a lot of early union history of their struggle against overwhelming odds and as a worker I saw the good they accomplished. Over my working lifetime I joined 15 different unions, mostly because I had to if I wanted to work.

I proudly accepted. I went to work the next day as the new union rep. I wish I had the brains enough to have asked what happened to the previous steward. As Manuel was my friend, I talked with him first and warned him that the union was aware of his play and it had to stop. Seemingly unconcerned he called my bluff. On the first shift I filed 32 violations . It was the most violations ever filed in one day in the entire history of the union. Manuel was furious. He insisted we talk. We made arrangements to meet after work.

I was the first one there. I was sitting at a table at George's Roundup bar on Pacific Coast Highway, close to Texaco drinking a Bud and a shot of Jack when in walks Manuel, his rigger brother-in-law, and the Master brothers. Manuel bought a round of drinks for everyone at the table. He spoke first.

"Kennedy, what in the hell are you trying to do? You know that you can't change anything. I'll be here long after you're gone. Be reasonable and back down."

"The union made me union rep....." I started.

"You didn't have to accept."

"Nevertheless, I'm the union rep now and they want you to stop hiring outside the hall."

"I don't give a rat's ass what they, you, or anyone else wants. I run this outfit and I run it my way. I always have and always will. There's nothing you can do that will ever change it. You don't see your last union rep around here, do you?"

"Look, Manuel. What you're doing is not only wrong, it's illegal."

"Are you threatening me?" About this time I was wishing that I wasn't alone. The other three men were strangely quiet and just staring at me.

"No threats. I thought you wanted a private civilized sit down, not with these three apes to back you up. Just a simple question, are you going to stop hiring outside the hall?"

"Not in your lifetime."

"This talk is over. I'm going to order another round."

"You may not live long enough to finish it."

"That's it!" I stood up. I had drank just enough Jack Daniels too fast that I was whiskey brave. "If you guys want to take this outside, one of you or all four of you at once, I don't give a damn. But I'll tell you one thing. I'm leaving my beer and money on the table and I'll be back to get it. I've never lost a dime yet."

While the Master brothers were ready to fight at the drop of a hat, Manuel raised his hand to stop them. "Sit down. We're leaving." And they left. I stayed there and got drunk. I didn't look forward to going to work the next day but I made it, hangover and all. Not a word was said about the previous evening.

Three days later the shutdown was over and Manuel laid off everyone including me and his own brother-in-law. The next day he called the hiring hall and they sent out his brother-in-law back to work. It seemed I had to be the last one laid off but not the first one rehired. No one at the union hall bothered to tell me this. The violations were filed. Nothing happened. Later, everything was settled in a back room with a handshake and the promise that Manuel would use the hiring hall in the future for all hires. I don't know if he ever did.

I was driving a motorcycle at the time. When we were laid off I managed to beat everyone laid off back to the union who were driving cars. This way I had a better time on my card and the right of first call for a job over anyone who didn't have a earlier time on their card. Every time I was sent out to Texaco now, Manuel would lay me off after four hours work. This would give me not only a half day's wages but it put be at the back of the line in getting called out again. There was nothing the union could or would do for me. Eventually I gave up throwing my card in for any job at Texaco. It was the closest refinery to Long beach and use to be worth 10 to 15 thousand dollars a year in wages to me.

Chapter 15

I went home for Christmas dinner and Medora was there with another boyfriend. This oaf was drunk, not happy to be there, and obviously wanted to get her alone. He ended up causing a scene. Rod made him leave. Medora stayed. After dinner I offered to drive her home. She agreed. I suggested that we stop and have a drink. Again she agreed. I was beginning to like this woman more and more. We talked and got to know each other. When the bar closed I drove her home and was invited in for a final drink. We stayed up all night talking and drinking. Her son, on leave from the Navy, was visiting and sleeping on the couch. I took an instant dislike to him the next morning when he woke up.

He was rightly upset that his mother was drinking and I was imposing on his Christmas visit. If he was the kind of man we had defending our country, we were in deep trouble. He was thin and pale, looked like a mild breeze would knock him down, and looked like a jerk. He was wearing navy flared wool dress blue pants, a dirty white t-shirt, and a tan corduroy sports jacket. Dirty combat boots completed his outfit. He shook my hand. It was limp. Medora fixed us both breakfast, I kissed her goodbye, and got the hell out of there. I went back to my mother's house where I had planned to spend a few days.

My mother had a fit. "Where were you all night? You slept with Medora, didn't you?"

"I spent the night there. We stayed up all night talking. Nothing happened, her son was there."

"I'll bet! The woman is a whore. Do you know Rod had an affair with her? She's slept with most of the men in the Valley."

"Nothing happened, Mom. I thought she was your best friend?"

"Not when she seduces my son. She's 39 years old, for Christ's sake. She's old enough to be your mother. I want you to stay away from her."

"I'm not sure I want to do that. I really like her."

"Then you are no longer welcome in my house. Get out." I packed my gear, threw it in my car, and drove over to Medora's apartment. She had to get out of bed to open the door. Her son was gone. She was absolutely the most beautiful woman I had ever seen in my life. I took her in my arms, kissed her deeply, and came in locking, the door behind me. We went to bed and I had the most exciting, satisfying sex in my life. I think for the first time in my life I was truly in love.

That night was a revelation. I never knew any woman who knew so many men. We couldn't watch TV for 15 minutes without the phone ringing, or a man coming to the front or back door usually carrying a bottle of liquor. Medora spoke to them all for a few moments and politely sent them on their way. After a while she took the phone of the hook but for hours men kept coming to the door. Many were drunk, insistent, pleading, but they were all turned away. I was actually beginning to feel pretty good about myself. We went to bed early and spent most of the night making love.

The next morning we made the mutual decision to live together. I told her the only way this could work is if we moved away and she didn't tell any of these old boyfriends where we moved to . To my amazement, she agreed. We moved to North Hollywood where we rented a new unfurnished apartment and registered as Mr. and Mrs. Joe Kennedy. I couldn't believe my good luck.

Medora was a registered nurse and preferred to work in a doctor's office. She found a job the very first day she went out. Two days later I became the night bartender at the Knotty Pine, a very upscale classy neighborhood cocktail bar. By this time I had become a good bartender. A sense of pride with me was to always look good behind any bar where I worked. I always wore a long sleeved white dress shirt, fancy cuff links, and a black bartender's vest. I was known for my extensive expensive cuff link collection. I never wore the same pair more than once a week. It was my signature vanity.

Being with Medora gave me an air of confidence I never had before. It radiated from me and all kinds of women became interested in me but I was only interested in Medora. As promised, she did not let her old boyfriends know where she was. What I did not anticipate was her amazing ability to attract new men friends. Every man who saw her, lusted for her and felt they had to possess her. She was that sexy and beautiful. She had a look in her beautiful eyes that seemed to challenge every man with the question, "Do you think that you're man enough to satisfy me?"

Medora would talk to anyone, was kind to everyone, and probably never turned down the offer of a drink in her life. While she didn't feel that she was doing anything wrong, she was possessive and jealous of me. The third night I worked at the Knotty Pine she came in with a group of new friends, all men. She was drinking and having a good old time. I lit a pretty female customer's cigarette and Medora threw her drink at me, got off her stool, and attacked the poor woman. Her friends broke it up and took her out of there.

The next day the owner informed me that if I couldn't control my wife, he would have to let me go. Two days later I was out of a job. Medora was so upset and sorry that she went on a bender, lost her job, and didn't come home. I wasn't there when she finally came home drunk, went out to look for me, and hit six parked cars on both side of the street.

It was my birthday. Shaun, my brother, came over to our apartment with his buddies and a case of beer. He wanted to take me out to celebrate. I wanted to stay at the apartment and wait for Medora who had been gone for three days with no word. After a while they talked me into going out. That‘s why I wasn’t home when Medora finally came home. If I had been there she would not have gotten in the accident. Thank God, she wasn’t hurt.

Shaun and his friends took me to their favorite watering hole, The Attic. The reason for the name was that it had all kinds of various junk hanging from the walls. After some serious drinking, Lenny, one of Shaun’s more criminal minded friends, decided it would be funny to see just how much junk we could steal from the walls before the owner noticed anything. We started taking pieces, one at a time, and stashing it in the car. It was when we were trying to boost a section of the booth that we got caught. We raced to the car and drove away laughing like crazy with our treasured haul.

We arrived back at my apartment just in time to see Medora handcuffed in a police car. No one was going to take away my girl. I was going to kill them all with my bare hands. It took Shaun and all his friends to gag me and hold me quiet until the Police left. As consolation they let me pick any two items I wanted from our ill gotten gains. I took a battered old dented French horn and a long horn steer’s skull with a rope handle. They took me to my apartment, wished me happy birthday and left.

I couldn’t stand the empty apartment and went to the closest bar, taking the steer’s skull with me for company. I put it on the bar and ordered a drink. A pretty black haired girl at the other end of the bar came and sat next to me.

"I like a man that is different." As I was getting short of money, I invited her to my apartment where I had liquor, to continue our interesting conversation. She came but made it clear that nothing romantic was going to happen. I told her I was in love and that the Police just took my Medora away. The last thing on my mind was sex. The girl told me that she was gay, had no desire for men, and technically was a virgin. Suddenly, it became the most important thing in the world that I seduce this woman.

I tried every stupid argument in the book. She was so into her homosexuality that she had her breasts surgically removed to look more like a male. Her hair was cropped short and she had just a hint of lipstick. I thought she looked rather cute but a little lost, somewhat how I was feeling at the moment. I must have worn her down because we ended up in bed together. It was the worst sex I ever experienced and she looked miserable. She put on her clothes and left with her sad haunted waif face. I never saw her again.

This was the first time I cheated on Medora. I never had another woman as long as we were together but when we were separated I hit on anything that moved if it was over two days. I had so much sex with Medora that I became a sex addict. Liquor and sex became the whole of our existence. Work was just an annoyance.

Medora lucked out. She received only 20 days in jail, and lost her driver's license for a year. Her car was totaled. Miraculously not one of the cars she hit sued her. We moved immediately when she was released and left no forwarding address. I didn't know what name she had on her driver's license but now she was using my last name. When she was released I decided that North Hollywood wasn't far enough away from her old drinking grounds and got her to agree to move to Long Beach. She was sorry for what had happened and promised that it would never happen again.

I chose Long Beach because I knew my way around and could be reasonably assured of finding a job. Medora found a job in two days. She hated Long Beach and the fact that so many women knew me. I got a job out of the union hall at Atlantic Richfield for a shut down. We both worked the same hours and had our nights together. For a while we had a happy life going. She seemed to love me and I was crazy about her.'

She was jealous of every woman I ever knew. I did not take her seriously enough for I felt that she was so superior to any woman I had ever known that she had nothing to be jealous of. Besides we had so much sex together that I could not possibly perform with anyone else without a long period of rest. She was more than enough woman for me but she didn't see it that way. She felt all women desired me and I was too weak to resist. She did not want to share me with anyone.

As long as she didn't do her drinking without me, she was fine. If she drank alone, she would meet some man and drink too much. She didn't come home sometimes and claimed blackout spells. I understood as I had them myself. I knew they were real but I could not stand not knowing where she was or if she was alright. She claimed that she never had sex with anyone but me, but how could I be sure? She didn't really know. She had her blackouts. All I knew was that if she didn't take that first drink we would never have to worry about the second one. The problem was that we were both alcoholics, she was a nymphomaniac, and I was a sex addict. It was not a workable solution to a happy relationship.

It was a mutual addictive attraction that kept us together. There was something dark about her past that she was hiding from me. I found out that she could not work in a hospital because her nurse registration had been revoked. She still wore her nurse's cap and worked in doctor's offices where they obviously didn't check backgrounds. She was a very talented and well trained nurse. She could do office work as well as take x-rays. Beautiful and intelligent, she was an asset to any doctor when she was sober. Drunk, she was still beautiful but unable to function properly.

Myself, they said drunk or sober I was the best worker they ever had but hung over I wasn't worth a shit. This was on the refinery jobs. As a bartender, I never really knew, as I was drunk most of the time. I lost those jobs by not showing up for work or quitting because I would rather party. We were a great couple indeed. We survived somehow. It seemed that one of us always had money.

We were surviving together. Medora wasn't happy about my oil refinery work. She felt I could do so much better. I tried selling Kirby vacuum cleaners. It was an interesting product but in my opinion vastly overpriced. I sold a few, got some excellent experience and gained valuable selling skills. Then I went to work for Public Finance Company as an executive manager. Don't let the title fool you. Every employee was an executive manager and started out in collections. I took a part time job with Western Auto Supply as a debt collector and did some out of area collections at the same time. This way I was paid double and got double car expenses when collecting out of area. I did not enjoy this kind of work and it did not last long.

Public Finance had me collect on a man with several small children. He had been out of work and was unable to pay his bills. I arrived at his home with the County Marshal. We actually removed the food from his refrigerator and set it on the sidewalk as we repossessed his furniture. The children were crying. The man asked me what could he possibly do? I was sick at my stomach. The next day I quit my job. Medora understood and I loved her even more.

It wasn't all bad. I knocked on a man's door to try to find out why he hadn't made a payment on a new set of tires that he purchased and financed with Western Auto. He was three payments behind and we hadn't heard from him. He came to the door roaring mad. A giant hulk of a man, he threatened me with bodily harm, if I ever woke him up again. He slept days as he was working the graveyard shift. I tried to be polite but he threatened to shoot me if I didn't get off his property. I left shaking. I went to the closest bar and had a few drinks to calm down. Then I got mad. About an hour later I sneaked back quietly, jacked up his car, removed all four tires, and threw them in my trunk. I let his car down on its axles in his driveway and got the hell out of there. I quit the job but I made a great impression on the boss Jim who said if I ever needed a job to come and see him.

Feeling that I had to hold up my end financially, I took a job back at the Sea King. It was a bad error in judgment. Medora was too jealous of me for me to be working around the type of women who frequented the Jungle. It is true that I had slept with many of them in the past but the past was behind me. Medora was everything I wanted or needed. She didn't buy it. She started drinking again without me. We fought and broke up for the first time. While she didn't live with anyone, she was seen with a lot of different men. Only she made sure I knew it. She was constantly coming into the Sea King and causing trouble. At least here she just fit in with the rest of the crowd, but I was miserable. I had to get her back or I would lose it.

The first step was catching us both sober at the same time. Medora had lost her job and I was drinking on mine. Eventually we had our chance and we talked. We agreed that the only solution was a fresh start. We moved to Newport Beach into a motel

During the off season. It was a two bedroom, living room, and kitchen with a reasonable winter rent. We were close to the water and it was nice and peaceful there, it was not destined to stay that way.

For seven weeks we were reasonably happy and got along with each other. It was like being on a romantic honeymoon. We both loved the ocean and took long walks together, hand in hand, along the sand. Medora got a job in a doctor's office almost immediately and I clerked at a local nautical hardware store that also sold yachts. We made the rounds of the local bars together where the people were warm and friendly. For once the local men didn't flirt with my Medora and I wasn't interested in any other women. Things were going so well that I just knew something bad was about to happen. It always did.

My friend Jim from Western Auto Supply was offered the job of manager of a new store that they were opening in Costa Mesa, and offered me a sales job on condition that I had my drinking under control. I accepted and worked ten days setting up and stocking this brand new store. I was working ten and twelve hour days. If things worked out well, I would be fast tracked to management training. I had less time to spend with Medora and when I did I was usually too tired to go out. This did not sit well with her.

The grand opening of the store arrived and all the big shots were there. I was the top salesman and the fair-haired boy. I was working 12 hours a day during the grand opening, seven days a week. The first week I was the top grossing salesman in California and 4th in their

Western division. I had an edge over the new hires in experience. I was not only a good salesman but I was smart. I worked more floor time, worked thru breaks, and concentrated on the higher priced items and suggestive selling. I had a future with them.

Medora, feeling neglected and lonely, started drinking too much again. She soon lost her job. With all the problems I had in the past, I had worked out a way to ace the system to collect unemployment insurance benefits. I shared this with her and she applied. I told her not to worry as I made enough money and that we would make it. The time came to pick up her first check in Santa Ana. I came home from work tired and hungry. She wasn't there.

There was only one bar in the area that we didn't go to together. I heard from friends that she had been drinking there. I went looking for her and there she was, sitting close to a strange man and drinking.

"Hi, Honey. I want you to meet........" the man stood up and offered his hand. I rudely pushed it aside.

"I had a rough day. Be home in 15 minutes or I'm gone." I walked away and went back to our motel. I waited an hour. She didn't come home. I was drinking whiskey on an empty stomach. I was tired and fed up. I packed my things and left. I got another motel room close by and fell asleep without eating. The alarm clock woke me early, in a foul mood, and suffering a hangover. I had forgotten something I needed for work. I went to our motel and let myself in with my key. Medora was in bed with the man from the bar. They were both asleep.

"What in the hell are you doing in bed with my wife?" I yelled rushing to the bed and pulling off the covers. She was naked and he was in his shorts. The man opened his eyes. He was totally confused. For a moment he didn't know where he was, let alone what was happening. I grabbed his pillow and as he tried to get out of bed, hit him with a mighty blow throwing him off balance. He fell to the floor. I was going to beat the living hell out of this fool when I was grabbed from behind. It was my brother Shaun. He was in town looking for me, picked up a girl, and spent the night in the other bedroom.

He effectively stopped me from fighting. Tears were running down my face. I broke away from Shaun and cursed him. She just wasn't worth it. I walked out. My brother threw on his pants and chased after me. I spied his car parked at the curb, jumped on the hood, and kicked out his windshield. He tried to stop me but when he saw the rage on my face he turned and ran. I went down to a bar and called Jim at work.

"Jim, I just caught my wife in bed with another man. I'm afraid I won't be in today."

"Have you been drinking?"

"What do you think?"

"Right, call me when you are ready to come back. Get yourself squared away. You're too valuable a man to lose. Is there anything I can do?"

"Just pray I don't kill the son of a bitch."

"You don't want to do that."

"I've had it with that woman. I'll try to be in tomorrow." I hung up. I had better stop drinking, get a hold of myself, and eat something or I would blow this job too. Just when things were starting to go so well, the same old shit again. When was I ever going to learn?

I did make it to work the next day. I had left our motel just in time as the manager had called the Police. Eventually I got the full story. The man with Medora was a marine on leave who was on his way home. She met him on the bus coming back from picking up her unemployment insurance check and offered to buy him a goodbye drink. After I caught them in bed together, he managed to get out of there just before the Police arrived. In his hurry he left his gear behind. Shaun disappeared and Medora decided to kill herself by cutting her wrists. She ended up in the Psycho Ward of the County hospital. They called me.

I refused to see them. I was informed that as her husband that I was required by law to talk with them. I was tempted to tell them we weren't married but I couldn't do it. No woman had ever tried to kill herself over me before. In spite of everything I loved this girl and she was in trouble. Against my better judgment, I took time off from work, and went to see them and her. She was sober and terrified that they were not going to release her. And they weren't unless I was willing to be responsible for her. Now, who had the hammer here?

Chapter 16

When the Police took Medora to the emergency ward, they secured the apartment. I wasn't about to pay rent on two places so I moved her things to my room. Several patrons of the bar approached me on behalf of the Marine. It seemed his sea bag was left behind in the apartment and there was no way he could get it. He was on leave, going to visit his family, and everything he owned was in his sea bag, war bonds, ID, photos, uniforms, and his personal clothing. His friends told me he was real sorry that he was drinking with my wife but nothing really happened, and that he would appreciate getting his things back. I had been in the service and my brother Shaun was a Marine on base with him. I told them that I never wanted to see this man. If he wanted his stuff, he could pick it out of the trash bin behind the motel. I threw his sea bag in there, poured gasoline on it, and set fire to it. He would think twice before picking up another man's wife again.

Medora was pathetic, lost, and beautiful in her hospital gown with no makeup. She begged me to take her back and give her another chance. She was sorry for what happened, swore that nothing had really happened between her and the Marine, and promised that it would never ever happened again. She loved me. She just drank too much and she was going to quit. All she wanted to do was to love me and make me happy forever and to please get her out of there. I took her back.

I rented a small one bed room white house behind a larger house in Costa Mesa away from our old stomping grounds in Newport Beach. Medora was released and I told her to rest up a few weeks before she looked for a job. I was closer to work. With the grand opening over, my hours were less and I was home more. I started a small garden and we adopted a small calico cat, Scaramouch. The cat was born wild and no one could touch him but me. I had the cat 3 days before Medora returned and that cat loved me.

For two weeks everything was wonderful between us. Medora didn't quit drinking but she drank at home and we didn't go out. I could sense that she was growing restless. Once a week she would take the bus to collect her unemployment check and I worried that she would stop at a bar but she behaved herself. Our only problem was her unfounded and unreasonable jealousy. If I was ten minutes late getting home from work, she would accuse me of having an affair. What she didn't understand was that I simply wasn't interested in other women when I had her for my own.

Our neighbor, an elderly lady had a pet white rabbit that was always escaping from his pen and attacking my vegetable garden. I talked to her but she turned nasty on me. I told her that if I caught her rabbit one more time in my garden I would shoot it. I borrowed an air rifle from work that looked real to show her that I meant business. Actually I loved animals and never would have hurt her precious pet. She kept Mr. Whiskers penned up.

Christmas season was upon us and I was working long hours again. I came home tired from work to find Medora drunk. Dinner was ready and the only way I could put up with her was to drink with her. I was fed up with her because everything had been going so well up to now. Then she started in on me running around on her. I told her I was in no mood to hear her crazy accusations and told her to shut up. When she didn't, I grabbed the air rifle, and threatened to shoot her if she uttered one more word. She believed the rifle to be real and that I was an excellent marksman. She dared me to shoot. Without seeming to aim, I shot out the light bulb next to her head. It was the only light that we had on. The room went pitch dark.

It was silent for a moment. Then I heard the door slam as she ran out. Now I've done it. I turned on a light. I had shot thru the lamb shade. I quickly replaced the bulb, flushed the broken bulb down the toilet, switched lampshades turning the small hole to the wall, went outside, and threw the rifle over my head onto the roof with the box of air pellets. I turned out the lights and laid down on the bed to wait for the Police. It didn't take long. Medora was with them.

I denied everything. She was hysterical and drunk. I claimed that there was no rifle, never had been, and that Medora was crazy. If they would check her record, they'd find she had just been released from the County mental ward. As there were no powder burns, no evidence, no rifle, they believed me. They let me go and took her away. The County called me at work the next day. This time I took my time getting there. I knew she would be mad and it was a stupid thing for me to do. Again she was scared and begged me to get her out of there. I did, of course.

It took her less than a week to get her revenge. I came home from work to find her gone. She took some of her clothes with her but not all. For three days not a word. It was a Sunday afternoon when she returned. I was outside watering my garden, with the cat in my arms, on a beautiful warm sunny day. She was in her bathing suit in a convertible with four marines. She had been drinking, of course.

"Hi, Honey, how've you been?" She got out of the car with a Marine who was wearing a bathing suit. "We've been swimming."

The Marine spoke. "What a beautiful cat! What's her name?"

"You like cats, do you? Here." I threw Scaramouch to him. The cat clawed his way from the Marine's chest all the way down and ran away. I apologized of course. Medora went into the house for 1st aid supplies and bandaged him up. No longer in the party mood, they left in a hurry.

"You're a real son of a bitch, Kennedy. Aren't you?"

"Did you come home to fight? If you did, you can just leave again. I just about had it with you."

"You tried to kill me."

"If I wanted you dead, you'd be dead."

"Where's the gun?"

"What gun? Did the Police find a gun?"

"So that's how it's going to be?"

"I'm not too happy with you right now. Get in the house and sober up. Just stay out my way for a while. I have to work tomorrow." She walked into the house and went to bed. I slept on the couch that night. I guess I showed her. The next morning I went to work before she got up. I didn't know whether or not she would be there or not when I got home. She was and dinner was on the table and it wasn't poisoned.

I asked Jim for a raise plus a 5% commission. If I had been on commission, I would have made seven times my salary during the month of December. Jim said not only couldn't he afford it but it was against company policy to give commission to anyone but tire sales people. I told him my wife wasn't working and I needed more money. He wouldn't budge, so I quit.

I took a job driving a dry cleaning truck. I got commission plus a bonus for each new account I brought in, plus an extra $10 per day for the driver who brought in the most new customers. Once I learned the system and my assigned route, I managed to complete the entire route in less than four hours. I religiously knocked on doors for two hours each day for new business and was soon making top wages. When I set my mind to do something it got done right. The problem was I was that dealing with a lot of lonely housewives and Medora couldn't stand it.

One day I came home to find that Medora had been arrested for drunk and disorderly. This time she had kicked a Policeman between the legs. I couldn't imagine why but she was sentenced to serve her time in the Long Beach jail. She got 20 days. The second time I took off from work to drive down to visit her I was hit with....

"You son of a bitch, I'm locked up here with all your whore girlfriends." She refused to calm down and talk to me and insisted to be taken back to her cell. Months later I got the story. Her seven cell mates were fed up with her constant bragging about what a wonderful husband she had. She had smuggled in a small picture of me and when they saw it, they broke out laughing. They all knew me from bartending in the Jungle and I had slept with five of them before I knew her. They teased her unmercifully her entire stay. When she was released and I picked her up, she refused to speak to me the entire ride home.

Medora got a job in a dentist office as a receptionist and I later got arrested when I later tried to run a yellow light. The newer car in front of me slammed on his brakes at the last moment and I hit his car. I got out of my car and saw that there was no damage to my front end. My older car was built like a tank. The other car was disabled. The driver, a giant of a man, came bursting out of his car with a tire iron threatening to do some serious damage to my skull. I had been drinking, fighting with Medora, and thought the prudent thing to do here was to get the hell out of Dodge. I got in my car, backed out, and drove away. When I arrived home, the Police were waiting for me. I was charged with hit and run.

While I was out on bail I got arrested on another hit and run. Again, rather than stay home and argue with Medora, I was at a bar drinking. A man conned me into driving him to a local night club. While making a left hand turn at a stop light, I miscalculated the speed of an oncoming car, and he hit me. I pulled away from the intersection and was looking for a place to park when the car behind me, on the turn, cut me off, and made a citizen's arrest. It turned out it was a Policeman who had just finished his shift and witnessed the accident. My passenger borrowed a dime from the Policeman who handcuffed me. He said he would find a pay phone and call the police. This was the last anyone saw of him. I went to jail and this time I didn't have the money to bail out.

While I was waiting to go to court, my first hit and run hearing came due. As I didn't have the paperwork with me, they wouldn't take me to court. Now I was a Failure to Appear and would have to deal with a most angry bail bond man, if and when I ever got out. Meanwhile Medora tried to kill herself again and ended up back in the mental ward. This time I was unable to help her get out. I was assigned a public defender and by some miracle, he managed to resolve both my cases and get me released for time served. I thought it best to get out of town. I didn't have the money to pay another month's rent.

I still had my car. I drove to Long Beach and rented a room. In packing our things I found eight bottles of liquor that Medora had hidden in various places in our apartment. I went to my union hall and as soon as I secured a job, I drove to Costa Mesa to see if I could get Medora out. During the doctor's interview she promised me everything. She admitted that she had some serious issues but was confident that we could work them out. I knew the suicide attempts were bogus but the doctors were taking them seriously. She would sterilize the razor blade before she cut her self not too deeply, and call for help she acted.

She got a job right away and in two weeks we had an apartment again. She just wouldn't quit drinking. It was fine when I was working in the oil refineries for she couldn't call and bother me. On any other of my jobs, she would get drunk at some bar and call me at work. She was always checking up on me and accusing me of running around on her. I tried talking with her when she was sober. She always promised to change but she never did. Finally, I had had enough and I moved out. I figured that since she didn't like Long Beach she would soon move out of town. But she stayed around to torment me and it cost me a few jobs.

I decided to use my brother's name. If Medora couldn't find me, she couldn't cause me trouble. I got duplicates of Shaun's ID. I got a new California drivers license. I was concerned as they took my thumb print, but evidently they didn't cross check it. I applied for a social security card under his name and they sent me a card with his number. I tried again, using a different birth date, and I scored a new number with Shaun's name on it. Basically, I took my brother's life up to now and branched off as myself with his ID. Shaun had a stable work record, excellent credit, and a college education, all of which I tapped into. This was great! If you had five sons and named them all the same, you would only have to send one to college. They could all share a college diploma and you'd pay for only one tuition.

I got a job using the name Shaun Kennedy, kept a low profile, and hung around new bars. Medora never found me and soon moved on. I was free of her at last. I missed her and tried to drown out old memories with liquor and more women. There wasn't a woman alive who could live up to what we had together and I could never drink enough to forget her. My life was a mess. I told myself that I was better off without her. I sat down with a sheet of paper to list all the reasons why I loved her and why we were wrong for each other.

Sex was on the plus side. She was the most satisfying sex partner I ever had. Her physical body temperature was higher than normal and that was exciting. Drunk, angry, ill, she never once turned me down and she truly enjoyed sex but was allergic to me. If I licked her arm, it would instantly break out in red welts. She had beautiful red hair, violet eyes, and was breathtakingly beautiful. If she had any faults it was in being short and sexy as opposed to classic beauty. This was a woman to enjoy. She looked as though you didn't have her, you haven't lived. There was a constant challenge that hung in the air surrounding her. "Do you think you are man enough for me?"

On the downside, she was possessive, insanely jealous, and drank too much. There was something dark in her past that was disturbing her. She couldn't seem to say no to a drink or a party and it was highly probable that she had sex with other men when she was drinking. Also there was the possibility that she might be married, as she never spoke of it. Her arrest record was growing at an alarming rate and she had no respect for authority. There was a hint that she might be taking drugs or even selling them. I realized that I knew very little about her other than what she let me know. I called our old phone number on a hunch to see if she kept the same number. She answered and I hung up without saying a word.

Medora and I had been together almost two and one half years. Living together was hard but living apart was harder. I was drinking too much, building up an arrest record, and going from job to job without getting anywhere but older. At the request of my mother, I moved to the Valley to help my stepdad start his new business. Tired of working for someone else and with the help of some investors, he had opened his own auto and truck paint shop. Prior to Rod's Truck & Auto Painting one had to drive to downtown Los Angles to get a large truck or semi painted. The shop was large enough to paint a small airplane. They needed a top salesman to get started. What they got was me.

No salary, straight 10% commission, with $25 a week auto expenses was all I was offered. If I wasn't collecting unemployment insurance I would have had to turn them down. I started visiting the big moving van companies. I got a few jobs, hardly enough to keep them busy. I decided that automobiles were where the business was. Rod charged about 3 times what Earl Scheib's did so I had to sell quality. I took a gamble and it worked. Soon I was making more money in one week without getting out of bed on Monday morning than the payroll for the entire shop. Rod decided that from then on I would only be paid on the business I brought in personally. I disagreed and so I quit. The shop was closed within six months, Rod lost the house he was buying and they moved back to Chicago. I moved back to Long Beach

Nine months wasted by. It was now 1962 and I was 27 years old. The Russians had put missiles in Cuba and backed down from President Kennedy, no relation. Medora was now a distant memory which no woman could ever live up to. When I was working in the Valley for Rod, I tried a few of her old stomping grounds. No one knew where she was. My mother hadn't heard from her since we started dating. I was afraid to call the last phone number I had, as I felt it was my last tie to her. I tried desperately to find some other woman who could help me forget. Nothing seemed to work but drinking, and drinking was keeping me from holding down a job. Something had to change and soon.

I had taken a sales job at Columbia Dept Store on Pacific Ave in Long Beach. I had been working there about six weeks over the holidays and with commission was doing quite well. Feeling alone and miserable I got drunk over the weekend. I blacked out and don't remember what happened exactly but it seems I kicked out the plate glass window of a filling station. Either I pay for the window immediately or I go to jail. I called my boss who came up with the money and paid my way out of trouble. Ashamed and hung over, I called work the following Monday and took a couple of days off. I went to the Seymour Sanitarium and Medical Clinic for the California Society for the Study of Alcoholism and inquired about how one stop drinking. After filling out endless forms and talking to several doctors, I left, not knowing anymore than when I went in.

I left the clinic, got drunk, arrested, and ended up in jail. Unknown to me, the clinic had contacted my father and he wired them the money to help me. They bailed me out of jail, kept me in the clinic three days, and then released me. I was sober and on a drug called Antabuse that prevents one from drinking. They had contacted my boss and I still had my job. I resented this entire business. I felt I had lost control of my life. I had no intention of ever involving my father in any part of my life, and If I was going to stop drinking, I wanted it to be my decision. I decided to play along with the program for a while. The drug protected me from drinking. If I never took the first drink, I would never have to worry about the second one. With sobriety came the strength that allowed me to believe that I was in control.

I was so confident that I took a relief job as bartender at the Sea King for extra money, to keep busy, and to prove that I didn't have to drink. Well, I was totally wrong. There was no way I could be around a bunch of drinking people and stay sober. Without the benefit of drink, drunks weren't funny, women weren't beautiful, and I wasn't having any fun. More important, I didn't like myself when I was sober nor did my friends. The job at Columbia Department Store which was to be the base to my sobriety, was more like an anchor around my neck. I felt they were just waiting for me to fail.

I had been warned about the drug Anabuse. No drinking period. It stayed in your system for72 hours. Being a hard head, I had to test it. I was sitting at the Sea King before going to work when a customer offered to buy me a drink. I took a small glass of beer. I took a small sip. Nothing seemed to happen. I took a bigger sip. This was silly. I called for a double straight shot of Jack Daniels. I figured if I drank it fast enough it would overcome the effect of the drug. I gulped it down.

Kennedy, what's wrong with you? You're all red and swelling up." I felt like I couldn't breathe. I tried to get up and fell to the floor. I couldn't get up. My heart started beating like a sledgehammer as if it was going o burst right out of my chest. I tried crawling. I couldn't even do that. I remember someone laughing and a group of people around me. It got dizzy and I must have passed out. I came to lying on a couch shivering and violently throwing up. Henry, a gay man, was holding my head gently and wiping my forehead with a damp cloth. I think I threw up on him. He covered me with some extra blankets. He told me that he brought me to his apartment and that I would be all right. He asked me if I wanted him to call the Paramedics. I said no, I just wanted to get home and tried to get up. I couldn't do it. I was weak as a kitten. Henry said he was going to the store to get something for me and that he would be right back. I was left alone. I shut my eyes and tried to control the shaking. If I could only die I'd feel better.

I don't remember too much about what happened next but two sailors came in. They seemed mad that Henry was not there. They asked me where he was but I could not speak. Then they got mad. One held me and the other slapped me a couple times. The bigger one of the two unzipped his pants and tried to force his ugly member in my mouth. I couldn't fight back. I gritted my teeth as hard as I could but I felt I had to throw up again. The large sailor got on to top of me and pinned me down. Grabbing my hair and my jaw he tried to force my mouth open. Two Policemen burst into the room and pulled him off me. Henry coming home, heard the two sailors abusing me and called the Police. They asked me if I wanted to press charges.

"I'm sick. I just want to go home."

"Come on, we'll take you home." And they did after getting the names of the two sailors. They already knew Henry. I stayed home for three days trying to get well. I quit my job at the department store, got my last check, and moved out of the Jungle. I made my decision right there. No more Antabuse, ever. It damn near killed me.

It was back to my original idea. First, no more drinking in low class bars. In the better bars I behaved myself, got into less trouble, and drank less. Two, I would only work in the better bars. Lastly, I would not get involved with any woman. From here on out, I would pay a prostitute. It would be cheaper in the long run with no emotional involvement. I took a job at the Navy Shipyard to get myself back in shape. I was hired as a Pipefitter (marine) WG-8. Without previous marine experience and skills I didn't qualify for WG-10. Basically I was a pipefitter's helper. It paid a little less than a maintenance pipefitter but it had some great benefits. It was a Civil Service job and I was hired as a permanent employee.

My last government job was the US Navy. I flashed back to standing guard over an empty garbage dumpster with an unloaded M-1 rifle. This was in the middle of an armed camp, at 4AM, in a cold driving rain in January 1954 at Great Lakes, Illinois. This was not what I had joined the Navy for. I also found it hard to have respect for less than intelligent people who had a higher rank than me. At least at the Shipyard I was a civilian and as a civil service employee, it was almost impossible to get fired.

My first day at the shipyard, I had to wait almost four hours for a man to show up to fix the Polaroid machine so I could get a picture ID. I tried to tell them that I had an appointment to report for work and that I was on the payroll. Couldn't they issue me a temporary ID and I could come back the next day when they were ready for me? It was not an option. Sit down and wait. Next, they wouldn't allow me to drive my motorcycle on base because I wasn't wearing a helmet. California law did not require one at the time but Federal law did. I wasn't about to park my bike outside where it could easily be stolen. I had to walk it on the base, plus three blocks for special parking. I received a coupon for a free lunch only to find after I ordered my food that it was an expired coupon. I finally met my foreman about an hour before shift end. He told me it was too late to assign me to anything and to just look busy. He walked away. This was day one.

On previous jobs working for contractors, the priorities were, do it right, do it safe, get it done quickly. Time is money. I could not, for the life of me, figure out what these people were trying to do. Day two I was assigned to a pipefitter who told me straight off that he wasn't a baby sitter. This man's advice to me was to look busy. He evidently graduated from the same success school as the foreman. It seemed most people were there to get away with the most they could without getting caught, blame the next guy when things went wrong, and rest up for when the shift ended.

If I needed material or a tool for a work order, I had to order it from a runner. I could not walk a block over to the warehouse and pick it up myself. It would deprive a man of a job. The runner felt he had the God given right to use the bathroom twice a day, an hour at a time, to catch up on his reading, do his personal grooming, or examine in detail his fascinating excretions. His main business was making book and helping his clients make important gambling decisions. When he found the time he would pick up stuff and deliver it, if it would fit on his bike. If it was too large for his bike, he would schedule a truck to pick it up. This evidently worked well for him but it paid hell with the few men who took their jobs seriously and were there to work.

The manager of my apartment house worked on the base for many years as an electrician. He had a company truck that he was able to drive off base and keep over night. His apartment was overfilled with stuff he had stolen from the base every day, not things that he could use, or even sell but just because he could do it. He kept trying to give me some of this junk. I had to laugh. Every day when we left work they made us open our lunch boxes at the gate to check for theft. My manager just drove out with a wave of the hand. They never checked his truck.

I was quietly getting fed up with all the waste and incompetence I was surrounded by. I was spending way too much time trying to look busy. Sometimes I could spend a whole day without seeing my pipefitter longer than 15 minutes the entire time. Finally he got a job he couldn't push off on someone else. After studying the blueprints for a half hour, he had me order a section of special nickel alloy pipe from the runner. We actually got it delivered first thing the next morning. He told me cut off a piece 10 and one quarter inches long and bevel it on both sides for the weld. I had been looking at the blueprints over his shoulder and asked, "Are you sure that's the right size?"

"You've been here one week, I've been on the job 12 years, and now you're going to tell me how to do my job?"

"No, sir. Where is the pipe cutting machine or do I have to send it out?"

"I told you to cut it."

"A shipyard this size and we don't have a pipe cutting machine?"

"They're all down for repair. Cut it by hand. You've been sitting on your ass all week. Are you afraid to get your hands dirty?"

I didn't answer. I got a hacksaw and went to work. It was a tough job. A pipe cutting machine would have cut and beveled it in about ten minutes. It took me over 3 hours by hand to cut and hand file the bevel. I took it to my fitter. He took one look at it.

"Too short." And he threw it overboard. I walked away. I found the foreman.

"I quit."

"Do you mind telling me why?"

"You don't even want to know." It took almost as long getting out of there as it did getting in. I was free again. No more damn Civil Service jobs for me.

Chapter 17

I couldn't survive without unemployment insurance. The way I quit jobs and got myself fired could impact my cash flow if I could not pick up my weekly checks. At first I would go work a day laborer job and use it as my last job to be eligible for unemployment insurance. It worked out fine, except sometimes I would get a very hard physical job for very little money. I bought myself a post office box, waited a day, and then used it as my last job. I figured that if I never answered their forms, I would not be committing mail fraud. It worked fine. I never reported the few days that I spent in jail as time being unable to work. If questioned, my argument was that I was always available for work, even if I had to bail out or pay a fine, I'd be there. Never asked, never questioned, no problem, I always collected unemployment insurance.

I started drinking again. True to my promise to myself, I drank in the better bars, behaved myself, and stayed out of trouble. I paid the occasional prostitute but I never took them home. While this worked better for me on several levels, the money spent faster. I was going broke so I sold my motorcycle. It gave me a few more weeks of drinking money. I evaluated my life to discover I was going nowhere fast, getting older, and accumulating a bad arrest and employment record. I really didn't have any friends left except for little Kenny. I did not see him often as he hung around those bars I was trying to avoid.

It was early December 1962 when I starting bartending at Tobo's at 14th st. and Long Beach Blvd which was formerly American Ave. The bar was owned by an ex-Vice Squad officer Tom and his partner Bob, a retired lie-detector technician. Tom had been working managing several large gambling casinos in nearby Gardenia. The grand opening night almost killed me. The place was packed and the only help I had was a midget bartender who couldn't quite reach the bar to be effective. The midget got drunk early and was useless. The bar was three deep when a man offered to buy the bar a drink. I almost quit then and there but I stayed the course. At closing time, they locked the doors, and shot craps on the pool table until daylight. I was given an extra $100 bill to stay on and serve drinks.

I held the job three weeks. They were just not my type of people. They were too fast, monied, and had a superior air about them. I was making good money but I would never fit in with this crowd. They paid more for one hub cap than I did for most of my cars. The women didn't look at me twice and this was something I was not use to. Prostitutes were good for sex but I was lonely and longed for something else. I had a terrible emptiness that drinking would not fill. I thought of Medora again. Even at her worst, she was better than nothing. I got drunk and lost my job. I got in a fight with two men at the rooming house where I was staying and was given until the next morning to get out. In desperation I called Medora. It had been almost a year since I saw her.

She answered the phone. I cried and begged her to give me another chance. She said she had missed me and would come and get me.

"Don't get mad now. I have to have a friend drive me down to Long Beach. He's just someone who has been helping me out, a good friend. He's not my boyfriend."

"Where are you living now?"

"I've got a small apartment in Sun Valley. Do you have any money/"

"A little, a few hundred. I don't have much stuff. I've been living in a small room."

"I'll be down to pick you up in about two hours. OK?"

"I'll be here."

"You better be. I've missed you." She hung up. I closed my eyes and tried to sleep. Everything was packed ready to move. I hoped I wasn't making a mistake again. If two people ever didn't belong together it was us. Well, all one could do is try. After you've done your best what more is there?

True to her word Medora showed up with her friend. George seemed like a nice enough fellow but he definitely was not happy to meet me. Nevertheless he was polite and helped me load my stuff into her car. It was her car but her driver's license only allowed her to drive to and from work. We got to Sun Valley, her apartment, and got me unpacked. We sat around and had a few drinks. I thought George would never leave. I wanted to talk with Medora alone. Finally he left. I had the feeling that it was really his apartment.

We talked for a while saying a whole lot of nothing. I just wanted to get her into bed and feel like she was mine again. She wanted to go out and celebrate our getting back together. Honey, I've had enough to drink for tonight. Let's just call it a day."

"I have to pick up some money that is owed me at the Stagger Inn. The rent is due tomorrow. We don't have to stay long. Now that you are here, you can drive me." Reluctantly I agreed. I followed her directions and drove to the bar. Before we got out she warned me.

"Now I don't want you to get upset. I know how you get. There are some men in here that know me. I've been coming here a long time. Don't be jealous. I'm with you now."

I had a bad feeling about this but I kept my thoughts to myself. Sure enough, within five minutes, some jerk grabbed her ass. I took exception to this and decided I had better stop this immediately. As I was laying down the word, he decided to be a man and show off by fighting me. As I fought him, Medora walked out the door with two other men.

I won the fight easily and left the bar. Medora and the car were gone. I walked into another bar and ordered a drink. I had never been in Sun Valley before and I didn't know my way around. I didn't even know where I was. I was tempted to get drunk and forget the whole thing but I loved this woman. She had warned me about the fact other men knew her. I lost my temper and acted like a jerk-off. She was willing to take me back over all the other men she could have. What was wrong with me? I decided that I would have a few drinks, give her time to calm down, and then take a cab home. I bet she thought that I couldn't find my way home having been there only once.

I had two more drinks, tipped the bartender, and called a cab.

I let myself into the apartment with the extra key that she had given me. There on the couch was George and Medora. There was a jug of wine on the floor, she was wearing a robe, and George was naked.

"All right George, get the hell out."

"I'm not going anywhere." He growled. He was a short muscular man about 45 years old and more than a little drunk

"Now George, this is my wife and I'm telling you to get out now or I'm going to have to throw you out." He took another drink and gave me the finger. I walked to the couch grabbed him by the neck and jerked him to his feet. He swung at me a mighty blow. I merely ducked and hit him with a three punch combination that left him lying on the floor. He just lay there and covered his head.

"You want to fight, you son of a bitch? Get up and fight like a man." He didn't get up. I kicked him three times hard. He still wouldn't get up. Medora got up and tried to stop me. I back handed her. She flew across the room and crashed into the wall. I noticed that George was bleeding on the white rug.

"You son of a bitch, you're bleeding on my rug." I jerked him up, slung him over my shoulder, walked to the bath room, and threw him naked into the tub. I should have stopped there but I didn't. I jumped on top of him, with one foot pressing on his throat, I kicked the living shit out of him. I took out on him every man who had ever slept with her. Suddenly I stopped. I was drained of rage. He was a bloody mess and unconscious.

Medora was sitting on the coach crying. "You want him? You got him." I waved graciously. I left the house, walked as rapidly as I could for a few blocks, spotted a night club, walked in and got drunk at the piano bar. I didn't particularly notice it at the time but no one sat next to me. I walked home to find two Police cars waiting for me. I went quietly. I was at peace with the world. Hell, it was less than two months to Christmas.

I came to. I was only wearing my shorts and a shirt. I had a hangover but thank God, I was Irish, my mind hadn't turned to mush. I couldn't find any paperwork. I was in jail but I didn't know why.

I called the first person I saw. "Hey, Badge, what am I booked for"

"Son, if you know how to pray, you better get on your knees. The man you beat up is in Intensive care. If he dies you're being booked for murder one." His jaw, left arm, and three ribs were broken, one rib had punctured his lung, and he had over 127 stitches on his face.

Hell, it was all a blank to me. The last thing I remember was at the piano bar singing, "Nevertheless".

George lived and I was booked with felony assault to kill with a deadly weapon. It seems that if you use your feet on someone in the state of Californian it is considered a deadly weapon. I pled not guilty and was assigned a public defender. He advised me that if I pled to the lesser charge of misdemeanor assault, with intent to do bodily harm, with my record, it would be in my best interest. It seemed every public defender I ever had had advised me to plead guilty rather than go to trial. My record kept piling up but I didn't have any felonies and they did not know me in this town. I pled guilty with an explanation.

"Alright, son, what's your story?" The judge looked decent enough. I told him the whole story. He listened intently. I ended up with, "I'm sorry I beat up the man so badly but he swung on me first. He was in my house with my wife and I told him to leave." I then shut up and waited.

The judge picked up some papers. "Mr. Kennedy, I have your complete record here. Who in the Hell do you think you are that you can go around beating up on people?" I remained silent and hung my head.

"I'm remanding you to 30 days in the county jail with a two year parole. You are not to go in or about a place that sells or serves alcohol. You are to be a good citizen and obey all laws at all times. Is that understood?"

"Your Honor, I'm a union bartender. How can I work?"

"Would you rather spend the entire year in jail?"

"No, Sir. May I ask a question sir?"

"What is it?" he asked, a little peeved.

"Your Honor, I thought I was right. The man was in my house about to rape my wife. I asked him to leave. He wouldn't go. What should I have done?"

"You call the Police. You never take the law into your own hands."

"Yes, Sir"

"Any more questions?"

"No, Sir". I was led away. Was this man kidding? By the time the Police would have gotten there, the rape would have been done and over with. Sometimes you have to act at the moment. This judge is totally out of it. He wasn't for real but he had the hammer. I was going to jail.

I spent three days in the Los Angeles downtown county jail being processed before being made a trustee and allowed to work on an honor farm. I don't know how these boneheads thought but in their wisdom they had me work as a tailor. Maybe when I said sailor the man heard it as tailor or maybe my past job experience at Lerner Shops got me the job. At any rate, I was a complete failure at running a sewing machine.

The three days in Los Angeles county jail was an interesting view of our penal system. It was impossibly overcrowded. In a cell designed for 20 men they would force as many as 60 people meaning most slept on the concrete floor. There was one open filthy toilet without a seat, and one sink in each cell. Usually there was no toilet paper. During the three days that I was there, a plain bowl of pinto beans, 2 slices of day old bread, and a cup of kool aid was our lunch. We all herded together and were treated like animals. Many of the guards were angry, impatient, and in generally foul moods. Outside phone calls were almost impossible to make. Fellow inmates were not the type of people you would want to associate with, smell, or be on the same planet with. It was like being in hell without the advantage of being dead.

The honor farm was clean, well run, and decent enough. We slept in a bunk house, ate in a mess hall, and had access to showers and clean washrooms. The work details were not too hard as there were more man then needed. It was more like an Army camp then a jail but the loss of personal freedom was hard especially on someone like me. And of course there were no women.

Visiting day was a complete surprise. Medora came. Surprisingly she was not mad at me. She explained that she had other men friends the year we had been separated, George was one of them, but none of them really meant anything to her. She loved me. George just didn't want to give her up. I beat him up so badly that he did not even want to hear my name. He refused to sign a complaint against me and wanted to forget the whole thing. He would never see her again. If I still wanted to, we could try once more. Certainly, we had been through enough so that we could still make a life together. She wasn't happy without me and evidently I still cared for her. I was totally shocked. I had no money left, no job, no home, and nowhere to go. I agreed to give us another chance. I would go to her when I was released.

Medora started writing me letters about three times a week. In each letter she would put two or three dollars so I would have enough change for the inmate's store, candy, and milk machine. Now I could buy a daily newspaper, get a decent haircut, and buy necessities like razor blades, soap, and toothpaste. It made my confinement easier. She was still working and George was still in the hospital. This was the only woman in my life who ever really loved me but was I man enough to handle it?

Forced sobriety and time alone to really think made me reach some difficult decisions. From 1957 to now I had accumulated 24 arrests all drinking related. The more recent arrests involved fighting and violence. Now I had almost killed someone. I abused alcohol, I have a bad temper, and little or no control when I'm drinking. For whatever reason I had a bad attitude and it was getting me in trouble. I hung around losers and inferior people, mainly because they looked up to me and it made me feel better. Also I could be an idiot and would not be noticed as I fit right in.

I loved women too much and might be a sexual addict. I never forced a woman, raped one, or thought about doing so. Being Irish, tall, and not ugly I always met more than my share of willing women and never went too long without one. Leaving home at such an early age, drinking at a very young age, and going with older and often times married women or prostitutes, left me unable to trust women or have a normal relationship. The way I lived, not having steady work, not saving money, getting drunk, and arrested, I was afraid to take on any responsibilities. I loved animals but I wouldn't have a pet because I was afraid I couldn't take care of it.

On the plus side, I did not have to drink, I had a sense of humor, I wanted to do better, and I felt deep inside that I really had a talent for writing. I was intelligent enough to realize that I rationalized all my faults and was doing nothing to change them. But all in all I was gaining some very valuable insights and life experience.

Now I had to examine survival and Medora. If I went back with her, tempting as it was, I would probably end up killing her, me, or someone. There wasn't much chance that she would change and I didn't have the knowledge or skills to help her. If I didn't really know what was wrong, I just couldn't fix it. She would not be able to change herself until she admitted that she had a problem, was willing to change, and did something about it. She attracted men and when she drank, she went with them. It wasn't that I wasn't man enough for her, I couldn't be with her every moment of her life. I was going to have to live my life without her. I refused to spend the rest of my life in prison. I would rather be dead.

Could I live without her. I would have to. That was all there was to it. I had a $900 IRS tax refund check coming that I had forwarded to her address. I was able to talk to the chaplain, explain the situation, and get a change of address so that I could receive my mail at the honor farm instead. I just hoped it would come in time before I was released with only a few dollars to my name. All my clothes were at Medora's apartment and I didn't want to stay there any longer than I had to. The longer I stayed, the harder it would be to leave. Once I made my decision it seemed that a weight was lifted off my shoulders. I concentrated on finishing my time as easily as possible. I caught up on some books I always wanted to read.

The weekend before my release, Medora came to visit me. I studied her carefully memorizing every inch of her. I knew after a week that I would never see her again. I was sad but I knew it was for the best. My tax refund check came. I could not cash it until I was released but at least I had the security of having some money. I had enough to catch a bus to Sun Valley where my things were. I would have to see her to get my stuff but my mind was made up. I was going to be strong.

The day came. I was released early. I hit the first bar I could find open and had a few cold beers. I waited until the banks opened to cash my check. With over $900 hidden in my sock I caught the bus to Sun Valley. I found the apartment and let myself in. Medora was at work. I didn't have the heart to leave without seeing her one last time. I waited. She came home with a beautiful cake and a couple of bottles of Champagne to celebrate my homecoming. She cooked me a great steak dinner and we stayed up late and talked for hours. We went to bed and made love. She got up early, kissed me goodbye, and left for work. I packed everything I owned, left, and caught a bus to Long Beach. I didn't leave a note. I caught a glimpse of her walking on the street from the bus window. It was the last time I ever saw her. It was the hardest thing I ever had to do in my life. The only way I could ever forget her was to tell myself that she was dead. It worked.

The bus pulled into Long Beach. It was the same old city but I was looking at it in a different light. I loved this city and this time I was going to do it right. Hang with better people, stay out of dives, and set some goals. The first business was to keep busy and find work. As it was close to Christmas I caught a sales job at Harris & Frank's Department store in the men's wear department. Things were tightening up everywhere and I was offered a salary only no commission. I rented an efficiency apartment off Third Street and Magnolia. My job was to last only thru the holidays. If I was careful with my spending, I'd start the New Year with about $800. This was quite a bit more than the $.37 I started with seven years previously when I first came to Long Beach. not knowing anybody.

The only thing I remember about Harris and Frank's was my lunch box and the security guard. Many employees brought their lunch to work in the usual brown bag. I lugged in my old oil refinery lunchbox everyday with an one quart stainless steel thermos bottle. At closing time the security guard sat at the employee exit checking any purchases and their receipts. For one week he never asked me to open it. Then one Wednesday he asked me to open my lunch box.

"You're kidding?" There was a long line of employees waiting to get out the door behind me. I usually just politely said "Good Night" and walked out.

"Not tonight. Open your box." My eyes fell as I nervously opened the box. It seemed as if everyone was expecting him to discover something. The box was empty of course! He waved me thru. It was difficult to keep from laughing. I was wearing a new belt, tie, cuff links, silk square, and tie bar. In my pocket was a new wallet and magnetic money clip. I had just walked out the door with over $100 of new merchandise undetected. It sure as hell wasn't in the lunch box.

Employee theft is a growing concern in our country. Basically, I don't believe in stealing but I don't believe in underpaying your help either. Most non-union companies that I've worked for seem to pay as little as they can get away with. I also know that if you don't like what they offer that you do not have to take the job. Why did I steal? I really didn't need to. I never stole a dime when I bartended. Maybe because when they set up elaborate systems they believe to be fool proof, I consider it a personal challenge to ace their game. Or maybe, I'm just a rebel at heart.

With too much spare time on my hands, I took some night work bartending holiday parties at some of our better hotels. Keeping busy didn't leave me time for commiserating over my lost love. I made some excellent tip money, got free meals, and met some new interesting people. One such person was Johnny Brennan, night bartender at the old Wilton Hotel Sky room. Johnny was considered by many in the trade to be the best bartender in Long Beach and was liked by everyone. After the first of the year there was an opening for a relief bartender at the Wilton Hotel and Johnny recommended me. I was now working for the top place in Long Beach. Unfortunately, it changing ownership.

On two of my shifts I was working a tiny bar off the lobby. It could seat only ten people at the bar and had no side tables or booths. It was only opened 12 hours a day and that is what I worked. It had no restroom. I'd lock the cash register, take the elevator to the 2nd floor, to go to the toilet. With very few customers, I had the place mostly to myself and I was bored to death. It was difficult not to drink but I maintained. I never got drunk on the job but I had to take many trips to the men room. Finally they decided to close the bar. There wasn't enough work for me so I gave my notice.

The Bartenders Union had combined with the Culinary Union and there were several advantages to being a member but the pension plan wasn't one of them unless you made it your lifetime work. I had joined many different unions as in the many jobs I had it was a requirement. I was a strong believer in unions until the way I was treated when I was a union steward. Benefits, hiring halls, health, dental, and pension plans were the obvious pluses. Dues and misuse of that money were the downside. I thought it was about time I took advantage of one of the stronger unions while I was still young.

It was 1964, President John F. Kennedy died Nov 22, the year before.

I was 29 years old, and in twenty years, I would be 49. If I could either get a good pension or manage to save $100,000 to have invested at 10% interest, I would be in good shape. It wasn't too impossible to have both. I had become a top bartender, I enjoyed the work, the salary wasn't great but with tips it was good. If I controlled my drinking there was no reason I couldn't make it. Two choices came to mind, Las Vegas and Cruise ships.

Las Vegas was a strong union town. So controlled that I would have to work a year as a bar boy before I could be a bartender. It was opened 24 hours around the clock, plenty of action, beautiful women, top entertainment, and constantly growing. The problem was gambling. I knew I had an addictive personality. I was fine as long as I wasn't around it but I had a bad feeling about it being available 24/7. I'd spent the last seven year trying to beat roulette. I had that kind of mind. I hated to lose.

Cruise ships on the other hand seemed perfect. The Merchant Seaman Union was solid, benefits galore, and a generous pension. Adventure, travel to foreign lands, and wonderful background experience for writing. The romance of the open sea appealed to me. Where have I been? This was the life for me! How do I get my ticket? I went down to the Merchant Seaman Union in Wilmington for information. First, I would have to have seaman's papers where I would have to apply to the Department of Transportation, Treasury Department of the United States Coast Guard. To apply I would need an endorsement from the union agreeing to hire me. I asked how one could get an endorsement?

Who are you, who do you know, and more importantly, who knows you? They gave me the papers to fill out. I took them home. As this was important to me, I gave it a lot of thought. I was currently a member in good standing in four unions, and had a honorable withdrawal in five. I had an honorable discharge from the Navy. I had worked casual labor in their sister Long Shore Union and swamped trucks in the Teamster Union. My arrest record was problematic but I had no felony convictions. I did not want to take work away from current members and was willing to wait for a job opening requiring my special abilities as an experienced and trained bartender. I filled out my paperwork and brought it to the union. Hardly reading it, they gave me a written job endorsement, first step down.

Next I contacted the Coast Guard who sent me the required paperwork. I completed everything truthfully and sent it in with two photos and a Police approved fingerprint card. I crossed my fingers and waited. About a month later I received the following letter:

"Dear Sir:

Reference is made to your application for original seaman's document filed at this office on February 14, 1964.

We are now in receipt of a reply from Coast Guard Headquarters regarding this application. The nature of your police record, which includes convictions for crimes of violence sufficient to warrant the belief that you are not a safe and suitable person to be entrusted with the duties of a seaman on board merchant vessels of the United States. This decision is made in reliance on the decision of the U.S. Supreme Court in the Case of Boudoin v. Llyes Bros. SS Co., Inc., 348 US 336 (1955), wherein it was held that the employment of a seaman with a propensity for violence could render the vessel unseaworthy.

In view of the foregoing, issuance of an original United States Merchant Mariner's Document to you will not be authorized.

Yours very truly,

T.V. Kennedy

Ensign, U.S. Coast Guard

By direction of Officer in Charge

Marine Inspection"

This was cold. Another dream crushed. I wasn't paranoid, God was really out to get me. Just when I finally got my head together and decided to straighten my life out, they pulled the rug out from under me. Hell, I'm tough, I'm strong, I'm Irish, I'll make it. From here on in, they all can kiss my royal Irish ass. I won't dream, hope, or love again. Don't trust anyone. They will only hurt you. I didn't ask to be here but as long as I am, the hell with it. To hell with everyone. I had to answer this asshole's letter. He had the same last name as me.

"Dear Ensign Kennedy,

It's men like me who win the wars for our country. Being tough doesn't make one a bad person. There was a reason for every fight I was ever in. I fought to win. With a name like Kennedy and being Irish, I'm sure you understand. I just wanted a job and a chance for a new start.

Yours truly,

Joe Kennedy"

I enclosed a copy of his letter to me and mailed it. I did not expect an answer. A month later I received an original seaman card, no letter, no explanation. I didn't believe it. I rushed down to the Union. Unless I knew someone, I would have to start out as a dishwasher, work up to a porter, and then maybe a bartender. The estimated time for this was eight years. I told them I had served my apprenticeship and there was no way I was going to start at the bottom again. I walked out, never to return.

Chapter 18

I heard of a job opening in Paramount, California, just next to Long Beach, in a bar called Mae's Café. I applied and was hired for the day shift by the owner, an old, old lady named Mae. The bar was on the outskirts of town and did very little business. It was rumored that it was a house of ill repute during the war and that Mae, in her prime, was the madam. The old building in the rear on the same property used to be a hotel of sorts where the working women took their tricks from the bar. It was a colorful story and I had no reason to disbelieve it. But the old days were gone along with the action, big money, and the beautiful women.

Mae let me have a free room in the old run down hotel. I was the only guest. As I didn't have a car at the time she offered to let me buy an old 1949 2-door Ford convertible she had for $50, on credit. It ran good and didn't look too bad so I bought it. My first working shift I had five customers, all men, the only females in the place were old Mae and an even older cat that liked beer. I asked one of the men "Who is the prettiest girl in town? He said it was definitely the woman who owned the beer bar "Penny's". I headed there as soon as I got off work. It was about two blocks down the street.

"Penny's" was packed. The owner, Penny, was a delightful surprise. Blond, tall, statuesque, sexy, blue eyed, and dressed in a brief old time saloon costume she was definitely eye candy. The bar was sparkling clean and the beer was ice cold. She was friendly with everyone and seemed to have a great sense of humor.

She was maybe ten years older than me. I introduced myself as the new bartender in town. I told her I was looking for the prettiest girl in Paramount and she was it. I certainly would not have to look any further.

I stayed there the entire shift, helped her close up, took her out and bought her breakfast. She spent the night with me in my room. Two days later I moved into her apartment, located half way between the two bars. It was perfect except I worked days and she worked nights.

The first crack in our relationship was my temper. I considered Penny as my girlfriend and I resented the way men grabbed her at her bar. When one man patted her fine behind we had words that led to a fist fight. I won the fight but lost the war. Penny eighty-sixed me from her bar. Unable to drink in there anymore I tried the only other bar in town. It was miserable, full of old drunks, and no action worthy of a man of my temperament. I started getting short with Penny.

Mae decided to close her bar and suddenly I was out of a job. Penny made it plain that she was not going to support me. Even the sex was getting bad. She acted like she was doing me a favor. I went to the Union hall and got a shut-down job at Arco Refinery. When I came home dirty with oil from work, one look at me and she told me to leave. Most of her furniture was hand rubbed white leather, she had white carpet, and she was always as sparkling clean as her apartment. I left. I never was one to hang around where I wasn't wanted. The shut-down ended in 12 days. I was alone and out of work again.

I was depressed and ready for something new and different. Times were tough and jobs were few. Remembering the good luck I had had with private employment agencies in the past, I applied to one. They had a bartender job opening in the desert in a small town called Baker, California, about 100 miles from Las Vegas. It was in a 24 hour coffee shop named the "Bun Boy", that was a stop for tour buses making their way to Las Vegas. The job paid little but it included room and board. I thought it would give me a chance to clear my head and maybe save a little money. I took the job.

On a hunch, I didn't give up my apartment and paid three months in advance. I just took what I needed and headed for Baker. It was summer and this was the desert. I was not sure how I was going to like it. To my surprise I loved it. I loved the clean dry air, heat, and burning sun. The solitude was refreshing.

I got off on a bad footing almost immediately. I was to be a bartender for only two relief shifts a week. The other four shifts were as a busboy. Not only did someone not tell me the truth but the salary would be considerably less than I expected. Living quarters were single bedrooms cooled by evaporative units in an old house across the highway from Bun Boy. A bed, dresser, sink, and closet was it, with a community toilet and shower on every floor.

The restaurant manager was a nice enough fellow and the work was easy. The only time we were busy was when a tour bus stopped. The food was good but the menu was small and never varied. The waitresses were few and not doable. The only possibility would never be caught dead dating a busboy. The regular bartender thought I was out to get his job and took an immediate dislike to me. The fact that he didn't know how to be a bartender probably influenced his insecurity.

There was absolutely nothing to do in Baker except watch the rust grow on my Ford. On the trip up I had a radiator leak around the top below the cap. I fixed it myself with a product called liquid steel. I could not see buying a new radiator for a fifty dollar car. It turned out later to have been an unwise decision. After four days I was bored out of my mind. The only other place to drink in Baker was a private veterans club which by showing my Navy discharge papers, made me a member. There was no bar business except for a few grizzled old men. Once you've heard their stories, wait around, they will tell you the same crap the next day. I needed a woman. It was time for a road trip.

The only close friend I made was a cook named Chris. He was one of the chosen few that knew there was a life outside of Baker, California. As he had been divorced twice, I assumed he knew what women were best at. On our first day off together we headed for State Line, Nevada, about an hour's drive. I had only fifty dollars that I could afford to gamble with, I had a roulette system I had perfected over the years, and the drinks were free. The first place we hit was Whiskey Pete's. They had a giant wheel of fortune as you entered. I put $5 on the $20 spot and it hit for $100. I was on my way!

I had first visited Las Vegas when hitch-hiking on one of my trips to Long Beach. I detoured from highway 66 and decided to check it out. The only previous gambling I had done at the time was playing a dice game called 26 which was played with ten dice in a Chicago nightclub, and hustling pool. I considered myself lucky at gambling, which was sort of stupid as I wasn't very lucky in life.

I was totally awed by the lights and glitter of the strip. I stopped in a casino After several free drinks on an empty stomach and a few exploratory bets I found myself at the roulette table with only twenty five cents to my name. The dealer winked at me and said "Try 28."

I put my last quarter on number 28. It hit and paid 35 – 1. "Let it ride." It hit again! I now had over $300. I loved this game. The rest I don't remember but from there on I couldn't seem to lose. I was wearing tight blue jeans and I won so much money that I couldn't fit it all in my pockets. I was downing all those free beers and I blanked out.

When I came to, I was lying fully clothed on a bed in the casino's hotel. They evidently comped me a room, Security escorted me and locked me in for the night. I woke up with all sorts of chips and money. I got up, splashed water on my face, had a steak & eggs breakfast, and went downtown to the bus depot where I had stashed my gear in a bus depot locker. Everything was there. I should have left then and there but I didn't. I walked into the nearest casino to break the bank. I lost everything but change. Heartbroken I hit the highway to Long Beach.

Since that time I tried to remember and analyze how I won at Roulette. I read books on gambling systems. I spent hours studying. And here I was again, several years later, back in a casino. Chris was a craps player, having honed his skills in private games when he was in the service. I watched him play a few games and I moved to the Roulette table. I bought $300 of five dollar chips. I bet #28 for luck and boxed it. On the third spin it hit for a total of $510. It was not too shabby for a 6 chip ($30) bet. The payoff averaged about 17 to 1. I cashed out. I now had over $800.

I went to see how Chris was doing. He lost everything. I lent him $100. We went to the bar for a few drinks and to rest up before returning to the tables. I went out and filled the gas tank just in the remote chance that I might lose. I love Roulette. Where else can you get a payoff of 35 to 1? My system was simple. Pick and play one number twenty times. If you are lucky it will hit. Betting a $5 chip you invest a $100 and rake in $175. When you can afford it, box the number, betting every other way it can win, and hedging your bet. Plotting your action on a graph, you will win some, lose a little more because of the odds against you, but when your number hits, all bets are winners and your curve shoots off the chart.

I have watched many players bet several chips all over the board. Sometimes they win and stay at the game for a long periods of play but eventually their luck runs out and breaks them. To me it is stupid as you are betting against yourself. You win on one or two numbers and lose on eight or more numbers on the same spin. To each their own, when my number hits, I win on all bets.

My system works until I get greedy and start doubling and tripling up. By doing this I play out my bankroll on a losing streak. It is difficult to have a real big payoff when there's a table limit. All gambling is luck. Good luck runs out. Your best option is to play smart. Years later I gave up on Roulette to play video poker. I made it my business to learn the game and cut my losses for more play. I have hit seven Royal Flushes in the same casino in Jean, Nevada. Not only is it good luck but it's also playing smart by knowing the odds.

Back at Whiskey Pete's my money was burning a hole in my pocket. The women in the casino were more interested in gambling than in men. I wanted to get back into the action. Chris had a goal of winning $1,000. All he needed was a little luck. He headed for the crap table and I made my way to the Roulette game. My number 28 hit just as I was sitting down. Considering this a token of bad luck, I bet #35. On the fourth spin #28 hit again. I put my next bet on #28 only to have #35 hit. I should have walked away but I didn't. I stayed until I lost it all. I didn't know what to bet.

I found Chris. He crapped out. Sadly we drove back to Baker vowing to return and break the bank. Back home things took a bad turn. I got drunk at the Veterans club and threatened some old drunk. They kicked me out. Nowhere left to go in town I went to our bar. The bartender refused to serve me as he said I had had enough. This pissed me off. I was the only customer, we were in the middle of nowhere, this was the only bar left in town, and I worked there. Who in the hell did this jerk think he was?

I went to the coffee bar and drank beer all night. The waitress wasn't going to serve me but my friend Chris was on duty and as acting night manager ordered her to give me whatever I wanted. At two o'clock when it was against the law to serve alcohol in California, I drank it out of a coffee cup. No policeman in town and no customers. Who gave a damn? I was still mad and more than a little drunk when the manager showed up at eight AM. I told him what happened and said that if he didn't fire the bartender, I would quit. Chris came out of the kitchen and told the manager that if he fired me that he would quit too. The manager did not like the squeeze play and fired both of us. A waitress, a busboy, and the dishwasher all quit because of Chris leaving.

Losing five of his staff at one time was quite a blow to his business. This was a man who used to cruise highway 15 looking for hitchhikers to offer them a dishwasher job. The manager wouldn't back down. He asked us to stay but he would not fire the bartender. We were out of there. He wrote Chris and me our last check but made the other three wait until payday. Without either of us getting any sleep, Chris and I packed our stuff in my Ford and drove off. Chris wanted to go to Lancaster, California. Hell, I had never been there before.

On the way there the radiator leaked, the engine overheated, and I blew a head gasket on the Ford. Grabbing our gear we started hitch-hiking. Our ride left us off in some small town in the middle of nowhere. He headed for the nearest bar for beer. It was blistering hot. Talking to two customers I gave them the pink slip on the Ford for two beers. They said they would tow the car off the highway and salvage the parts. I didn't want to mess with it nor did I want a ticket for abandoning of a vehicle on a public highway. We drank until late afternoon when it cooled off a little and we were on our way. We made it to Lancaster early in the evening and got a hotel room downtown. The next morning, reasonably sober, we cleaned up and went job hunting.

Chris found a fry cook job starting at midnight within two hours. It took me all of four hours to find me a job.

I lucked into a night bartending job at one of the finest places in Lancaster, the Caravan Inn. Not only was I paid top dollar, but I was offered a free motel room until I could get my own place. It was a busy dinner house with a piano bar, far too busy for one bartender to handle. The regular bartender put me at the waitress station to see how I handled it. With all my previous banquet experience it was easy. I was in and they were glad to have me. Chris sort of drifted away as my friend. My bar was too classy for him and too expensive. I was grooving with the moneyed people. Coffee house action was in my past. This was what I was looking for. All I needed now was a woman.

Valerie came into the bar one evening escorted by two older well dressed business, men. I was instantly smitten. She was breathtakingly beautiful, tall, blond, and curvy in all the right places. I caught her eye and she smiled. She knew exactly what was on my mind. The next evening she showed up alone, near closing time and sat at the bar near my station. When I had a free moment we talked and she agreed to have breakfast with me. She spent the night in my room. We had sex but except for the fact that she was so beautiful, it wasn't all that great.

Until Valerie I was trying to hit on the day maid who cleaned my room. She was Spanish, didn't speak English, and had a huge bosom. We did some heavy petting and kissing but she would not go any further. It seems that she was married, couldn't take much time for a break, and probably was waiting for me to offer her some money. I knew something better was bound to come along. I didn't want to waste my drinking money on sex.

The night bartender introduced me to a man who owned a car dealership. He insisted on giving me a nice car and told me I could make payments when I got paid. He also put on four new tires. I refused but he insisted that I had to have a car. Public transportation was almost nonexistent in Lancaster at the time. I didn't want to hurt his feelings so I took it. I paid him $100 out of my first paycheck owing him $200.

I was getting up in the world. I was meeting interesting moneyed people, drinking in the best places, and looking good. Shep Gub came to town and bought a beer bar. I had met him briefly in Long Beach a few years before. Shep was a big flamboyant man, flashy dresser, and big spender. You just could not buy a drink when you were with him. He was always buying the house a drink. Within a week, anyone who was anybody, knew Sheb Gub. The rumors were spreading. Shep was going to open a girly bar, something that Lancaster had never seen.

Shep took his existing beer bar and completely remodeled it. Lots of lights, mirrors, and a raised platform behind the bar, so that when the women served you they had to bend and you could look down their blouses. He hired ten beautiful busty young girls to work for him and dressed them in skimpy costumes. The doors opened for business and the place was packed, Shep would still buy the house drinks like it were going out of style. Beautiful girls, ice cold beer in the hot high desert, what more could any man want. He really pumped up the cash register.

Shep had three offers to buy the bar before he opened but he waited 6 weeks and sold it for five times what he paid for it plus the costs. He explained later that he wasn't in the bar business, he was in real estate. The day he sold the bar he had ten girls working there and the bar was so packed that you could hardly squeeze another customer thru the door. I visited the bar three years later. It had one bar girl and three customers. Shep knew how to make a buck and then get out.

Valerie was a school teacher by trade. During the summer break she worked as a cocktail waitress at a bowling alley in nearby Palmdale. She liked to dress up and date older men who would take her to the best places. With her great looks, she could pretty much get what she wanted. I was not what she was looking for and she stopped spending a lot of time with me. I liked Valerie. There was a direct honesty about her that I admired. She knew what she wanted but I had to find another woman.

Then I broke my long existing rule of dating women where I worked. I should have known better, but I just couldn't resist Sandy who worked the reception desk for the Caravan Inn. She was Irish, attractive, full of life, and looked like a nice person. I talked to her a few times and felt there was a mutual attraction. Sandy was a single mother living alone with a small baby girl. Some holiday was coming up and I invited her to dinner on my night off. She said that she would have to bring her baby as she could not afford a sitter. It was fine with me as I love children.

We arranged to dine at the Caravan Inn where we both worked, and like a jerk I showed up late and drunk. I ordered dinner, had a few martini's, and ordered a bottle of wine for the both of us. Sandy had one cocktail and drank a half glass of wine. She had dressed up for the occasion and looked very pretty. After desert I finished the wine and asked for the check. I was told that the management had taken care of it. I left a $20 tip and asked Sandy to come to my room for a drink. She refused and said she had to get home.

Pissed off, I grabbed the baby. "If you want your girl, I'll be in my room." I left, taking the baby. About five minutes later there was a knock on my door. There was Sandy with our security guard. He did not look too pleased.

"Come in, we were just getting acquainted." Sandy took her baby and left. Not a word was said. The next morning I got up and went out. I drank beer most of the day. My usual practice was to come to work early and have a good meal before getting behind the bar. That night I went directly behind the bar and started working. Within minutes the security guard showed up and said the manager wanted to see me. He escorted me to the manager's office. He had my final paycheck made out.

"Be out of your room by check out time tomorrow." He didn't say another thing. This Irishman doesn't stay where he's not welcome. I packed my clothes, loaded up my car, and headed back to Long Beach where I still had my apartment. As I was coming over the pass my front tire came off. I managed to stop the car just inches from going over a steep cliff. I locked the car, walked until I found an emergency phone, and called the Motor Club. The tire was gone. They put on the spare and checked the other tires. All the lug nuts were loose. Whoever put on the new tires did not tighten the lug nuts. It almost cost me my life.

When the man who sold me the car finally contacted me in Long Beach, I not only refused to pay him the balance owed, but told him he was lucky that I wasn't suing him for risking my life. There wasn't anything that he could do. I hadn't signed any loan documents and he had signed over the pink slip. All in all, I was in pretty good shape. I had a nice car, an apartment, and money in my pocket. I lost a good job but there are plenty more. I'd get it right one of these days. Working seemed to be interfering with my drinking and my sex life. One had to work once in a while. I never had a problem getting a job or working, just keeping it.

Chapter 19

The year was 1968. Robert Kennedy, Martin Luther King, and Malcome X were gone. Protests, anti-establishment, love-ins, civil disobedience, dropping out, and the psychedelic 60's were here.

I hadn't changed much but I was now 32 years old. My arrest record had risen to 28 drinking related arrests in the City of Long Beach alone. Nothing to brag about to be sure but I was after all, Irish. But as one judge pointed out wryly "You're old enough to know better."

My last arrest for public intoxication, New Year's Eve, I was twenty-five cents short of cash to bail myself out. Not one person in the drunk tank would lend me a quarter. I called my brother Shaun, who was now married and working as an engineer. His first words were that I had never repaid the five dollars I had borrowed from him.

"Shaun, I'm sorry. I don't remember. I must have been drunk. Why didn't you remind me? All I need now is thirty-five cents to bail out. I don't want to go before Judge Anderson. He gave some man a year in jail once for plain drunkenness. Can you be here soon?"

"I'm sorry, Bro, get it from one of your drinking friends. I'm not driving down to Long Beach tonight. I need my sleep," He hung up. The next morning they took me to court. When they asked me to plead guilty of not guilty" I replied:

"I'd rather not enter a plea at this time, Your Honor"

"May I inquire why?"

"I just need thirty-five cents to pay my bail and forfeit out, Sir. I'd rather not appear before the court."

"Plea is postponed for thirty days. You will remain in jail or post bail. Is that understood?"

"Yes Sir, thank you." It was back to jail. Would you believe that it took three days before they arrested someone who knew me who had a dollar to lend me."

When you drink as much as I did lack of money is always a problem. I found a day shift bartending job downtown at the Roman 1V that was in probate. I worked under my brother's ID. Two weeks later when I went to collect my unemployment insurance check under my own name, they said I had to have a special interview. The interviewer happened to be my customer at the Roman 1V the last two days.

It was obvious that I was caught. The investigator was nice enough. He explained that they were more interested in how I was able to collect two checks at the same time more so than the money. If I cooperated with them they would not prosecute. They were far more interested in fixing the system. It made sense to me, so I told him in detail how I was able to get a false ID and a new social security number. He got up, went into an office, and returned with:

“I’m really sorry, Joe, but they decided to make an example of you.” Two local cops came in, hand cuffed me, and took me directly to jail. The charge was making a false statement with 52 counts. I went to court, was assigned a Public Defender, and in exchange for pleading guilty the charge was reduced to two counts. I was sentenced to serve 30 days in the county jail with a year’s probation. The court did not order me to make restitution. The State of California was quite a different matter.

Every day that I was in jail they sent me a bill, each bill for a larger amount. I estimated that I had taken them for over $20,000 over a period of six years. I called my attorney who got the state to agree to a final sum of about $700. I got off easy because I had many jobs, some of these companies were out of business, and my union refused to give out information. I also argued that if I had worked under my own name only, I would have been eligible for a larger amount each week. I could not collect unemployment insurance benefits for one year and no benefits until I paid them back.

County time was easy. I was sent to a minimum security farm. I only served 20 days as I got 5 days off for donating blood and 5 days off work time. When I got out, I had some hard decisions to make. Without unemployment insurance I would have to pretty much work steady. Previously, six months was the longest that I had ever held one job. I didn’t mind working, I just enjoyed partying and drinking more. My run of bad luck continued. Jobs were few and hard to find. I was out of money.

I took a job as a busboy at Hof's Hut in North Long Beach on Long Beach Blvd. I immediately got food and tips. Again I was hurting for a woman. There were several good looking waitresses but to them I was some kind of a loser. They couldn't see beyond my busboy persona. I never blamed anyone but myself for my situation. I always believed that one made his own luck. Whatever job I had, I worked hard at it and did my best without complaining. I was probably the best busboy they ever had but not one waitress would date me. If I had been hired as a bartender there, I would have had to beat them off with a club.

Twice a day a pretty dark haired girl would sit at the counter and have a cup of coffee. I often felt her staring at me but when I looked at her she averted her eyes. She was short but had a cute figure with a full bust. She wore expensive conservative clothes, very little makeup, and no jewelry but a small gold watch. I made it a point to ask her a question. I got a polite answer. It took a week before she seemed comfortable enough to exchange small talk with me. I asked her if she would meet me after work so we could talk and get to know one another better. Two days later she said yes.

I met Shelba after my shift and we took a walk along the beach. It took forever to get any information out of her. Her story was that she worked for her rich father as a dental assistant and that she had been married. She put her husband thru both law and medical school. Once he graduated, got his two degrees, and a doctor's position, he left her. It turns out he was in love with another man the entire time. But he left her with two small children. Her self esteem was shattered. I had never met anyone so sad and so hopeless. I fell in love immediately.

Two days later we had sex. I sensed then that she was not the right woman for me but I didn't have the heart to tell her. She liked me! Everything I did enthralled her. She had never met anyone like me. Her parents were from the old country and she had lived a very sheltered life. I was the second man she ever had sex with. She was rich, classy, good looking, generous, but she was boring. She would go to a bar with me but would only have one drink all night. I don't remember ever seeing her laugh.

Shelba was always buying me gifts and things I never asked for. She never gave them to me, she hid them where I would find them. Once I came home and found a new stereo system in my living room. Finally she told me that she didn't like the bars I was frequenting and she wanted to go to the better night clubs. When I told her that I couldn't afford it, she said that she would pay. I refused. She asked me if I would rather she went by herself. I gave in. We went to the best places and she would slip me the money. She always refused to take the change back. I felt like a gigolo. This Irishman always paid his own way until now.

It was about this time I met Jocko Butler in a local bar. Jocko was a smooth talking, charming, incredibly handsome man who always got any woman he wanted. Jocko liked women and drinking in that order. He was a successful women's shoe salesman and not only made good money but seemed to have an endless supply of beautiful women to date. His problem was that he had just been paroled from state prison for armed robbery. It seemed he broke into a store with an unloaded gun, set off a silent alarm, and was caught. He was high on narcotics at the time. All this didn't bother me as he bought me drinks and introduced me to some fabulous looking women.

I never ran around with other women when I was in a committed relationship and I considered my affair with Shelba as being serious enough not to cheat on her. In the course of meeting my friends she met Jocko but I never told her about his personal life or how I felt about him. I wasn't much for passing on stories. People were always telling me the most intimate details of their lives but I had learned that the best policy was to keep my mouth closed and my mind open. Jocko was always telling me what a treasure Shelba was and how I ought to marry her before someone else got to her. "She's rich, pretty, educated, and loves you. What more do you want?" I just didn't see it that way and did not have any intention of settling down yet.

Shelba and I had a date one night. I was drinking and got home late. She wasn't there. I did not see or hear from her for four days. I figured she was just peeved and would get over it. Then I learned the truth. Jocko ran into her when she came to pick me up and took her out for a drink while waiting for me. Two days later they were married. Shelba bought him a new sports car as a wedding present. I never saw Jocko again. More then15 years later I ran into Shelba again and learned that the marriage lasted less than a year.

Two brothers lived in my apartment building, Bob and Bill Brooks They both worked at the StarKist fish canneries in San Pedro. They both smoked a lot of pot. I got to know them and they seemed like nice enough guys but they always stank of fish. Their whole apartment stank of fish. There were those people who worked there, especially the women, who claimed that the odor wasn't of fish but of the chemicals used in the processing. Who cared? They smelled so bad I wouldn't go out drinking with them and they had a difficult time attracting women.

Both these boys worked hard for very little money. When they decided to close down the fish cannery they were laid off. Neither one had a trade nor an education. I took it upon myself to help them. A big shutdown at one of the oil refineries was coming up. I took them down to the union hall and after all the regular members were hired they got on. I made sure they both signed up for the union. They made more wages in one day than they had made working for a week in the canneries. It was hot, hard, dirty work but they loved it. Both being hard workers, they soon were promoted to helper status with even more money. I was their god.

I would not join them smoking pot. I never was a smoker. With their first paycheck they bought me a case of beer as a thank you. Once they didn't smell like fish we went out drinking together and became good friends. They envied my easy way with women and tried to be more like me. It was like having two younger brothers. Their mother bought me a book that I wanted and inscribed it "Thank you, Joe, for helping my boys". I think they would have killed someone for me if I had asked. I could do no wrong.

I liked Bill, the older brother, a lot better than Bob. Bill was smarter and seemed to have some class while Bob was a loutish fellow with a foul mouth around woman. Bill had the desire to better himself and get ahead in life. Bob was happy just smoking pot and leering at women. I found out that Bob had a couple of previously sexual related arrests involving women. He believed all women liked it rough. He was always asking them to his apartment to get high but they were instinctively afraid of him and turned him down. Bill had a problem with getting a girl because he was almost always with his brother and Bob ruined his action. None of the girls I knew would double date or help me get dates for the two brothers. I finally gave up.

Bob was popular with the workers at the refineries. He was generous with his pot, was a hard worker, and volunteered for the toughest jobs. He was always sucking up to the bosses and asking for overtime. He was strong as an ox and just about as dumb. In less than two years he had a top union card and classified as a #1 pipefitter. It took me four years to become a pipefitter and seven years to get my white card. While I wished him the best of luck, I told him that if I was ever called out to work as his helper, I would quit on the spot. He was just too dangerous to be around and he really did not know his job. He thought I was joking.

Shelba had been the last straw with me. I refused to let any woman get close to me again. I didn't trust them. The truth was that I had no sense when I was drinking. All my brains were between my legs and at times I did not think at all. I managed to keep working pretty steady for the year that I was ineligible to collect unemployment Insurance. After one year when my probation period ended, I was once again able to apply for unemployment benefits.

Then I used the benefits to pay back what they claimed I owed them. I refused to use earned income that I was paying taxes on to pay them back. Eventually they were paid off and I could collect again. I was back in business. I was very careful as I had been warned that if I ever tried anything like this again, I would be charged with a felony.

Bill Brooks and I stopped into El Torito Restaurant and Bar about an hour before the afternoon happy hour where we would score free munchies. Bill had been bothering me for several months to tell him the secret of picking up women. When two attractive women came in by themselves and sat at the end of the bar I decided to shut him up once and for all.

"Bill, what I'm going to show you is only known by a handful of men in the entire world. You must promise never to tell another living soul, even your brother. Do you so swear?" I thought he was going to wet his pants he was so excited. He nodded his head.

"Just watch and learn. We're going to pick up those two women." I called the bartender over, "Give those two ladies a drink."

They acknowledged our presence with a curt thank you and resumed talking. When they had finished their drinks and started on the ones I bought them, I called the bartender again. I sent them two more.

"The secret, Bill, is that you buy them a drink when they still have a full one. It just sits there and they can't help but notice it and think of us."

Again they thanked us. "Where are you boys from?" asked one.

"We're both from Long Beach and you? Do you mind if we move over so we don't have to shout?"

"Come on." I was amazed. I had never tried this before. Soon we all were talking like long lost friends. They were Lucy and Betty and had just gotten off work. Lucy suggested that we go to her place, drinks at the bar being so expensive. We could be more comfortable. I offered to buy us a bottle. She said she had plenty to drink at home. They didn't have a car so I drove us all to Lucy's one bed room apartment. Lucy and I did some hot and heavy petting. Bill, as usual couldn't get started. Betty just plain didn't take to him.

Lucy and I announced that we were going into the bedroom, Betty decided to leave. Bill was left alone. Lucy and I undressed, jumped into bed, and had hot passionate sex. When I was finished, I got dressed, and was looking for a way to get out of there fast, when Lucy said. "I really must apologize for my friend Betty. She's a little uptight. I really feel sorry for your friend Bill. If you're thru, why don't you send him in here?"

I went out and told Bill he was next. He didn't believe me. I told him, "Don't be such an ass and get in there before Lucy changes her mind". He went into the bedroom and shut the door. When he came out he was wearing a big stupid grin. We both got out of there. I was the king and all it cost was the drinks. What were the odds?

My single apartment was on the second floor right above the Brooks brothers. At the other end lived a married couple, the husband worked at the Navy Shipyard as a welder. The wife Lanette was young and beautiful. The husband, Raul, was quite a bit older, short, Samoan, and huge. He did not drink. I saw him once without his shirt and his back was covered with knife or chain scars. He was a quiet man and rarely spoke. I always said "Hello" when I saw them and Lanette was always pleasant. She had a body to die for but I didn't have a death wish. Raul looked dumb, but dangerous.

Lanette occasionally would knock on my door and ask to borrow a few dollars. I always lent her money and she always paid me back. One morning she caught me drunk, moved in close, and we kissed. We tumbled into bed. It became a regular thing. Raul would go off to work and she would come over and climb in bed with me. While her husband was at work she would go out drinking with me. As he didn't drink it was unlikely he would hear about us but I still was uneasy.

Lanette's story was strange. She was the only daughter of a Texas multi-millionaire who spoiled the hell out of her, but would not let her have her own way. She married Raul to spite her father. He especially didn't like non white races and thought Samoans were on par with Mexicans. Raul made good money, worked a lot of overtime, but it was never enough for her. She swore she didn't love him and that they were not having sex.

Raul was insanely crazy about her. He turned his entire paycheck over to her and she gave him an allowance of $5 a week. He didn't drink or smoke. It was rumored that he once had a terrible temper and had killed several men in fights before he quit drinking and came to the United States. He looked mean and tough enough for anyone to believe it.

One bright morning, as Raul left for work Lanette came over and climbed into bed with me. We heard Raul coming back up the stairs. He had forgotten to take his lunch bucket. Lanette sprang out of bed and made a mighty dash back to her apartment. Raul saw her in the hall just before she got her apartment door open. She was in her night clothes. He came storming over to my apartment and pounded on my door. I opened it wearing my robe.

"Was my wife here trying to borrow money?" He asked.

"She heard you coming up the steps and ran home. She didn't have time to ask for anything." I replied. "I've loaned her a few dollars now and then. But he always paid me back."

"Don't give her any more money. I give her enough. I can take care of my own wife."

"Right." He left and I shut my door. I was shaking like a leaf. This was getting too dangerous. I moved out that same day and didn't leave a forwarding address. Lanette knowing where I drank, tracked me down, went to my new apartment with me, and when I was asleep, had her own key made. I was back in harm's way. It didn't take long.

Again my apartment was on the second floor. I heard loud arguing in the downstairs hall well one morning when I was expecting Lanette. I opened my door to check it out to find a very angry Raul. He was shaking with uncontrolled rage. "Have you been sleeping with my wife?"

"Just a moment please, I have some biscuits in the oven." I turned and walked into the kitchen and pulled a tray of biscuits out of the stove. I was almost paralyzed with fear. I couldn't think. Just then Lanette sprang on Raul's back and started hitting him. She was yelling about getting back some letter that he had written to her father. Raul, distracted tried to get away from her and ran and down the steps. Lanette followed screaming at him the whole time. I shut and locked my door. When it was quiet I went down to the bar. I didn't go back to my apartment for a week.

It eventually died down and I found out what happened. Raul had hired a private detective to document his wife's affair with me. He wrote a letter to her father, and they separated. Lanette's father sent her some money and she got her own place. We agreed not to see each other for a while. I started drinking in different bars so that I would not run into her. There were too many women in the world to get myself killed over one. Again I vowed to myself not to date married women. It seemed a good idea at the time.

Lanette would not give up on me. She would look up my friends and find out where I drank. When she found me drunk, we would end up in bed. That was the way it was. She probably would have married me but I didn't make enough money for her. She was just too pretty and sexy to turn down. She was always giving me money when I was broke. I thought she was great until Little Kenny told me that she was returning my own money she took from me when I was drunk. She said she loved me and I figured that I would at least have one person show up at my funeral when her husband caught us.

I met a bartender while working a banquet at one of our local hotels who invited me to a big party in Hollywood. I thought it advisable to get out of town for a few days and I accepted. It was one giant drinking party that kept moving from one party to another for about a week straight. After two days of partying I was drunk and stayed that way. You'd fall asleep where ever you were, wake up, and someone would shove a new drink in your hand. I didn't know any of these people nor do I remember any of them.

At one party a group of young students were discussing how all the homes were built alike and looked the same. If you moved one bush, the owner might never find his house again. One man claimed that his uncle lived next door and if we rearranged his furniture, he would think he came home to the wrong house. Everyone thought it was a great idea and worth some laughs. The young man let us in the front door and a large group of us went in and moved all this man's furniture. Everything that could be moved was moved. Then we went on to the next party and so on.

All good things come to an end. I finally ended up back in Long Beach with an enormous hangover. When I went out I was told that the police were looking for me. It seemed that when the man came home and found his furniture moved he called the Police. When they questioned the people next door as to who had the party, they blamed it all on me as I was the only stranger there. When the Police learned that I was an Irish bartender named Joe from Long Beach, they called the union, got my address, and found me. . Detectives in the Valley wanted to talk to me.

I told Lanette the story. She promised to wait for me while I went to straighten things out. Detectives questioned me but to no avail. I couldn't remember anything that except it was supposed to be all in fun. It seems the man who claimed his uncle lived next door was not a relative, nor did he have a key. He broke in the back door to let us in the front door. Thank God, nothing was stolen. I cooperated the best I could. I was arrested for felony 2nd degree burglary. I didn't have the money to bail myself out.

The plaintiff testified that he arrived home to find his TV set in the bedroom upside down. The attorney asked "And where is the TV set usually?"

"In the living room, right side up." I had to laugh. The Judge gave me a dirty look. During the break, my attorney made a deal. I pled guilty to misdemeanor trespassing, was sentenced to ten days, and was to pay a fine of $100. I was the only one on trial. When I tried to tell the Judge that it was just a harmless joke, he said that he didn't think it was very funny. Courts are seriously conservative. When I got back to Long Beach,

Lanette was dating someone else. I was somehow relieved. I had to change my ways. Now seemed like a good time.

Chapter 20

Times change and life moved on. Lanette married her boyfriend. Kenny showed me a news article, "Didn't you know this woman?" It was Valerie, the women I dated, from the Caravan Inn. An ex-boyfriend had beaten her to death with a bowling pin in the bowling alley in Palmdale where she worked as a cocktail waitress. Beautiful, fun loving Valerie, who just wanted to marry a rich man and live happily ever after.

I received a letter from a partner in my father's law firm. My father had passed away. He didn't leave me or my brother a dime in his will. I always thought that when he passed on that I would be rich. I was his first born son and I felt that he was sorry about the way I was raised.. Evidently not, another dream down the toilet.

While working for the Purple Heart Veterans soliciting donations door to door, I knocked on a door in Cerritos. The beautiful lady who came to the door said that she had some clothes to give. When I was filling out the pickup slip she gave her name as Pat Caswell. "You wouldn't happen to be married to my friend Bob Caswell from Chicago?" I asked.

"My husband's name is Bob Caswell and he is from Chicago" She looked at my identification badge. "Why, you're Joe Kennedy."

I hadn't seen or heard from my friend Bob for about eight years. I told my crew boss that I was taking the rest of the day off and called Bob at work. I stayed for dinner and met his family. He had five beautiful little girls and this great wife Pat whom I had never met.

It seemed that Bob had met Pat over the telephone when he was working at the bank. She was also a teller at another branch. They met. Bob didn't introduce her to any of his wild friends as he didn't want to take a chance of losing her. He left the bank, got married, and joined the Army where he spent four years mostly in Germany. He was now working at an oil refinery as a tool man. He seemed glad to see me again and was really proud of his beautiful wife, children, and the home he was buying. I was happy to see that at least one of us had made it and it was good to see him again. We were good friends until he died seven years later.

I wasn't doing too well at the time. I was living in a small room in a house with a community kitchen and bath on each of the two floors. There was a public phone on the first floor but there was no one I could depend on getting my messages as almost everyone who lived there was drunk most of the time. They were all older was older than me and retired on social security or disability. There were a few who had a small pension. If they didn't have an income they all probably would have ended up on skid row. Almost to a man they drank wine at home and seldom went anyplace.

It was here that I met an Irishman by the name of Jimmy Harrigan who lived in the room next to mine. Jimmy was retired and had been married seven times. He knew all there was to know about women and he had a great sense of humor. He was also a man of all trades who could fix just about anything, and he had the tools to do it with. With his social security check and by doing odd jobs he got along just fine. We became great friends. Jimmy would drink anything and would always share what he had. He was a very giving and generous man with anything he had, especially advice.

I was never much for drinking alone. I craved companionship and someone to talk to. I was going to the better bars when I went out and I usually invited Jimmy along. Jimmy had a beautiful singing voice and knew all the great old Irish songs. He was always clean and the women just loved him. He was old fashioned, well mannered, and charming. A lot of people thought he was rich. I met a better class of women when I was with him.

It was about this time that I was asked to join the Moose Club. Up until now I had never given anything back to the community or belonged to anything but unions. As part of my overall plan of self respect I applied and was accepted. Now I belonged to something and had a new place to drink. I met some great people who did more in life than drink all the time. I even brought Jimmy in as a member.

I was offered a job at the King's Victoria in North Long Beach as a swing shift bartender. It was a busy coffee house restaurant and cocktail bar owned by five brothers who also owned the Lakewood Country Club. It was considered a prime job and I grabbed it determined to make this work. My hours were 11Am to 3Pm and return and work from 5Pm to 8PM, five days a week. We were located next to a busy factory that manufactured thermal controls and had a huge government contract. We got most of our customers from the factory during lunch and dinner. I was to help the regular bartender and I was led to believe it was a permanent job. The previous bartender went to the hospital and it was said that he would never be able to work again.

My problem was that I didn't have a car at the time and I had two free hours between shifts. My options were go home by bus and return (about an hour), stay there and drink beer at a close by bar, or play miniature golf. As I didn't want to take a chance on getting drunk, I elected to play golf. It worked well for about a week until I aced the course. It was too easy and became boring. I decided that I had to make a decision, either buy a car or move into a nice local apartment. I decided on the apartment.

The Shangri La Apartments was a swinging singles, wild party, expensive compound rumored to have beautiful young working women. It had a pool room, Olympic size swimming pool, and tennis courts. It was exclusive with only the best people living there. It also had a waiting list. I put my name on the list. Within two weeks a single apartment had a vacancy. I signed a six months lease paying 1st and last month's rent plus a security deposit. Two days before I was to move in I was laid off. The regular bartender was released from the hospital and wanted his job back. They gave it to him.

Here I was stuck with the a high rent apartment that unemployment insurance wouldn't begin to cover, no job, and in a part of town where I hardly knew anyone. The Shangri La turned out to be mostly men who were looking for the same beautiful women I was hoping to meet. I needed a job. I went down to the union hall and got hired for a shutdown as a pipefitter. After two weeks on the job I injured my back and was forced to apply for state disability. It still wasn't enough money for rent and living expenses and now it hurt to move unless I was drunk which I couldn't afford.

I was hanging at a busy local bar, close to the apartment complex called the Back Door. When a job opened up I asked the owner, Jack, for the job. He only knew me as a customer but he decided to give me a chance. I asked to be paid under the table because of the disability insurance. Jack agreed.

"Joe, I'm going to hire you under one condition. If you work for me, I don't want you drinking in here. You're pretty much of an asshole when you're drunk. If you can accept that I'll start you at $15 a shift." I agreed and we shook hands on it.

After my first shift Jack said "Joe. I really didn't know if you were a bartender. I took a chance on you because I like you, you're a good bartender. I'm going to pay you the same as everyone else. As of now you will be getting $22 a shift. Keep up the good work."

I worked three days and had a day off. I got drunk. When I returned to work the next day Jack called me into his office. "Remember when I told you if you work for me that you were not to drink in here? I heard that you got drunk yesterday?"

"Yes, sort of. I didn't come in here, did I?"

"No, but I have to make a new rule for you. From now on when you drink in other bars, don't tell them you work here. I had complaints from owners that you were drunk and tried to steal their customers. I don't want you spending your money to get me customers. Your job is just to take care of the customers we have. Understood?"

"Yes, Sir." God, you had to love this man. He worked the Alaskan pipeline, saved all his money, and bought his dream of owning his own bar. He was the only man I ever met who could dance with a woman, remove her bra without her knowing it, and win side bets doing it. Jack, if you were Irish, you'd be dangerous.

I made enough money to buy a Saab car and drove downtown to see Jimmy and Kenny. Jimmy was doing fine as always. But with Kenny it was a different story. He was jobless and drank himself to the bottom. He was living in a flop hotel and three weeks behind in his rent. I went to see him and he could not even get out of bed or stand on his feet. He was shaking so bad he could hardly speak. He was unshaven and filthy. I had never seen my friend like this before.

I told him that he could come home with me and sleep on the couch. I would get him back in shape and help him find a job. I packed what little dirty clothes he had left and carried him to my car. When I got to my apartment I had to sneak him in the back way. It took me five days to get him in reasonable shape and where he could keep food down. I didn't try to lecture him but I did attempt to find out what was bothering him. Basically he had lost his job of many years thru his drinking. Being uneducated or trained in anything else he could not find any work. He started drinking and just gave up. Another worry gnawing at him was that he had not filed his income taxes for the last 12 years.

With a few inquires, I found a tax accountant who would help Kenny. Even with penalties and fees he owed, he got a check for over $800. He was now even with the government. Before this, when he was well enough, I found him a well paying job with the gas company as a laborer. Afraid he would cause me trouble by staying with me, he got a nice place of his own. In two months he had his own car. He got his tax refund about a week before he was laid off. He decided to go back home to Massachusetts. I was sorry to see him go.

My six month lease was up. I had lost my job at the Back Door by getting drunk and not showing up for three days. My life at the swinging singles apartments was a big disappointment. I didn't get to sleep with one woman who lived there. The few I met were already involved with someone or looking for someone rich. I managed a few casual one night stands with local talent but no one really interested me. I decided to move back downtown. I got a room where Jimmy lived. At least it was cheap at $8 a week.

Pat Caswell, Bob's wife, came down with a high fever and was rushed to the hospital. They could not find what was wrong with her. Three days later she died. Bob was left with his five daughters to take care of. The first thing he did was get rid of all the household pets which really upset his children even more. Then he started drinking. He was on bereavement leave from work. I went to see him to see what I could do to help but there was little I could do. Vickie, his middle daughter, was missing. Bob assumed that she left because he had gotten rid of her pet cat, and that was staying with a girlfriend.

I questioned her sisters and they claimed that they didn't know where she was. When I found that she hadn't taken anything with her, not even her money, I was worried. I tried to talk with Bob but he was so into his grieving that he wouldn't, or couldn't, listen. "If she doesn't want to live here, the hell with her."

They found 11 year old Vickie 3 days later in a shallow ditch. She had been raped and strangled. It took them a year to identify her from dental records. Bob never mentioned her. Years later, when Bob died, I attended his services and had the opportunity to meet his four girls. They were all grown up and beautiful charming women. Two were married and had children of their own.

The years passed and I didn't change much. I had a lot of casual girl friends but I really couldn't get close to anyone. Jimmy turned out to be a good friend who was always after me to find a good woman and straighten out. He thought I was too good a person to live the way I did. In 1974 a pretty woman, Jeanne Marie, came into my life. She was originally from Canada. She was a divorced mother of two grown children and worked in the insurance industry. We started dating regularly and really hit it off together.

Jeanne was a fun woman who had a talent for playing the piano, drinking, and partying. She had a great personality and everyone seemed to like her. A short, large breasted woman with dark hair and deep dark sparkling eyes she drew attention whenever she walked into a room. She took a liking to me and we became exclusive. Sometimes she got drunk but she never missed work or got out of line. We had a lot of fun together.

Jeanne lived in a rented house with her 20 year old son, Bob. Bob's only goal in life was to have as much fun as possible and surf. A tall, handsome, well built, sun tanned, lad, he had many girls chasing him. He loved them all but refused to get serious or worry about anything. He believed that something would always come along tomorrow. I found him a good job. He lasted three days. He just wouldn't take it seriously. He was there to have fun, not to actually work.

His beautiful 18 year old sister, Jasmine was married to an older hippy who wore strange clothes, had a heavy beard, long hair, sideburns, and was stoned on pot most of the time. Rollo, her husband, adored her and worshiped the ground she walked on. He was easy going and I got along fine with him.

I was not allowed to have women in my room and Jeanne would not let me stay overnight at her house as long as her son was there. Our sex life wasn't as frequent as I would have liked but I remained faithful to her and did not date other women. I had made up my mind to always be faithful to anyone that I was dating regularly. I thought it only fair as I would not appreciate a woman cheating on me. Also I did not want to take a chance of losing someone I cared about.

Drinking, the times, and living the way I did gave me a casual attitude towards sex. All I required was that women were they willing and warm to the touch. Feelings played very little part. As I grew older I began to consider the other person's feelings. I was slowly evolving. I've always used the excuse of being Irish for my drinking, brawling, and whoring. It was an image I had built up in my mind. I may not be perfect, but I'm Irish. I believed I was supposed to be tough.

One night Jeanne showed up at my room drunk. She left early as she had to go to work the next morning. The thing was that she did not remember it. As I had had blackout periods from drinking myself, I accepted it. I was glad she spent the night with me instead of another man. However, it planted a danger sign in the back of my consciousness. Maybe she had a drinking problem. I found out later that she always carried a half gallon of Vodka in the trunk of her car to have it close.

Our relationship progressed. I accepted a night bartending job at the Moose Lodge. Jeanne would come in after work and play piano gratis for the customers. We were soon the most popular couple in the club. I especially liked the fact on week nights the Lodge closed early so we had time to go bar hopping. Jeanne and I were always together. We were considered a team. She never flirted with other men, she always had her own money and paid her own way. She always looked great and except for a few flashes of temper she was just about perfect.

Then Jasmine, Rollo, and Bob were involved in a terrible car accident. Bob and Rollo were fine but Jasmine, who was driving was taken to the Intensive Care Ward. Her head was swelling and brain surgery was necessary to relieve the pressure. Her mother, Jeanne, was going to pieces. There was very little that I could do to console her. Jasmine was near death. A pickup truck had run a red light and slammed into the driver's side of Rollo's Volkswagen in the middle of an intersection. The Volkswagen was totaled. It was a miracle that the two men escaped injury. The pickup driver had insurance.

For a week we didn't know wither Jasmine was going to live. Jeanne took off from work to be by her side at the hospital. Finally, Jasmine pulled thru. She was alive but she was never the same again. It was not only the scars but her whole personality changed. From a beautiful soul she became an ill-tempered foul mouthed bitch. Her brain was impaired and she started smoking, drinking, and swearing. Rollo stood it for about nine months, then left her to file for a divorce.

It was 1975 and I was going to turn 40 years old. Jimmy was after me to marry Jeanne. "It is a very special thing to find a woman who loves you as much as she does. You're not getting any younger. I've never seen two people who are so perfect for each other. What are you waiting for? Do you want to end up old and alone, like me?"

Jimmy made a lot of sense. I was ready for a change in my life. I wanted to settle down and be someone before it was too late. I knew I could quit drinking anytime I wanted to. If I didn't take the first drink, I would never have to worry about the second one. I liked women a little too much but I never cheated on Jeanne. Evidently one good woman was enough to keep me satisfied.

I asked Jeanne to marry me. She said yes. The die was cast. We decided to get married by a judge and have the reception at the Moose Lodge where we both were members. We got the banquet room free, and the lodge supplied the wedding cake and champagne as a wedding gift. It was a grand affair with many members and friends attending. There was a four piece band, dancing, and a giant buffet donated by the Ladies' Elks. We must have received over 150 wedding gifts.

For our honeymoon we went to Disneyland. More than twenty years in California and I had never been there. Jeanne had not been there since her children were small. We stayed at a small motel within walking distance of the park. I limited Jeanne to opening our wedding presents to four a day. We dined in the best restaurants and all in all, had a memorable time. After three days we went home to a one bedroom apartment that I had rented in downtown Long Beach close to Jeanne's work. I purposely rented a one bedroom so that her son Bob would not be living with us. He moved in with one of his many girl friends. My new life began.

I decided to apply for a real estate license. This was my original plan 20 years ago. It was one of the few professions where you could make a fortune without a formal education. I received a letter of rejection from the Real Estate Department committing the crime of moral turpitude, evidently making a false statement to the unemployment insurance department. During the last ten years I had been arrested only three times, all on major holidays, and for public intoxication. Of course a total of 36 arrests in Long Beach did not indicate a stable person. I had the right of appeal. I thought I had better get a lawyer to represent me and my wife agreed. I was a changed person and now all I had to do was to prove it.

I hired a local attorney who agreed to represent me and also, he would try to get my arrest record sealed. He filed an appeal for me and a hearing was set. The trick was to prove rehabilitation. This is not an easy task when one is Irish and as hard headed as I am. We got letters of recommendation from prominent people, both Jimmy and Jeanne agreed to testify on my behalf. At the hearing Jimmy portrayed me to be a saint and Jeanne brought tears to one's eyes when she told of how when her daughter was almost killed in a car accident how I was there for her and what a truly wonderful, caring person I was. . Listening, I could hardly believe it was me that they were talking about.

The opposing counsel acted as if they knew me personally and hated me. There was no way in hell I was ever going to get a real estate license in the State of California if they could help it. My attorney showed how

I served my debt to society, paid restitution, was now married, and completely rehabilitated. He offered 32 letters of recommendation attesting to my good character. The hearing ended and I would be notified of the results. I was issued a two year probationary license. My lawyer committed suicide before he had my arrest record sealed. It turned out he was suffering from cancer.

I put my real estate license with a Century-21 broker in Paramount. I started out with the handicap of not knowing the right people, not being from the area, and not graduating from a local school. There were way too many people in the business at the time and the part timers were killing us. My broker was too busy to give me the attention and guidance I needed. All he seemed interested in was making a million dollars before he turned 25. He was too busy to talk to less than three people at one time.

I got excellent training from their available classes. I bought everything they had to ensure my success, from themed apparel to advertising materials. I even purchased a new portable VHS player to show clients listing and selling films. When it quit working I took it in for repairs and found out I was the ninth owner. The broker was selling it to agents as new for $250 and buying it back for $50 to sell to the next new agent. This was the last straw, I quit. I had three listings but hadn't made one sale. Working on commission only just wasn't my thing. I went back to the union hall.

My new wife didn't want me to tend bar anymore and I agreed with her. The temptations were just too much. I didn't particularly like working the oil refineries, chemical plants, and shipyards but I couldn't expect Jeanne to pay my way. I had to hold up my end. It was what I knew and it paid well. My first job was as a pipefitter during a shutdown on graveyard shift. Jeanne worked days and I worked nights, not a great arrangement for a newly married couple.

I worked hard, slept days, and got up in time to fix dinner for us when Jeanne came home from her job. One Friday, dinner on the table, Jeanne did not come home from work. My first thought was that she had to work overtime but it was strange that she did not call me. I called her office and it was closed. After about an hour of waiting I went looking for her. I found her drinking with another man at a local bar that was also a dinner house and motel. I tapped her on the shoulder and told her that she had 15 minutes to get home. I totally ignored the man who was obviously with her. I went home and waited. She never showed up.

I called my job and took the night off. I started drinking at home. The more I drank, the madder I became. I went this route with my ex-girlfriend Medora. I just was not going to put up with this nor did I want to end up in jail for the rest of my life. I made a decision not to lose my temper, no matter what. When the bars opened at 6AM I went looking for Jeanne. She was at the same bar with the same man. It was all I could do to control my rage but I walked away. I went down the street and got drunk at the first opened bar. When I finally made it home Jeanne was passed out in bed. I laid down next to her and passed out too.

When we both were rested and sober we talked. She swore nothing happened between her and the other man. She stopped after work with a couple of the girls and just drank too much. She apologized and promised that it would never happen again. I told her that this is the one thing I will not put up with. I almost killed a man once and I couldn't take the chance of losing my temper. I couldn't live like an animal locked in a cage for the rest of my life. It would drive me insane. "Please, if you love me, don't run around on me. I might even hurt you."

She swore on her life that she did not do anything wrong. She promised that she would never do anything like this again. If the girls wanted to go out, she would call me and I could join them. I realized that this woman I married had a drinking problem. How could I have missed it? Everyone deserves a second chance and I had too much invested in this relationship. I would have to trust her. I forgave her and we made up.

It lasted exactly one week. The following Friday she did not come home from work or call me. I had dinner waiting on the table. I packed what stuff of mine that I could carry and left. I rented a room where Jimmy lived. I made one more trip back for another load of stuff. She still wasn't home. I left a short note, "I'm sorry. I told you I can't put up with this. Goodbye and good luck, love. Joe". I didn't tell her where I went. It was the end of our marriage....

EPILOGUE

All my hopes, dreams, aspirations lay dashed on the rocks of reality. Everything I ever tried to do in my life ended up useless and hopeless. Twice in my life I had tried to kill myself but that was the coward's way out. I will go on but I will never trust anyone again or let anyone get close to me. I will live below the radar and keep out of harm's way. I won't fight anymore, only defend myself if I have to.

Jeanne wouldn't admit that she had a drinking problem. There wasn't any way I could help her. After I walked out, we didn't see each other for several months. I got suspended out of the Moose lodge for throwing a drink at the bartender. Screw them, I joined the Elks lodge. I never filed for a divorce as I was afraid of getting drunk and getting married again. After about six years Jeanne asked me for a divorce. I filed the papers. She never showed up in court.

My good friend Jimmy died. I got to visit him in the hospital the day before he passed. To this day I still have two beautiful table lamps that he made for me. I have nothing to remind me of Jeanne except a photo or two. It was 14 long years before I met a woman I could trust and care for.

The Irish are known for telling stories and embellishing the truth. Names have been changed to protect the author from getting sued, beaten up, or killed. This book is fiction. If you want to know what happened to Joe Kennedy, our hero, read my book "Honesty, Is It worth The Hype" and check out the adventures of Joe Murphy. They shared a very similar life. Thank you for reading ....The Author

Twenty-Six

This is a banking game which was popular in the Midwest of the USA between the 1930s and 1950s, played with ten dice. It was often found in taverns, which would make payoffs in drinks, until anti-gambling legislation killed the game off to a great extent. An operator will often provide a score sheet which states the rules and payoffs made on bets. Of course the odds are always in the operator's favor.

Play:

The player chooses a number from 1 to 6 as his point number. He then throws the ten dice 13 times. His score is the number of times that his point number is thrown.

Payoffs made by the operator vary but the following is considered to be the normal.

Score	Pay-off Odds
10 or less	10 -1
13	5 -1
26	4 -1
27	5 -1
28	6 -1
29	8 -1
30 or more	10 -1

Any other score loses.

Cover By Jeff Glover

This book was published with the expertise of

Richard Jarvis of Alchemy Computer.com

Richard@
AlchemyComputer.com

This book was written by Joe Sullivan he can be reached at joe@joesullivanrealestate.com

www.ingramcontent.com/pod-product-compliance
Lightning Source LLC
Chambersburg PA
CBHW070638310726
48982CB00001B/325
9781938845017